With Be[illegible]

THE PRISONER
and
the
PEARLS

Mel Flavell

MEL FLAVELL

authormelflavell@gmail.com

ISBN NUMBER 978-0-9956302-0-8

NICHOLAS' JOURNEY

Table of Contents

CHARACTERS IN ORDER OF APPEARANCE

Nicholas Baron (Baronski)	Son of Stefan Baronski
Janice Murray	Secretary and flatmate to
Carole Semele	Secretary and flatmate
Anna Romane	Neighbouring flat dweller
Joe Southgate	Commisionaire
Harry Bailey	Carole Semele's boss
Alex Counter	Son of Commander Counter
Boris, Georgiou, Barbara, and Sheila	Friends
Sir Charles Willingham Wright	Head of M15
Commander Tashaun Counter	Guardian to Nicholas Baron
Minka Counter	Mother of Alex
Peter Swayne	Friend of Carole Semele
Steve Southgate	Son of Joe Southgate
Doris Southgate	Wife of Joe Southgate
Captain Aaronovich	Captain of 'The Ice Maiden'
2nd mate Leibviev	Second in command
Otto Strauss	American CIA

Buckland Berkeley Redfern	CIA
Mr Ponsonby Brown	Ambassador Geneva
William Wardour	Attache Geneva
Karl Danesoff	Spy Chevaliers de Russie
Captain Malekoff	Captain of Northern Crane
Captain Zetrov	Captain of Barge
Dimitri Baronski	Uncle to Nicholas
Babeta Baronski	Aunt to Nicholas
Mikhail Baronski	Cousin to Nicholas
Igor Petronovich	Neighbour to Uncle
Nina Petronovich	Daughter of Igor
Jan Gorki	Carter in Siberia
Mrs Gorki	His wife
Commandant Sokorski	Governor of Gulag
Stefan Baronski	Russian dissident

PROLOGUE

Two distinguished gentlemen of middle years, sat deeply ensconced in their respective leather high-backed chairs, in their London club. On the mantelshelf, above the cheerfully flickering fire grate, ticked the clock. It had held its place since the beginnings of this venerable establishment and, as far as anyone knew, still kept the same idiosyncratic timekeeping that it had always displayed. The logs that had burned brightly when these gentlemen came into this hallowed space, were at a critical point. Those mighty oaks, that had warmed them fiercely two hours ago, now displayed a fiery cavern which was on the point of collapse. But no one dared to interrupt the peace of this moment. They had reached that time of day when gentlemen were apt to do a lot of contemplation and did not like to be disturbed. They had eaten a very satisfying lunch, with the appropriate wines to compliment it, and had discussed a proposition of mutual interest.

Now they sat, with brandy in hand and cigars lit, and only the telltale smoke curling up into the afternoon air of the Smoke Room, betrayed their presence. At this time of day members respected the privacy of their fellow diners, as they, were also apt to 'contemplate' after a large lunch.

But the stillness of the two gentlemen, belied their very active minds indeed. There had been a serious topic discussed, and both were thinking how to further their plan.

They had been men of action, having served in their respective Navies, and they were both used to solving problems. Things happened quickly at sea and a flexible approach to decision making was all part of their training. Now they had an idea that needed careful planning and execution and the men were able to discern what their plan required. Absolute discretion was essential at this stage as they were both familiar with the world of 'Intelligence.'

They had known each other a long time, since the last days of World War II, when they had served their countries respectively in Secret Intelligence Ops, and their paths had crossed many times since. Initially, they had seemed to have very different ideologies. But over the years. things had changed, and they had found a more mutual point of view. Now they just had to put in place the nuts and bolts of their joint venture and, through the cigar smoke, they were beginning to see how to operate.

****

Later that week, a young man with a fincly chiseled face and dark brown curly hair, severely curtailed by the exigencies of National Service regulations, had been summoned to a meeting in Kensington by the organization called Chevaliers de Russie. He had finished three years serving his adoptive country and had just returned from Cyprus to London, where 'Civvy Street' beckoned.

He was being guided by his Godfather, who had been his guardian since coming to Britain as a child, from Russia.

Commander Tashaun Counter and his wife Minka, had taken him into their home when he had been left an orphan and he had been a companion/brother to their son, Alexandre. They had been educated together at Winchester and had later studied at Oxford and Manchester respectively. Now they were free. Free from the Army and free from University. Their father had told them that they could take twelve months to decide where their interests lay but he dearly hoped that his own son, at least, would want to join him in his marine engines business.

In the meantime, the young men were to be interviewed about a project that sounded mysterious. Nicholas knew of the organization Chevaliers de Russie, as his guardian was a prominent member. They understood the nostalgia of such an association but did not feel in any way that it was their country, although Nicholas, in particular, had ties to that country still.

He had arranged to meet his 'brother' at Knightsbridge Underground Station as the offices of the Chevaliers were housed in a large red brick block of flats, at the back of Harrods. He shouldered his rucksack and stepped out of the brightly lit Underground Station into the busy street and looked around for Alex, with a frank blue- eyed gaze.

****

A young lady with fiery curly red hair, stepped off the night train from Edinburgh and looked around her. So far so good. She had never been to London before but her desire to become part of the wider world had carried her to the Capital.

Janice Murray was a tall, slim girl, with hazel eyes, a pert nose and determined mouth and her smile came only after a thoroughly appraising look.

She had left her home in Scotland to work in London Whitehall, having been recruited by a guest speaker whilst at Durham University. Now, here Janice was, ready to take up her post with Sir Charles Willingham-Wright of the Foreign Office. She turned into Old Brompton Road and then found Onslow Gardens where she saw the entrance to the YWCA. Entering the porticoed entrance to the building, the smell of boiled cabbage assailed her. The familiar odour of Halls of Residence and Boarding School, and was at once comforted and repelled by such reminders of communal living that this bright young hopeful had known since childhood.

"Ah, you've arrived at last, Miss Murray. We weren't sure when you would be here after such a long journey. Said a severe looking lady with hair pulled back into a bun. I am Miss Welsh. Let me show you to your room." And it was quite obvious that this formidable lady was in charge as she led the way up some wide stairs which opened out onto a generous landing with doors leading off in every direction.

She was left to put her belongings into the large room that was to be shared with three others. Miss Welsh had fired several instructions at her and Janice was relieved to find herself alone again. A sigh escaped her lips. She was not leaving childhood behind but could see that all the rules and regulations were the same. "Where then was freedom?"

PART I

THE LONDON LIFE

CHAPTER ONE

New Beginnings – Autumn 1961

A young woman walked eagerly along Cromwell Road and into Harrington Gardens. It was a crisp autumn late afternoon. Carole Semele was feeling pleased with herself for her life was about to change. By now she felt like a fashionable Londoner with a black Cossack style fur hat, a short emerald coat, and most especially, long black boots, which she handled with reverential care, her step confident. Nobody in this city was going to say 'another provincial' ever again. She was a real 'Georgie Girl' waiting for something to happen.

Carole had spent all her childhood years near to the River Avon, in the Vale of Evesham. One day she and her teenage friends had taken beer, up to the top of Bredon Hill, for a party. On the way home, the car had skidded off the road in the dark. By the time the accident was discovered, her brother was dead

Her parents were devastated by their loss and somehow her presence had felt like a reproach and she had decided it was time to leave and to see something of the world.

She had come to London three months ago, and had found accommodation at the Kensington YWCA where Carole had made friends with one of the girls Janice Murray. She was about to share an apartment with her new friend. Having left her home in the Midlands to gain her independence, this was the key to a whole new world.

Carole turned into the entrance portico of a Georgian terraced building and looked for the caretaker who sat in a small side room.

"Good afternoon, I'm here to pick up the key to Flat 4 booked in the name of Janice Murray." She said politely.

"Oh yes, Janice explained to us yesterday that you would be along this afternoon. Here you are." She nodded her thanks, took the key and entered a large vestibule where a broad grand staircase wound around, up to the first floor. She found the flat and was about to enter when a small lady, with wild curly grey hair and dressed in black, greeted Carole.

She turned to say hello and was startled by a pair of violet eyes appraising her from a face that still held a vestige of, what must have been, a very beautiful face. From her drab appearance and petite figure, the little lady could easily be overlooked. But once held by her eyes, it was easy to see that she would command attention in any gathering.

"Welcome to your new home. The lady greeted her.

I am so pleased to meet you, as I live across the way." She said as she waved vaguely in the direction of the door opposite, although there were several other doors leading off the stairwell.

"Perhaps you would like to take coffee with me one morning to welcome you to our community."

The voice held a slight trace of what seemed a European accent.

"That is very kind of you, perhaps when my new flat-mate arrives, but now I must see to my home." She murmered.

Slipping into the large room that was to be her new domain, she set her basket down, put her coat and hat on the bed and pirouetted across the tiny carpet in front of the electric fire.

It was a high-ceilinged room, long and narrow, which had probably been twice the size at another time but had quite clearly been divided, and the room contained everything needed for two people. Twin single beds dominated the room with bright bedspreads. Set beside them, in front of the electric fire were arranged two small armchairs. Behind a curtain was, an iron bath with a toilet and washbasin.

On the opposite side of the room from the fire, cupboards and a bookshelf were neatly arranged with all the necessary additions for their comfort. A shiny new electric kettle and 'Baby Belling' oven beside it, sat on top of a sideboard, completing their needs. But, in addition, they had one luxury, a balcony. She was immediately drawn to the French windows overlooking the gardens in the small square.

The lights of a London winter evening shone mistily, casting shadows into the trees but leaving the garden shrouded by darkness. She idly thought of what the square would be like when Spring opened the buds on the canopy of plane trees. It would be a fine evening with that smell of autumn leaves that heralded the winter to come. Birds were roosting in the half bare trees and a flight of wagtails swooped down to find a home and to add their voices to the chatter while they all settled for the night. Carole was content to stand there and soak up the magic of dusk as a whole new atmosphere pervaded the square.

She noticed a figure standing almost in the shade of a doorway and his stillness was only betrayed by the occasional pinprick of red light moving upwards towards a concealed face and traces of smoke curling away to join the misty air. From the safety of the balcony wall she watched, and he watched, neither certain of the other's presence. Carole was startled out of her reverie as the door key turned and, her new flat mate, walked in. She stepped back into the room and greeted her friend. A new life was beginning.

"Hello Janice."

"Hi there Carole. Have you been looking at the view?"

Carole laughed. “Indeed, I have. It looks lovely and a bit mysterious too with the lights and shadows under the trees.”

“I agree.” Said Janice. “But have you put the kettle on yet?”

Carole ruefully shook her head, “I am afraid I was carried away by watching the light fade, but at least I know where the kettle is.” She offered and turned towards their shiny new kettle, to boil the water Soon they were sitting cosily in front of their electric fire, feeling free at last from all the strictures of communal institutions.

Janice was a softly spoken Scottish lassie, whose independent spirit had led her from her home in the Lowlands of Scotland, to the Foreign Office, where she had been for some months. Carole thought that she would be a bracing tonic after being surrounded by students at the YWCA. Janice was part of the real world, the ‘Toilers and Weavers’ of the city existence and instinctively Carole felt sure that they would get on.

****

Carole sat down with a sigh. At last she had a seat to finish her journey to the City. She had woken earlier than usual that morning but because of the change of the clocks to wintertime, had allowed herself a little bit longer to stay cocooned inside her warm blankets. ‘A wink had become a nod’ and sleep had overtaken her again and, very early, had become, very late. Now she was travelling with all the rush hour commuters with only the lateness of the trains as her excuse.

She looked around at the other passengers and sighed again, encountering the blank withdrawal in all their faces. Carole had come to London with all the curiosity of a puppy but her natural friendliness would not be met with any response in this carriage. She supposed that this air of distrust was all part of the life in a city which had no other kind of privacy, amongst so many other people. Back home there had always been a friendly nod of greeting by those around, which, if not kept in check, resulted in an interrogation as to your place in the universe and as likely as not, in discovering a mutual acquaintance. Here, the only distractions to the daily routine, were the billboards along all the stations' tunnel walls, advertising the next exhibition or West End show.

Her thoughts were halted by the realisation that she was nearing her stop at The Monument. She joined the fast flowing, flood of people that burst forth from the train trying to navigate the stream, which was made more difficult by the shoes she had chosen to wear in her haste. Her stiletto heels were far too high, and threatened to sink into every metal grill or manhole cover she passed. She had already nearly come adrift as one of her heels began to submerge, leaving her balanced on one leg as she retrieved her shoe from a grid.

Inwardly Carole cursed the prevailing fashion which had all the office workers teetering on four inch heels and wearing pencil skirts, to emulate Marilyn Monroe in

'Some Like It Hot.' This was fine for sashaying across an office but took no account of the daily battle with the commuter trains. Every secretary in town knew that their key to success lay as much in the maintenance of a trim appearance as a grasp of Pitman shorthand. An indulgent boss was more likely to forgive a few mistakes in the filing of important documents.

Arriving at the entrance to Messrs. Bailey, Bailey and Whigstaff, Importers of Antiques, just three minutes late, she mustered the widest smile and slid past Joe Southgate, without comment. If lucky, he would mark her arrival time favourably, in the sign-in book.

Joe was a retired firefighter from Southwark who had swapped the uniform of the Fire Service to that of Commissionaire. When all the excitement of wartime bombing had ceased, he chased an entirely different kind of warm seat, in the heart of the City. No more excitement for him – that would likely be accompanied by a little too much heat for his comfort, and he sought his own kind of Peace, now that War was over. He was born and bred on the South Bank and his knowledge of London was encyclopedic.

"Good morning Miss, delay on the Underground again, is it?" He called to her retreating figure.

She turned. "Oh yes Mr. Southgate." She said breathlessly, meanwhile flashing him another dazzling smile. Of course, he realised her ruse but was happy to play along with her excuses, as she at least brightened his day. Not like those cheeky office boys who were more likely to 'give him lip.' There was nothing like a London lad for knowing all the excuses.

Joe knew all about wise boys. He had sons of his own all trying to make a living in the square mile and one of them, Bill, now worked for the Port Authority. At home, he would recount many of the tricks that were used to move goods illegally. There were many London gangs that terrorised the dockside and most contraband was moved by well-organised masters. It made him gasp sometimes when his son told him these tales.

Up in her office, Carole was glad to see that she was first in, despite her lateness. Most of Messrs. Bailey, Bailey and Whigstaff's trade was in importing antiques from Europe as the diaspora of Eastern Europeans filtered westwards. Years ago, there had been many émigrés that had fled both Revolution and War from the crumbling Empires of Europe. More recently this flow had become a trickle as the borders between East and West were closed, but some goods still found their way to the City of London. Indeed, Britain's own Empire was also splintering and artefacts of a more exotic kind were reaching the shores of Britain, as the Boxwallahs of India and the Far East came home with their reminders of past glories and their Oriental treasures.

Carole loved to be involved in listing and cataloguing all these wonderful objects. She had left Art College in Birmingham with a reverence for many of the artists' work that now came through her doors and felt privileged to be seeing some of these things in her own hands. Her greatest joy came when looking at beautiful jewelry that came to be valued. Occasionally a miniature painting or locket came in, which aroused in her a curiosity and wonder about the owners of these fine pieces.

She looked down the list of new ships in port and saw that a Russian and Finnish ship had arrived overnight. Both were likely to handle passengers as well as cargo, into Surrey Docks. The Port Authority was very vigilant about illegal immigrants but there were always some who came with apparently genuine credentials.

Occasionally goods were brought in under their noses, landing them in the stomachs of fish or carcasses and once, even inside a tin of caviar, which was brought to Billingsgate Market, right on their Office doorstep, by the Russian Merchant Fleet that traded in the Baltic and North Sea. This especially pleased her boss as he had spent much of his time during the War plying these waters, all the way to Murmansk. It was a well-established trade route and had been vital in keeping Russia fed during the darkest days of the Second World War.

Such was the life of the Waterfront, and Carole loved to wander in her lunchtime to the Tower of London and beyond to St. Katharine's Docks which were alive with seafaring barges and large shipping. The red sailed wherries that had plied their trade from further down on the river, were long gone. But the derricks disgorged the cargoes of every ship from every nation around the world, as they stretched away downstream.

All the riches of trade found their way to the Port of London. On the south side were the Surrey Docks and more and the lighters crisscrossed the river to take cargoes to the bonded warehouses to await Excise Duty. With all this traffic, it was not surprising that a little 'wastage' was experienced and the Dockers of London had rich pickings.

Overseeing all this was the Port of London Authority which kept a sharp eye on any misdeeds but who knew that their most vital role was to keep the traffic moving. The tide wouldn't wait and the life of the Capital throbbed to the lunar imperative.

All this bustle made work in the City very vibrant and Carole loved it. She thought about the lives of all the people using this waterway and had no idea that she was to be more intimately engaged than she could ever have thought possible.

CHAPTER TWO

The Plot – The Christmas Soirée

That night she arrived back at the flat after listing and sorting all the relevant cargo from the Russian ship and, as she climbing the stairs, was met by the little lady who had spoken earlier, her neighbour Anna. She was inclined to talk and Carole was ready to listen so put down her basket.

"I saw you go out in a rush this morning. Are you well?"

"Oh, yes we're fine!"

"Where do you go to, are you working nearby?"

"No. I work in the City in Great Tower Street at an Importers."

"How exciting." Said their new neighbour. "Do you ever deal with my own country? I am from Russia, but it is many years since I left my homeland." She averted her face but Carole could see the sadness that had been there in her lovely eyes.

"Oh, I am sorry to hear that. I do hope you still hear from family or friends."

There was a pause in which Anna looked at her. Of course, She reflected. She is young and doesn't realize the heartache that brought me to England. Young and completely unaware of the complexities of the world. But, sympathetic.

"It was very difficult. We were all scattered I don't know whether they are still alive but I don't seem to find any news however hard I try." The anguish in her voice left Carole unsure how to respond but her heart was moved by Anna's plight. What she had dreamed at work, looking at the articles she handled, was romantic and unworldly. But here was a real person with a real story to tell. Her fantasy shattered, she pondered on the individuals, like Anna, who had lived through times bad enough to flee their country.

Anna seemed to collect herself, "Of course I have many friends here and we even have a Friends of Russia Émigrés Society. At Christmas, we have a Soirée at the Embassy, a very special evening. It is full of young people. A very grand occasion." She paused. "Would you let me take you both, you would enjoy it so much? There is music and singing and perhaps, yes perhaps, some dancing as well."

While Carole prepared the supper, she recalled the conversation to Janice. and said.

She seems a very mysterious lady. Not at all what I

had imagined when she first introduced herself."

"I know what you mean Carole, I also thought she was a poor old lady, but I heard from the caretaker that she has a large flat, the rest of the floor in fact, and that it has eight rooms!"

"Good heavens, that makes her position entirely different." Carole said, "so that makes her boast that she is connected to the Embassy entirely plausible." And thought again of the possible invitation that their neighbour had made to a Christmas event there.

This made them see Anna in a more subjective way. Not as a lonely old lady in straightened circumstance. She now appeared to be someone who had influential friends and who may have led a quite different life when she had lived in Russia

Janice speculated whether the rental of their own room was actually a sub-let, so that she had some company near at hand, and had perhaps been used by a servant at one time.

Anna had insisted that they come to tea on the last Sunday in November. They knocked on their neighbour's door and were led into a quite different flat to the one they had imagined.

"Hello my dears, I am delighted you found time for an old lady like me. Do come in and make yourself comfortable." She led the way from the large vestibule into a lovely lounge with double windows, and a balcony, leading out into the square. In some ways, it was the same as their own as the main features were the French windows but there the similarity ended.

Instead of the long high ceilinged room, which had the feeling of being truncated in the one they rented, here was a room with handsome proportions and with a sense of elegance immediately apparent. The main colours of the room were cream and gold, furnished in the style of the French Second Empire. The most striking thing to behold was a large bold picture in reds and pinks, turquoise and blue that hung over the fireplace. This was echoed by several smaller, but similar pieces, on other walls. All, were rich in colour and danced with movement.

Carole exclaimed with admiration. “Oh, what a lovely flat you have, so bright and airy” She stopped herself from exclaiming further for everywhere she looked was a feast for the eyes and she did not wish to appear too nosey. She was aware, that the pictures had echoes of Matisse paintings and wondered whether her knowledge was accurate. She had particularly loved this fauvist artist and had studied his work at Art College and she was delighted to see a copy of his work in such a lovely setting.

“I’m so glad you like it,” And, as she urged them to sit, they saw that the table was laid with fine bone china and exquisitely made cakes. Lemon and milk were offered and the whole table arrangement was the height of refinement.

Their hostess seemed to be transformed in front of them. Instead of the rather drab little lady of the stairs, she had become an elegant woman. She had fashioned her greying scattered curls into a chignon and had added some crystal beads at her neckline. Her cheeks no longer sallow, had a faint blush and her lips were pink. Carole and Janice were openly impressed by the transformation and tried to conceal their astonishment. They realised that here was a lady with no idle boast about her connections to high society.

"Are you still enjoying your position Carole?" Anna asked politely. "Have you managed to be on time since I saw you?"

"Indeed, I have, but changed my footwear for using on the Underground as I nearly fell headlong in my stilettos when they caught in a gap in the paving stones." And she recounted her dilemma standing on one foot.

"Have you seen very much of the City yet?" Anna asked again politely and Carole mentioned her trips to the ships standing in dock for re-loading.

Carole said, "I saw a ship from your country this week and they come from all over the Baltic.

"I love to wander through the little alleyways that crisscross the City and to see into all the lovely Wren churches."

"I suppose I shall see more of the City soon as I understand there will be a strike on the Underground."

“Dear me.” Said Anna alarmed. “But that is a long way to walk, isn’t it?”

“Well I am not too worried as I have had to walk that far when we had a thick fog a couple of years ago, when I was working in Birmingham and the buses weren’t running.”

“Yes,” said Janice, “I come from Scotland and bad weather often meant that the only way home was by walking. I am better off than Carole as I only need to go to Westminster.”

“Oh, do you work in Parliament?” Exclaimed Anna.

“Indeed, not quite,” she laughed. “I am in the Foreign Office but I often see Members of Parliament and Ministers.”

“What lucky girls you are to have such interesting positions.”

“Yes, I think I am.” Janice said. “Especially as I work for the European Affairs Department.”

“You are lucky to be able to lead such independent lives, the world must beckon you.”

“Yes,” said Janice, “I hope shortly to be able to get a European posting. I don’t know where yet although there are lots of places I would like to visit.”

For some minutes, Anna was silent, perhaps

wrapped up in her own memories of Europe. It did not seem that they were happy thought as the sadness was again on her face. The brightness of her cheeks seemed to pale and with an effort at cheeriness said, “Now girls I mentioned to you that I would like to take you to an evening at the Embassy and I meant what I said.” She jumped up to look for her invitation. The two girls looked at each other and nodded.

“Now let me see. Ah, here it is."

The Chairman of the

CHEVALIERS DE RUISSE

Invites You To

A CHRISTMAS SOIRÉE

on Wednesday 6th December 1961

at the Russian Embassy from 7.30 pm - 9.30 pm

Evening Dress RSVP

“That is very kind of you Anna, I am sure we would love to come. We had planned to go to The Hammersmith Palais de dance but we can go at another time.”

Three days later Anna knocked on their door and said, "I have arranged a taxi for us to go to the Soiree, will you be ready to go at 7.00 pm?"

"Yes, that's fine but could we have another ten minutes as it will be difficult to be ready before then."

"Well if that is all you can manage, but we want to be there before the Ambassador's Party arrives."

They assured her they would be as quick as possible because they did not want to cause offence.

Carole arrived home at 6.30 pm to find Janice almost ready. "Fine, at least we don't have to fight over the bath," She thought.

Janice had brushed her short hair to form a lovely halo on her head and her green tartan silk dress set off her red curls.

Carole had chosen to dress her long blonde hair into a French pleat. This made her feel very sophisticated, as she had just learnt how to do this, from her visit to a hairdresser in Knightsbridge, called Michael-John. It had taken all her spare money but she looked very elegant in a short black cloqué cocktail dress and her very high heeled Italian Bally shoes. They would probably make her suffer for her vanity but, if necessary, she hoped there would be some squashy sofa to sink into.

"Hurry Carole, the taxi is here." Urged Janice.

“Coming.” Said Carole, as she picked up her evening bag and they clattered down the stairs just in time.

The ride to Queen Anne’s Gate was not very far and they arrived just before two Rolls Royce drew up to the Georgian Mansion.

They entered a wide tall reception hall ablaze with lights and a wide broad staircase led up to a large drawing room. This was draped with crimson velvet curtains and a carpet of Middle Eastern design intermingled with a tree of life, curling flowers and exotic beasts. All, were in strong contrasting colours of red and Prussia blue dominant, on a cream ground and was the most breathtaking carpet Carole had ever seen. The colours reminded her of the Matisse painting of a lady sitting in a chair with rich red drapes and sinuous flowers that she had seen at Anna’s flat and was quite unlike any English furnishing she had ever seen.

As they took the glasses offered to them by the waiter, the Ambassador was announced, followed by his wife whose spectacular bosom was graced by a large beautiful necklace. She might have amazing sapphires at her neck, but her husband sported a diamond encrusted insignia that outshone everything in the room. The only other gentleman to compete, was the Naval Attaché, who seemed to come straight out of a novel with such a handsome sunburnt face and military bearing. His sun crinkled eyes gave an inkling of his sea life and he walked like a sailor with a rolling gait.

Carole and Janice were introduced to many people before a young man took his place at the grand piano. He began softly with an Etude by Beethoven and built up gradually through Tchaikovsky and finally with Shostakovich, which reminded them of home and the struggles they had lived through. A young woman next took her place by the piano and in a heart stopping voice sang folk ballads. Of course, the words were strange to the English girls but they instinctively knew that the girl had touched the hearts of these people so far from their homeland.

Afterwards the two girls were introduced around and were surprised to find two other girls from the Hostel who had been invited. They were students at Le Lycée Français who were acquainted with Russian students who had escorted them here. They were glad to find someone they knew, as the whole experience was becoming rather overwhelming. Janice was able to hold her own more easily as she had already attended receptions at the Foreign Office but for Carole it was the opening of a whole new world. She realised that London held many layers of society but she had landed like someone from Venus into this glittering galaxy. Once her shyness had disappeared, this lovely young woman's personality, opened up like a morning rose, fresh and dew bespattered, who was transformed by the evening into one of the heady tuberoses that were gathered in all the vases. She was not aware of the affect she was having all around her but such loveliness stood out amongst the bejeweled ladies and diamond studded insignia of the military gentlemen, with no need for any other adornment than her youth and innocence.

Carole was not the only person to have newly awakened thoughts about the Soirée but of an altogether different kind.

Whilst Carole and Janice were enjoying the music, a band of young men were watching them. They formed part of a group of Russian emigrés, who had spent the greater part of their education in England at some of the major English public schools and would not normally be taken for foreigners, but they were members of the Chevaliers de Russe. They had been called into the Office of the Commander to be briefed on a plan to help imprisoned dissidents leave Russia. The role that they were to play seemed harmless, even promised to be enjoyable, and their task tonight was to observe the young women in question, and recognise them for some future opportunity to affect a meeting.

One watcher in particular was singled out to be the major player. Nicholas Baron was an engaging young man of attractive appearance with dark hair and fine eyes. His smooth-talking tongue ensured more than his fair share of attention from the ladies. That he had taken advantage of his good looks was perhaps an exaggeration, but he certainly enjoyed the company of the fairer sex and was familiar with the eternal dance they played with each other. He would be a good catch for the most discerning female, having a fine mind and influential contacts to add to his other attributes.

They were to observe the two young women with

Anna Romaine and he, in particular, was to commit to memory the fair young lady and his friend Alex was to observe the redhead. They were allocated the task of wine waiters and to discreetly hand around the drinks. The glamour of the occasion and the lovely musical focus was enough to disguise his special interest and it was becoming gradually more enjoyable, and he chuckled to himself at the thought of such a plum job.

By the end of the evening his interest had quickened to such a degree that, although he did not know it then, he was already halfway in love with the vision he saw before him.

"Well Alex, what do you think of our orders to become acquainted with those two beauties at this evening's party?" "That won't be too difficult, will it?"

"I thought the blonde was lovely. Such perfect skin and green eyes, and"

Alex interrupted, "Hold on there, Nicholas, we will have plenty of opportunity to appreciate their finer points but we first have to set up a casual meeting."

Alex was amused with the transformation in his friend when he walked home with him. His enthusiastic babbling about the task ahead was so out of character that he realized the situation immediately. He was well aware of the affect his friend had on the fairer sex but had never seen Nicholas smitten with the same starry-eyed posture before. "Things were looking up." Thought Alex, whose engagement with the ladies was altogether less successful.

****

Next morning it was more difficult than ever to get to work on time but Carole was able to work her magic on Joe and arrived at her desk before her boss Harry Bailey. He was a jolly man of robust stature, about 50, who had worked in the City since he had come out of the Navy after WW2. He had worked on the North Sea minesweepers and had even been as far north as Murmansk. He had come back to a city drastically different to that of his childhood but was happy to join his father in business and his knowledge of shipping proved useful over the years. Naval men, like military men, are proud of the trade they have plied and are happy to deal with like-minded seafarers and traders whatever their country of origin. The trade with the Baltic countries was a natural consequence of that seafaring knowledge. He was a bluff, no nonsense boss and he quickly saw that Carole had her mind elsewhere.

"Carole, this won't do. We shall get nothing done if you carry on in this sleepy fashion." He expostulated.

"Oh, I'm sorry Mr. Bailey but I was out ---- not very ---- late. I had such an extraordinary evening."

Mr. Bailey sighed. He decided to humour her on this occasion as she had certainly been very efficient up to now, so perhaps he had better let her tell her story as she had intrigued him sufficiently to arouse his curiosity. She recounted all the unfamiliar proceedings of the last night. As each new aspect of yesterday's events emerged, he was surprised and then strangely disturbed by what she had to say.

"This all seems extraordinary. Who is this lady in your apartment building? She certainly seems more important than you had imagined."

"Yes, that's what I am beginning to think," She said thoughtfully.

"Well this is all very fine for you Carole, and I am glad that you are able to enjoy yourself, but be careful where this could lead. Just remember, I am here if you need any advice. My experience tells me that all is not as it seems," He paused.

"Now, can we get some work done today!"

****

The following weekend they had a knock on the door very early on the Saturday morning.

"Peter," shrieked Carole as there, outside their flat, was her teenage friend who was doing his National Service at Gravesend.

"I thought it was time I looked you up in the big City. I have a 48 Hour Pass and thought perhaps we could 'hit the town'."

"Come in and meet my flat mate. Janice meet my

friend from home, Peter Swayne."

Janice was delighted to meet an honest seeming Englishman after all the foreigners they had experienced lately.

They decided to go the West End first, and tomorrow maybe a trip down to Greenwich to make best use of his available time.

"Oh, hang on. I don't know how Janice will think about you staying overnight." and she raised her eyebrow.

"Oh, that's OK" She said, having a brother of her own. "Providing you can sleep anywhere as I am not giving up my bed for you. Perhaps the bath might be more comfortable." As she gestured towards their magnificent Victorian brass-legged monster.

He laughed, "My dear girl, when you have been where I have slung my hammock that is luxury!"

They set off and were soon in Piccadilly.

Carole was delighted to see Peter. She had first thought about coming to London when she knew she might have a friend in the City. They had been good friends. They had spent most of her teenage years with a group of friends in the Vale of Evesham. Most weekends were spent 'messing about" on the River Avon. It had been their natural playground. If the river was swollen with floodwater there was always a chance of a walk over Bredon Hill or tea and cakes at Broadway and a climb up Fish Hill. This care free life, was cut short when her brother, David, was killed. Peter had been one of the party that had been in the car, in the misadventure. With too many squeezed into their Mini car, it had upturned into a ditch trapping them all, and became David's watery grave.

Her parents had found it hard to reconcile themselves to his death, especially her mother who had seemed in a 'far off place' ever since and her father had taken to long hours at work and had very little contact with his growing teenage daughter. Even amongst her friends, things were not the same as the sobering reality of David's death permeated their friendships. Soon after, they began to drift away as the call of study and National Service claimed two or three years of their lives and so Carole had resolved to leave her home for a life in the City.

After their trip to town they had come back to the flat exhausted but had lots to discuss and sat around with tea and cakes that had been purchased at the French patisserie at the corner shop.

Usually a trip to the West End would have suited Carole best. Saturday shopping would have been part of her weekend plans, but she had not felt entirely focused today. She was glad to see that Janice was enjoying her friend's company without too much input from her. She had started to think about what her boss had warned earlier in the week, and began to think that he was overreacting to her night at the Embassy. So, it was good to get back to earth with Peter's visit. Carole looked at the young man and saw how much he had changed. Peter was of medium stature with brown, close cropped hair and his time in the Navy had turned the youth into a man. It was obvious that he had been put through his paces as he was now a sturdy young man of muscular frame. The surefootedness that she remembered, was emphasized by his stocky physique and it had turned him into a real man of the soil. His steady eyes returned an honest gaze.

She had been glad to see him but hoped that he did not find her too offhand. It was funny how her time away from old friends altered her prospective. They had spent many happy days together and had generally been accepted as boyfriend/girlfriend. Indeed, she reflected, he would always be a real pal but no longer seemed to be more than that.

Janice was finding his company entertaining as they seemed to be laughing a lot and this made the altered relationship easier to handle.

Peter had many stories to tell of his time at Gravesend and the antics his friends told of the 'London gangs', some of which were hair-raising. One of his mates was from South London, across the river at Southwark. He had a brother with the River Police who was always telling of the tricks played on the Customs and Excise Officers down on the docks. When he realized that Carole was working in that part of the city he was immediately interested.

"Hey, I didn't realize you were working by the Tower. What luck, I expect you get down to the bridge quite often. I'm jealous, I don't have any freedom to call my own except on shore leave but that isn't very often." He continued after a breathless pause. "I could chase up some of those stories my mate tells me about the East End."

Carole offered, "Next time you come up I will take you to some of the Sunday markets, especially Petticoat Lane but you will have to be up early!"

Peter envied her the job on the riverside while he was stuck out at shore base but he enjoyed the life by the River Thames as there always seemed something different going on. Each day brought problems to solve and river surveillance brought new challenges and promise of action right there on the water.

If only he could be part of the life of the City, he would be satisfied. Gravesend didn't quite seem to be the heart of the Metropolis and from the tales he had heard from his friends, he was rather missing out. Still he only had three months more to go and he would be out of uniform at last!

CHAPTER THREE

Meetings – Invitations

The following weekend they had decided to go to the Hammersmith Palais for the Saturday night dance. They had been told by the girls at work that it was a venue they must try. There they could dance to all the popular Bands, especially Chris Barber and his Jazzmen.

When they emerged at Hammersmith Station there seemed to be total chaos around, with roadworks stretching out to the West at the beginning of the new flyover that was to dwarf all the existing buildings around it for many decades. Tucked behind this chaos, was the Dancehall where, it seemed, all of the youth of West London were on a Saturday night out.

****

During the next few days, Nicholas was anxious to engineer a meeting with this lovely creature he had seen at the Soirée and he explored several avenues in his search for a solution until on the Wednesday following, he learnt that the girls had planned to go dancing at the 'Palais' This seemed a perfect place to affect a casual meeting and his natural love of dancing made the prospect very pleasant.

Nicholas prepared himself for the evening out with more than his usual care. He was dressed in Italian style with a short one buttoned jacket and streamlined belted trousers in a dark shade. His shirt was sharply white and slim in shape and a thin knitted tie was fashioned in a Windsor knot. His narrow hips and broad shoulders were shown to advantage by the continental style. His friend Alex dressed in a somewhat more conventional suit which had the quality of personal tailoring, which in other circles would have gained complete approval but, in the world of sharp dressers, was rather ordinary.

They arrived at the dancehall and looked around for signs of the girls they sought but could not see them, so looked for suitable partners to dance with, and were soon enjoying the rhythm.

Carole and Janice entered the ballroom to find that the dance floor was already packed with dancers jiving to the Chris Barber Band which made a very lively beat. Girls were seated all around the ballroom on hardback chairs looking out at the dancers. The men clustered around the bar pretending not to be interested in the dancers whilst all the time eyeing the girls sitting around the room. They paraded in their Teddy Boy suits and winkle picker shoes. Some favoured the Transatlantic style of Levi jeans and blue suede shoes. Some of the girls were dancing together as the spirit of the dance was more important than anything for it gave them the opportunity to show off their dancing skills to the watching boys.

For the moment, Carole and Janice were content to watch. Then they decided to purchase a drink and moved to the bar. On the way, Carole was aware of a fantastic dancer with dark curly hair and a lithe, supple body, which was perfectly in tune with the music and expressing great innovation. Her interest was so acute that it communicated itself to the dancer. He glanced towards the watcher and knew that her interest had been caught and when the dance ended, sought her out, near the bar.

"Would you like to dance?" Said a deep, well-modulated voice beside her, and turning found she was looking into a pair of smiling moonlight deep eyes and realized that it was the dancer she had been watching. She followed him to the dance floor bereft of speech.

"I'm Nicholas, thank you and what is your name?" Introductions over, they started to dance and the skill of both perfectly harmonized.

They pulsated to the rhythm and she lost track of the time. She surrendered to the twists and turns of the jive and was surprised when the last dance was announced and the music slowed. She had misplaced Janice in her surrender to the beat and to the intense masculinity of her partner. He played his part to perfection as he increased and decreased his effect on her with the skill he knew how to exert over the opposite sex. He did not realise that his weaving was spinning himself into the web and wrapping them both in its silken threads. He pulled her close as the tempo changed and closed his eyes. Her initial resistance relaxed, as he knew it would, and drew her closer still.

Minutes passed in close embrace and two hearts beat faster with the intensity of awakening passion and he kissed her pearl-like ears sending shock waves through her. Soon, oh so soon, the dance was over and they stood arms apart but still held in the magic of the dance. The lights brightened and Carole was aware that Janice was coming over the dance floor and the spell was broken.

"Are you ready to leave?" She said and Carole turned to her partner and said "I'm afraid I must go."

"But don't go yet, I was going to ask you something," Protested the young man.

She introduced Nicholas to Janice and he said, "Hello, I see you are dancing with my friend. Splendid, as I wanted to ask Carole to the Chelsea Arts Ball. Perhaps you might like to come too. What do you think Alex?" He nodded enthusiastically and the stage was set for their plans.

"Have you come far?"

"Not really, Just along Kings Road, from South Kensington."

"South Kensington? So, you are going our way and we can make some arrangements while we walk home." The girls were delighted with this arrangement and innocently fell in with the schemers plans.

It was a fine, crisp night full of stars and perfect for a long walk along King Street and they had the opportunity to get to know each other. At last the two girls felt part of the London scene and they cheered at the thought their social life was looking up.

Carole let herself out onto the balcony to recall her special moments of the evening. She looked for Nicholas but the square was silent. She smelt the leaves that had fallen from the trees with a heightened awareness of the melancholy of the winter evening which was certainly not matched by her own mood which held a sense of excitement.

Reluctantly she turned to join her flat-mate and in that instant again saw the movement of a red spot of light. As she thought again of the evening she realised that there was something familiar about her new friend and wondered where she had seen him before.

She withdrew from the balcony and shut the window and the emotions of the evening calmed.

On Monday morning on the underground journey she was floating on a cloud of memories. She was also thinking of what she should wear to the Chelsea Arts Ball as it was to be a fancy dress, theme, the Roaring 20s. She thought about going to a new shop in Church Street, Kensington High which her office friends had been talking about as rather interesting. "I might be able to get a feather boa there as that would be very 20s."

She went into the office with a dreamy smile on her face. Joe enjoyed the pleasure of her appearance and thought that she glowed. He hoped she would never lose that special quality; that the cares of the world would not shatter her smile. It cheered Joe up for the day to see her bright face and golden hair and he wondered how long her open face, full of curiosity and zest for life, would last. Innocence shone from her green eyes. He feared the moment when the shuttered look, peculiar to the toilers of the Underground train became part of her mask.

He had begun to take a fatherly interest in her and wished that his sons could find such a wholesome girl. Steve had taken to his role in the Port Authority with much enthusiasm but it had taken its toll of him. His cynicism had begun to give him a very jaundiced view of humanity. 'She was just the sort of fresh-faced innocent that might restore it!" He shook his head, "Who was he kidding," He thought.

When Carole returned from work she remembered that they had invited Anna for drinks that evening and she hurried to be back early at the flat. This had seemed the right compromise, to thank their new neighbour without getting too involved, and was looking forward to it. Anna arrived and stepped into their tiny domain. They gave her one of the two chairs in front of the electric fire and they took turns in the other chair and the divan next to them. They had bought a bottle of sherry and some new glasses from Habitat as their cupboard didn't have such things.

"I hope you enjoyed your evening out on Saturday?"

Anna asked.

"Oh yes, very much," said Janice with enthusiasm, "and we have been invited to attend the Chelsea Arts Ball." Carole sat there with a dreamy smile on her face saying nothing.

"It's to be a fancy dress Roaring 20s theme," Continued Janice.

"How lovely for you both, how exciting to be going to a Ball," she exclaimed, "but what are you going to wear. Have you got something in mind?"

"Well no, not yet," said Carole "but we were going to a shop called 'Biba' to buy some feather boas.

"My dears, you mustn't spend all your money. I have an idea." She looked appraisingly at them both and said. "I know I am a fat old lady now, but I used to be regarded as beautiful and I have many lovely gowns still hanging in the wardrobe from my young days and I am sure they may fit you, if you would like to look at them?" The girls looked at each other and accepted the proposition.

When they had finished their drinks, they all returned to Anna's flat and spent the evening trying on such lovely gowns, just the style they would have wished, but were obviously all designer made, and they were thrilled at this generosity.

When Carole got to work, after seeing Anna again

and her most generous gift, she began to dream of the forthcoming Ball. Their social life seemed to be rather more exciting and was rather distracting. She was brought back to earth next morning when Mr. Bailey came waltzing in rather late saying "I hope you are fully recovered from your excitement last week because there is a lot to do. We have to work and concentrate today as there is a Finnish ship due in today and there is an Auction to be catalogued for viewing tomorrow. I hope that we shall find a few 'treasures' in the new cargo."

"Yes, Mr. Bailey, I shall try to concentrate today." She said demurely and she looked at him with such an exquisite purse of her lips that he was unable to continue in his severe tone.

"Although I realise how many distractions there are to be had in this City." She said as an afterthought.

He laughed, "Yes I should say so, especially when you are young. But don't let it run away with you Now back to business!'

For the rest of the morning they concentrated on cataloguing all that had arrived. She had no time to dwell more on the weekend.

"That's enough for this morning, Carole, I shall be out for lunch but will be back before you leave."

At one o'clock she was able to set aside her work while her boss went out with the Captain of the Finnish ship and she supposed that he would not be back very early after their liquid lunch. She picked up her sandwiches and hurried to the riverfront to eat them while watching the boats about their business.

She thought about her meeting with Nicholas and compared him with Peter. She was glad that Janice had liked him. He was now part of her childhood, more as the brother she had lost, and her feelings for Nicholas were quite different. What had been like a singing gladness in her teenage years with Peter had changed into an insistent beating of jungle drums when she thought of Nicholas "My Christmas gift" He had said.

"How appropriate." She thought, as she fantasised about the forthcoming date.

That evening there had been a lot of people on the train and she felt less unhappy about the impending train strike. She decided that any change from this daily crush would be welcome. It was a fair distance to her work from South Kensington but she supposed she could manage it for a day.

Back in the flat she flung her things onto the chair and flopped down on the bed. Janice had not returned yet. Although she had less distance to travel, she often had to stay late depending on what the day brought. She worked for an advisor to the Minister for War and any emergencies had to be dealt with immediately. It seemed to Carole that there was always a crisis in Foreign Affairs and that the country was living on a knife edge in its relationship with the Soviet Union. She couldn't think why, they had seemed such nice people, when she had met them at the Soirée. Of course, she had been with people who had needed to flee their country so things were different for them, she thought.

Carole had heard talk of a March on London to Trafalgar Square in protest at Britain having a Nuclear Bomb and realised that this was a serious issue. In her talks with Janice they had discussed Nuclear Disarmament but did not think there was anything she could do. After all, that was what we relied on Government for, wasn't it? She reasoned.

All this introspection somehow took away her enjoyment of the moment, peeling potatoes! Just then Janice arrived and such thoughts were forgotten.

"Oh, I picked up this message in the lobby," said Janice. "It's from Nicholas."

Carole was all attention. "What does he say?"

"He asks us to meet him at 'The Prince Leopold' in Sloane Street at 6.00 pm as they are meeting friends there and he sends kisses to you Carole!" Said Janice, looking at her friend mischievously, seeing the light in her eyes.

****

Nicholas had gone about his duties and engagements with only half his mind and, despite pushing his thought out of the way to concentrate on the work at hand, he had been unable to think straight. He had agreed to this adventure with little thought of the consequences here in England. His main priority had been the furtherance of his father's release from the Gulag and that was enough.

It did him credit that he had developed a conscience towards Carole but was far from understanding his motive. His relationships with the fairer sex had been that of young men of his age, who had found willing consorts, but his education was far from complete, because he had never found his deeper emotions even remotely stirred by these encounters. To be subjected to these new feelings and strictures of conscience were new to him and bore all the hallmarks of infatuation. That he was completely unaware of the consequences he was about to unleash in his life made for an amusing spectator sport for Alex, and Nicholas was looking forward to Saturday more than he would admit.

Every day seemed to drag by as they counted the days off until the end of the week. Carole had managed to keep her level of concentration up, but Mr. Bailey had looked hard at her on a couple of occasions. She was lucky to have such an understanding boss but she couldn't count on his indulgence forever.

He had a family out at Pinner and had taken an avuncular interest in her welfare, after all he had three daughters himself and he thought he knew everything about the female mind or at least he was learning that they were too soft hearted for their own good.

At last the day of the Ball arrived and the two girls had spent most of the day getting ready. There was much prancing and preening as they flaunted their costumes at each other. Their visit to the 'boutique' had proved very fruitful and they had dressed their hair in 20's style with a headband to match. They had entertained Anna the previous evening. She joined in their excitement and suggested she had just the thing for them to wear with their dresses.

"I found these in the drawer which I remember wearing. I insist you wear them to the Ball. I wore them when I was young and I would love to see them being put to good use again" and she gave them two sets of pearls to wear.

"Oh, how lovely," said Carole as she could see that the large pearls would be perfect with her cream and gold beaded gown, "but you have been so kind already lending the dresses."

"No, no, I insist. I realised afterwards that I had just the jewelry to go with the dresses and they have not been worn them for 30 years!"

"They will give you extra sparkle and allow me happy thoughts instead of sad ones," And suddenly there were tears and a look of anguish passed over her face. They were all silent as they thought of the sad events that had brought her to England. They knew enough about the horrors that had engulfed the Royal Family to realise they were desperate reasons. They could not imagine what had turned Russians into such barbarous people that could murder their Royal Family, the Tsar, Tsarina and their beautiful children. Such had been the reality of Anna's world.

By the next morning, they had forgotten such reflections as they prepared for the evening ahead with great excitement.

They wrapped up well with thick coats to keep out the night chill and headed for the underground and Sloane Square. They wondered what the new friends were like and were reassured by the good manners of the two young men they had met. The evening entertainment was due to go on all night and was to have two bands playing alternately so there was no hurry to be at the Ball and it had been suggested that they start at the nearby pub.

They pushed open the ornate crystal window glass doors into the saloon bar. It was already full but still not too noisy so it was possible to make themselves heard over the hub of noise. To their surprise, two of the other girls were known to them from the earlier Soirée, Barbara and Sheila, who were at Le Lycée Français. They were accompanied by two fellow students, Boris and Georgiou, and all was set for a great evening.

All the ladies exclaimed over their frocks and agreed that the gentlemen looked very impressive in their white tie and tails. Barbara joked. "So, who is going to show us the dance steps? You all look the part as Fred Astaire but can you dance like him?" At that Boris jumped up and began to dance a waltz around the room, with an imaginary girl.

Carole remembered the dance steps her father had taught her for the Charleston and the Black Bottom. Her mother had recounted how, as schoolgirls, they had practiced waiting at the bus stop, squeezing their knees together and kicking up their heels. Up she stood and, humming a tune, started to dance. There were whoops of approval from the rest of the group. Soon they were all trying to outdo each other in some way. Nicholas was a high-stepping Cossack and Alex found the piano and began to play Music Hall tunes. Janice, at some point, had given a few instructions in 'The Gay Gordons" and after whispering into Alex's ear, began in a clear piping voice, "My bonnie lies over the ocean, my bonnie lives over the sea."

Next, Boris took his turn at the side of the piano, and in a full baritone voice, began to sing a Russian folk ballad about a snow sweeper. At this the party seemed to become melancholy, as the song had somehow touched the hearts of the students who were far from home.

"Come on, we've been here long enough." Said Nicholas briskly and they all collected their things. It promised to be a lively night and it was obvious that Boris was going to be the life and soul of the party.

Carole was surprised at the amount of alcohol they were drinking but she had no intention of following their lead. She intended to stay sober. There was more fun to be had in dancing and her family tragedy had been the result of youthful folly in that direction.

The pub was already hazy with cigarette smoke. On the air, she smelt a strange new tobacco more pungent than she had known before. It was not cigar smoke but something infinitely more noxious and exotic.

When they arrived on the doorsteps of the College of Art they found the party in full swing. They found seats not too near the bandstand and watched the dancers whilst drinks were ordered. After their exuberant display earlier, the boys seemed to be egging each other on to start the dancing. The ballroom dancing was a little formal for some of them but Nicholas swept Carole onto the floor at the first quickstep and Alex followed close behind with Janice. Here they were in perfect unison and she surrendered to his practiced touch. The memories of their first dance came flooding back and also the feelings he had evoked. There was a hunger in her that she had never felt so strongly and the dancing heightened this sensation. She felt giddy with the spell and everything seemed perfect. When she looked into his eyes she saw a responding excitement.

She had thought long and hard about this evening and was prepared to let the evening take its course. She now knew, that Peter had been just a teenage romance. Here was a man full grown who would perhaps have more serious passions. There was a hint of danger in every glance he gave her. He also seemed more assured and popular with his friends and seemed to be the one organizing the group. It was pleasant to be in such good hands and she surrendered to the pace of the evening. The party became more lively, as the evening progressed. They had changed to a jazz band. Chris Barber and his Jazzmen now held them in thrall as they jived, twisting and turning in endless computations as the pace of the music unbuttoned their inhibitions.

Their friends from the 'Lycée' were egging Boris on to even wilder extremes. They seemed familiar with this routine and knew the affects that the alcohol would have on him as they plied him with drinks, especially strong spirits, and his capacity seemed boundless as he entered into the party atmosphere.

The evening had turned to morning some while ago and couples began to pair off and she and Nicholas continued their mutual exploration. They realised that the last dance was about to start. They took to the floor once more.

This time it was a slow waltz with the band playing 'Moon River.' 'How much more romantic could it be.' She thought. As the dance ended Carole went to the cloakroom. She needed to tidy up and she had made up her mind that tonight might be the right moment to pass into womanhood and she was not about to go unprepared.

She walked off the dance floor. idly running the pearls through her teeth. They looked beautiful but once or twice had nearly caught on a button of Nicholas's jacket and had thought to take them off and store them for safekeeping. As Carole was about to do so, she registered a sensation of grittiness through her teeth and gasped. She couldn't believe what she had felt and ran the pearls along her front teeth once more. Yes, there it was again a sharp grit sensation, confirming that what she had thought to be artificial pearls were genuine and of such a size that they would be worth a fortune.

Her dismay was followed by fear that they would either break or be lost before the night was out. She had no idea that her neighbour could possibly own such a precious piece of jewelry. She now suspected that what she had taken to be a copy of a Matisse, was probably genuine. So why not pearls as well? They had been given the jewelry with such casual generosity that they were unaware that special care needed to be taken. But she was acutely aware of their possible value for didn't she handle such items that came to be auctioned at Messrs. Bailey, Bailey & Whigstaff.

Carole carefully took off the pearls and thought what to do with them as her handbag didn't seem safe enough. She was still reeling from this knowledge when she returned to the dance floor to tell Janice of her discovery. What on earth had possessed Anna to lend her such precious pearls?

She desperately wanted to talk to Janice but hid them quickly in the double lining of the bodice of her dress. Before she had an opportunity to take Janice aside, Boris came over with a tray full of drinks for them all. "Just a little nightcap to see us on our way." Whilst he was talking to the others, with her head in a whirl, she began to sip her drink. Oh no, she grimaced, this is gin, I don't even like it, so perhaps someone else would like it instead, and she moved the glass to the other side of the table, picking up her old glass which was still half full. Boris picked up the glass that had been given go Carole and raised it high. "To a lovely evening and to our fair maidens." And his eyes, looking across the table at Carole, held a strange glint. He tossed it back and they all began to gather their belongings. There was a sniggering sound coming from Barbara and Sheila and they seemed to be taking special notice of Boris.

They reached the front door and, as the cold air flooded in, Boris staggered and reached for the pillar then slid to the floor. The girls laughed out loud and gestured to the boys to put Boris on a bench conveniently nearby.

"Oh, true to form," said Barbara, "Boris is great company but he can't hold his drink. Let him sleep it off. What a head he will have in the morning after all he has drunk tonight." Carole felt rather sorry for him especially as he had probably added her drink to the rest.

However, at this point she was not feeling too good herself. She had gone pale and faint and was beginning to feel sick. Nicholas, who had helped Boris to the bench, came back in deep thought and saw her state. He gave one more look at Boris and took Carole by the arm.

"Don't worry, I will look after you, you look pretty faint. Perhaps it is better that you come to my place as it is much nearer."

"Fine." she murmured as everything around danced and swayed and fought to stop the sickness that assailed her. He hurriedly explained what was happening to Carole to his friend Alex, who agreed to help, took Carole around the shoulders lifting and half carrying her wilting form along the road with Janice in tow.

By this time. Carole was semi-conscious and when they reached the river at Chelsea Harbour, the threatened sickness overwhelmed her. She sank onto the pavement totally mortified at the turn of events. What had happened to her all of a sudden Boris might have had too much to drink but she certainly hadn't. The grave look of concern on Nicholas and Alex faces helped her overcome embarrassment. Feeling slightly better she was able to walk the hundred yards to Nicholas's place, a motor cruiser moored nearby. Still slightly queasy, she negotiated the gangplank but needed all her sea legs to make it to a bunk. She felt someone lifting her onto a bed and then nothing.

CHAPTER FOUR

Consequences – The Arts Ball

Carole was dimly aware of a knocking and a squawking that seemed to come from above her head. She tried to raise herself but fell back onto the pillow as the knocking began again. It must be all part of the awful pain which made her head feel as though something was trapped inside. Suddenly the pounding stopped and she surmised that a bird had been knocking on the roof.

"Where am I?" As the events of last night came back to her, a sense of acute embarrassment washed over her again. What had happened? She did not even have the same excuse as Boris for her sudden illness. How could she ever look Nicholas in the face again?

Whoever was knocking on the roof, seemed to have decided to go away and the invalid struggled up to survey her surroundings. It was a neatly ordered cruiser with everything in its place. Supposing the heads were in the bows as usual she clambered through to that compartment. There was a sound from the gangplank and the opening of the hatchway. "She's gone." Alex's voice shouted in alarm and Nicholas also clattered down the step into the galley.

"No, I'm not, I'm here." Carole replied in a strange croaking voice. "What happened and how did I get here?" She feigned, to stop her embarrassment.

The two men looked at her with relief and a strange look of foreboding. "At last, you're awake. Alex said. We began to think we might have to carry you out in a box."

"A box, what are you talking about?"

Nicholas came over and took her hand. He looked earnestly into her eyes. There was a look of tenderness but also fear as he stroked the back of her hand. "Things were not as it seemed last night. We all thought that Boris was up to his usual Saturday night excesses but it was not the case. We went to get some bread this morning and ran into Barbara and Sheila who were in a state of some shock. After we left, someone looked more carefully at Boris and it seems he was not just intoxicated but dead!"

"Dead," Carole repeated in an astonished tone. "How can that be? What was the matter with him?"

"We don't know yet," said Alex, "but it seems he may have been poisoned."

"Poisoned." She croaked, again unable to take in such an enormous fact. "Was it something he ate?"

Nicholas and Alex looked at each other gravely. "No," Nicholas said slowly. "I think it was something he drank and perhaps," he paused unwilling to shock her further.

"Yes, and?" She prompted him.

He took a deep breath, "and it may be that you also were poisoned." She stared at him in horror as the implication of his words sank in.

"Do you mean that someone wanted to kill me, as well as Boris?" She stopped. Her brain was getting back into gear. What if…what if the drink she had been given was the one that had been poisoned? What if she had killed him! But no, she could not be held responsible but perhaps it <u>had</u> been meant for her. The fact that she had not drunk the glass meant for her, didn't mean that she had killed him but she might certainly have been the agent of his death. She began to feel dizzy again and struggled to master her frailty.

Nicholas had seen her distress and put his arms firmly around her shoulders. "I think that is enough for now. This young lady is lucky to be alive I think and the best cure will be a cup of builder's tea," he said jokingly "and then something nourishing inside you. Janice perhaps you can get that stove working and we can re-assess the situation over breakfast!"

Soon they had the kettle boiling and the cabin ready for eating with all the relevant parts assembled, over or under in a wonderful origami of folding tables and chairs. Despite misgivings, Carole was able to eat some scrambled eggs and wonderful strong sweet tea and her thought processes began to function again. She began to piece together other things about her evening and realised that there might be much more to the events than she had first thought.

Firstly, she had discovered that she was wearing very valuable jewelry, then secondly, she may have been poisoned. What for (jewels?) Thirdly, there was an undeniable Russian thread running through all this. Why had Anna loaned them the jewelry? (What threat did they pose?) She had been very eager for her to take them to the Soirée at the Embassy but was she a poor emigre or still part of the Soviet system? She had not told them exactly when she had left her homeland but they had supposed that it was during the revolution. As she pondered this rapidly, she thought that another visit to Anna might be the best course of action.

"At this point I think it will be best for you both to go back to your flat, you will both feel better when you have had a chance to think about all this," said Nicholas.

"The College was crawling with police when we bought the bread and I expect we shall all have to give them our statements for last night's events." Said Alex.

Carole looked at Nicholas and blushed. They had the perfect alibi for most of the evening and her appearance in his boat spoke volumes about their relationship. She shook her head sadly. Her evening had not ended as she had hoped. She felt Nicholas touch her cheek.

"Don't look so sad, we had a lovely evening, didn't we?" "What might come of this might not be all bad." He looked steadily at her and whispered, "my little English rose."

Janice had already borrowed a jumper from Alex and the chill wind over the water brought the winter reality to Carole and so she also needed another jumper to keep out the cold morning air. They had lost track of time but it was now mid-day and the usual strollers were out. The sight of two girls in partial night finery was not too unusual to the passers-by on a Sunday morning. One or two smiles were exchanged as they passed but their walk to Sloane Square Station was fairly quick and their journey was uneventful. Janice had been unusually quiet on their way home and her mood matched her friend's reticence. Carole was dying to tell her friend about the pearls but felt they must be somewhere private before she told her.

As they approached their flat, they were conscious of a disturbance on the pavement ahead of them and two policemen on the steps of their apartment block. Their police car was outside and the policemen seemed to be taking statements from passers-by.

Janice went to hurry to see what was happening but Carole held her back. She was reluctant to speak to the police on any matter until she had been able to order her muddled thoughts. If the police were waiting for their return she wanted to have her story firmly fixed in her head before she had to give a statement. Some of her thoughts were very dark and Carole felt she was out of her depth about last night's events.

"Good afternoon Misses, are you tenants in this building?"

"Why yes officer, what seems to be the matter?" Janice asked.

"We are investigating an incident on the first floor! Could you tell us which is your flat?"

"Well, we are on the first floor, Flat 4. I hope it isn't something too serious?" Carole asked.

"That's as maybe. I am afraid the elderly lady from No. 1 has had a serious accident and has gone to hospital." Carole held her breath and waited for more.

"She appears to have fallen downstairs and we are here to find out if it was an accident or not."

"Can you give us some proof of your identity and where you were about seven o'clock this morning. We should also like to see inside your flat."

"Why is that," said Janice.

"Because it appears to have been burgled and your door lock is broken."

Carole and Janice both gasped. "But what for, we have nothing of value?"

“Well they were looking for something valuable because they have also been in the old lady Miss Anna Romaine’s flat too.”

They hurried up the stairs and found their flat in complete chaos. Every item of furniture appeared to have been turned over and all the drawers of their bureau had been ransacked. Every handbag and shoe box was cast asunder. The only item that appeared untouched was the iron bath resplendent on its cast iron legs and upon inspection even had dust underneath undisturbed.

“Well I don’t know what they were looking for, officer, as we have only recently taken over the flat,” said Janice indignantly. Carole remained silent and steered the conversation back to the other flat “Have they taken anything from Anna’s flat?”

“That we don’t know yet as Miss Romaine was unconscious and can’t tell us anything until she regains her senses if ever.”

They both echoed their concern, “Where is she, what hospital is she in?”

“Well for the time being she is in the Royal Brompton Hospital but the Caretaker thinks she may be moved to a private clinic when her friends hear of things.” The policeman was inclined to be a little bit more forthcoming than he should be but he felt that they were really concerned about her. He had just learnt of the possible identity of the unfortunate lady and was feeling rather important.

“Well ladies, I will leave for now but would you call at the Police Station sometime soon to make a statement and a report can be made out.”

When he had left, the girls re-ordered their chaotic flat and sat before the fire to settle their agitation. Again, the kettle was to hand and a cup of tea steadied their nerves. One traumatic event this weekend was enough but two was getting rather too close for comfort. Janice listened with dread to the story that Carole unfolded and it was not long before she realised how close to home these events really had been, that Boris had drunk the glass of wine meant for Carole. Janice broke the silence that had descended upon the room.

“One thing we must keep in mind. All of these events are connected and we must be careful whom we trust. It is hard to imagine any of these friends being involved but we must be on our guard and not tell anyone from the party what our suspicions are. There is a very real possibility that someone in our group wanted you dead or drugged and we must look as puzzled as we can until we can see more clearly. The exception to this, I suggest, would be to tell my boss who might be able to look at this from the security angle. There is a lot of information that he might glean from diplomatic channels that might have a bearing on the case.”

“Although Anna might seem a perfectly harmless old lady, she has certainly surprised us with her international and political status and more information on that front, would be useful.”

“I suspect we will also be asked for a statement about last night. If the two incidents are logged close together with the same officers, they will be asking some very particular questions. We might be very reluctant to reveal everything we suspect until we know more.”

Carole was impressed by the calm and clear headedness that Janice had displayed in just those few minutes. Carole had been mixing her emotions about the murder with her relations with Nicholas and had not stopped to think of him possibly being implicated. Her heart contracted at the thought that Nicholas could be involved but his final words to her now struck a strange note with her. Outwardly he was the very essence of a well-bred young Englishman but he had called her “my little English rose,” as though he was not English. Although she had been attracted from the first moment of their dance, there had been a nagging thought that she had already met him before but their mutual regard seemed to stifle any other reflection. Her boss had misgivings about their involvement with Anna, hadn’t he? She now realised that this might be a very misplaced trust and her foolishness might put them in even more danger.

At six o’clock a note was slipped through the door with a message saying that due to developments Nicholas and Alex couldn’t see them later but would meet them at The Prince Leopold the next evening. Carole and Janice turned in for an early night having fixed up a warning system on the top of their outer door of a jar of water to alert them of any intruders. They sighed with relief as they realised that events had taken an even more sinister turn and help from Sir Charles would be reassuring, in the light of everything that had happened.

The next morning Carole joined the commuters to the City and had time to reflect on the weekend. She had slept badly and was still feeling pretty rough. Her usual trim figure had an air of neglect and her eyes were dull. She hoped to slip passed Joe Southgate but he spied her from the corner of his eye. Her untidy appearance was immediately noted and he frowned with concern. She sped on with her head down and he made no comment. He kept a sharp eye out for Mary Currie, the tea lady, who usually knew most of what happened in the building. “Good morning Mary, I have a little job for you today. See what is up with Carole if you can. She doesn’t look her usual self.”

“Oh my, I am sorry to hear that. She is usually such a happy young lady and so friendly. I hope it is just usual tribulations. It’s alright for those that live at home in London but these girls that come from elsewhere need a bit of an eye keeping on them.”

Later in the morning Mary brought the trolley into Carole’s office and said. “Good morning. I have some lovely doughnuts for you today”

“Oh, nothing for me.” Said Carole absently.

“Why what’s wrong with you, honeybun, you’re usually one of my regulars? What’s the matter, are you going down with a cold? You've got to keep up your strength if that is the case You certainly look peaky this morning." May asked

"Oh Mary, thank you for your concern but it's nothing you can help me with. I have to sort this one out on my own."

Mary opened her mouth to say more but remained silent, thinking that she had said enough already but was concerned at Carole's appearance. Mary hoped she had not "got herself in trouble, but somehow, didn't think so. Carole was touched by Mary's concern. Some of the girls in the office thought she was a 'nosey parker.' Carole thought of her as kind heart and didn't resent her enquiries. This was the nearest to what she was used to at home and through Mary she saw that not everybody in London was unfriendly.

When Carole passed Joe at lunchtime her heart lurched. He was deep in conversation with a young policeman. She heard Joe gasp and say, "well I never." but did not stay to hear anything else. She needed to clear her head for when she eventually was called to give a statement.

When she returned to the office Joe called out. "I need a word with you, Miss."

"Oh yes? What's up Joe you look very serious?"

"Well I have just had my lad in here from his Manor and West London Police have asked him to trace the whereabouts of Miss Carole Semele. There was a young man who died at the Chelsea Arts Ball. You were there, weren't you? Did you see what happened? Anyway, they are interviewing all the people who were there that night." Carole looked at him, her face going pale

"Yes, Joe I was but I didn't know anyone had died. Did your son say how he had died, was it a drug overdose or something? Some weird things were being used but mostly, purple hearts were around. You know, to keep us all awake throughout the night." She feigned a certain knowledge of these things but she had not taken them herself. She had seen such things being passed around at Art College but it had never appealed to her. Life was exciting enough without such things and they seemed to be a substitute for anything in life that was better. She had seen one or two incidents in her years at College and didn't think much of them. The more she elaborated her story the more she wondered if indeed she had imagined all her suspicions.

"I don't think they know yet but they would certainly like you to pop into Chelsea Police Station when you get home." Her heart sank but she knew that she couldn't put off her story any longer.

That evening there was no way that she could avoid the headlines in the paper as there was a picture of Boris, there on the front page of the **London Evening Recorder** '*Balladeer sings his Swansong.*' 'Boris Ustinov sang his last sweet ballad hours before he was struck down, in the middle of enjoying dancing the night away at the Chelsea Arts Ball. Hours earlier, he and his friends had been singing merrily in the 'Prince Leopold Tavern' where he had sung a tribute to his home country, 'The Snow Sweeper,' a well-known Russian folk song. Although Boris had been schooled in England his parents were Russian Emigrés, living in Paris but he still had family in Russia.'

Well that was news to her as, apart from his name, he had no discernible Russian accent and she had not realized his origins, with his blond hair and blue eyes. Indeed, the only trace of Russian she could think of was his ability to drink hard liquor. But that was surely shared by every nationality. Someone very close had obviously not minded telling all they knew about him but it gave even more credence to her own theory of Russian connections. Somehow those pearls were connected and her hasty disposal of them before she knew of the murder seemed as foolish now as it had seemed inspired when she had hidden them earlier.

Carole phoned Janice later in the day and agreed to meet her to go to the police station together and to agree upon their version of events during the evening of the murder. That someone had spiked his drink was a possibility but she had withheld the fact that it was meant for her from Janice as it had seemed an unnecessary complication. Now she wondered if that had been wise. It had seemed an appalling thought that she might have been the instrument of his downfall but the alternative, that it might have been meant for her, was even more frightening to contemplate.

"Thank you, ladies," said the Sargent, "for coming

in to make a statement. Of course, there were many people at the event but you were both part of the same party so your statements were most useful. Just don't leave London, as we may wish to speak to you again."

They walked away much relieved that they had not been asked any awkward questions and made their way to the 'Prince Leopold.' They found the same party of revelers that had been there on the Saturday night, minus one.

Nicholas spotted them coming through the door and jumped up to greet them. He gave Carole a big hug and kissed her on the cheeks. "We are so glad to see you both and relieved to hear that you are alright." His obvious relief seemed at odds with what he knew and he appeared to be better informed of the burglaries than expected. "When I came around to see you on Sunday, the caretaker told me of the happenings in the apartment block. Have you seen your neighbour yet? Is she alright now?"

"We don't know as our time has been taken up at the Police Station, so we haven't heard any more. But it sounded serious so we shall try to go to see her tomorrow."

"Poor lady, perhaps we should all buy her a bunch of flowers to cheer her up." Suggested Nicholas and Carole agreed to take them. Again, he appeared to have a kind heart and she thought that admirable.

Janice had brought the **London Evening Recorder**

and put this in front of them all. "Look at this headline everybody. Someone was quick off the mark with this amount of detail to the story." Barbara and Sheila looked uncomfortable and hung their heads.

Barbara piped up, "I suppose you'll hear it from someone sooner or later. I did it. There was a journalist on the spot pretty quickly and, when we heard that Boris was dead and that our assumption of his being drunk proved to be false. We hung around and somehow this journalist got all these details from us."

"So," said Janice, "how did you know all about his background?"

Sheila and Barbara looked at each other, then over to Nicholas, Alex and Georgiou. Nicholas nodded and Sheila explained.

"Didn't you know we are all Russians? We were sent to English public schools to get us as far away from Russia as possible. Most of our parents live in Paris although Nicholas had family in Montpelier."

At that moment of shocked silence, as they digested yet more news about the Russian connection, Carole looked over to Nicholas as he casually poured some beer into his glass with his left hand, showing his slender wrist with a Rolex watch above it. At last the jigsaw was complete and she remembered where she had seen him. It was at the Soirée, serving champagne, and he had topped up her glass. The elegant wrist and watch and the serving of the wine from a different angle had meant that she had glanced up at his face as he bent towards her. If their eyes had met of course she would have remembered him. Carole gave a sharp intake of breath and this time, as the glass was filled, he glanced up and their eyes met.

So, there we have it, thought Carole. The pieces of the puzzle are falling into place. Much thought had gone into this elaborate plan. she realised. It was slowly dawning on her that there was perhaps more at stake than a pearl necklace. It seemed that a simple burglary would perhaps have served the same purpose but why was she set up to take the pearls away from Anna's house? There seemed to be no clear reason why she should have been dragged into it. Even her supposed accidental meeting with Nicholas could have been designed to attract her attention and she couldn't face that thought. That all his actions had been a calculated charade. She swallowed back a sob and held his gaze.

"So, I suppose you all know Anna Romaine as well and your gesture of flowers is because of personal knowledge. Why don't you all come to visit her since you have obviously made her acquaintance" She said drily.

"Oh no," Alex explained "we couldn't do that. She is far too elevated for us to presume, although we obviously know who she is." Carole caught a slight shake of the head from Nicholas and Alex said no more.

The party seemed to sink into their own thoughts until Nicholas spoke up. Gently he took Carole's hand

and put it to his cheek. "You see we are all émigrés but we are all from a different stratas of society, not obvious to our English hosts," He paused, "And for some of us, the old life is still real. There are still family members who live there. We have to think of them when we show our loyalties in England. There are always people who will report any actions that they consider compromises our allegiances." He looked her straight in the face with a wistful smile. "Not all our actions are calculated and unforeseen consequences result." She tried to control her beating heart but her distrust was melting away.

At that it seemed enough had been said and Carole and Janice had to be satisfied with their explanation. Nicholas and Alex walked them home through the dark streets. They seemed to have explained much that had puzzled them and they walked back home without misgivings but they were no nearer to knowing what Boris's involvement in his own death had been Carole still held back from telling Nicholas about her suspicions and did not mention the reality of the string of pearls.

They arrived back at their flat and Nicholas drew her close to him. "Don't think that meeting you is unimportant. You are special and I shall always be glad that duty has brought me to know you." He kissed her with passion and her restraint was abandoned in that moment as she realized the power he had over her.

CHAPTER FIVE

The Secret – Suspicions

The next day the girls were able to get to work on time but the questions still remained. Why had Boris died? Who had put the poison into the glass and how much did the others know about the pearls? It seemed that Anna had intended the pearls to be out of her house for some reason but so far that had not become clear. They decided that they would visit Anna in Royal Brompton Hospital that evening and perhaps find her awake and able to tell them something of this mystery.

When she arrived at work, Joe Southgate was looking out for her. "I hope you managed to get to the police station yesterday. It must be very upsetting for you. Remember you can always come to me if you are in need of help. I know Steve is not involved in the case but he can always be there if you need to talk to someone." She thanked him for his concern as she surmised that by now the whole of the office knew of her involvement in this drama.

Mr. Bailey was already in very early that morning and again repeated what Joe had said. "If you think you would like some time off during this week let me know but, in the meantime, we have an auction to get organized so we need to concentrate." For the rest of the day she was hard at work dealing with all the matters attending and was looking forward to Auction Day as it was always fun to see how the prices ebbed and flowed. There were several important galleries represented and it was whispered that the Queen's Art Advisor might be looking at some Romanov art that had come in from the Baltic.

After such a busy day Carole was eager to get home. She had grabbed a couple of sandwiches from the local sandwich bar in Pudding Lane as there would not be a lot of time before she went to see Anna at the hospital. Janice had already arrived when she returned and had lots to tell her but just mentioned that her boss was very interested in what was happening.

When they arrived at the hospital they were directed to a private room in the Neurological Department. They were surprised to see that there appeared to be a guard on duty. When they asked at the desk whether they could visit, the nurse looked rather worried.

"Well," she said, "I don't think so as she is still in a coma. We see signs of returning senses but it is far too soon to allow visitors." They gave their flowers to a nurse who said, "Would you like to sign the visitors book?" They bent to sign their names and saw that most of the names already there were of Ambassadors and Politicians, including Foreign Ministers and Attachés from European countries. Who was this woman who seemed so insignificant and yet was someone of some stature? As they prepared to leave they could hear an altercation between the nurse and a heavyset man in a black suit, who appeared to be telling her off. It was clear that she had allowed them beyond where they should have been taken. They thought it was best to slip away while the argument was still in flow and before the man saw them.

By the time that they had arrived home, Janice had brought her up to date on the interest her boss had shown in their Russian friends. He had ordered profiles of the people in their group at the Ball. This was fairly easily come by with his authority and, although he did not disclose any more to Janice, it was clear that they were of particular interest to him. He urged the girls to maintain their friendships with the group but cautioned them about what they might tell them. Janice had told him that they were all émigrés so their credentials could easily be checked.

"I told him that they were mostly students at Le Lycee Francais and the school should have decent records of their students. For the time being he said we should act normally and work as usual." So, they were left to make sense of the puzzle.

"Carole, you will be surprised to learn that he was very attentive to what I had to tell him. He seemed very interested in what had happened to Anna and ordered profiles to be produced of the members of the group."

"Really Janice? I wonder why such people would

interest him rather than the police."

Carole was beginning to see that her role in the evening of the Ball had been more significant than she had been prepared to tell anyone. But questions would soon be asked as to the motive of the killing and who stood to gain by his death? No one so far, had connected the pearls with the death but she knew that the real victim was meant to be her. She tried to work out who had access to their drinks before sitting down, after her discovery of the authenticity of the pearls. Boris and Georgiou had been standing at the table watching the dancers but he was very attentive when she returned to the table in offering her the drink. However, she did not know who had been at the table when the glasses were brought or, indeed, anything that could have happened at the bar. She felt it imperative to discover the motive.

She could probably rule out the two other girls, Barbara and Sheila, as they wouldn't have been to the bar and could not direct the drinks to be certain of reaching her. They were certainly amused at Boris when he downed his drink but drew attention to themselves so it was unlikely behavior if they wanted to escape detection. Alex and Janice, who were not very far from the table when she returned, had fetched her coat, so were unlikely to have had time to put anything in the drink before Carole had returned. Anyway, she had seen them coming from the cloakroom. That left Nicholas and Boris himself, if she discounted the bar staff. As they had little connection with anything else she felt she could rule them out.

With a sinking feeling, she realised that the same was not true of Nicholas. Oh Nicholas, her heart raged, it can't be you. All her instincts were to trust him but already she had learnt that there had been calculation in his actions. He had also been very anxious to get her away from where Boris had been laid on the bench. Had he already discovered that his plan had backfired and that the wrong person had been killed? "My illness was the perfect cover for him to take the pearls but that had not happened. He had certainly had opportunity when she had lain prostrate in his boat but perhaps there were too many witnesses.

Had Alex and Janice been with him all the time? If so, it would have accounted for him having no opportunity to look for them as they had been right there under his nose. She laughed mirthlessly when she remembered what she had done. His obvious care and concern had blinded her to his possible involvement and she had jeopardized any possible proof of her innocence by her hasty hiding place. When she had been told of the full extent of the evening's events on the Sunday morning, she had hidden the pearls in the heads amongst various nautical clutter of ropes and anchor and had thought them safe until being able to retrieve them.

Now her only hope of proving her innocence was to get the pearls back and return them to Anna. Well that was not going to be easy. They had seen how serious her injury was and it seemed there was now an armed guard. The very possession of the jewels could be seen as a possible burglary by us, made to throw the police off the scent and might even be a reason for murder. She prayed that Anna recovered her senses and shed some light on why she had really given them the pearls as someone knew that she had this valuable heirloom, as indeed they must be.

The following morning Carole arrived at work looking even more careworn, much to the alarm of Joe. That morning the headlines in the paper had announced that the death was now subject to a murder enquiry as it had been established that Boris had been poisoned by a substance not usually found in either alcohol or recreational drugs and the wild 'goings on' at the Arts Ball could not be blamed as the cause of death. There had followed many reports of licentiousness by the partygoers but she knew that the accounts of such behaviour were out of the imagination of the reporter rather than anything she had seen or experienced. No, she certainly couldn't put her sudden illness down to purple hearts or cannabis, etc., although she had certainly smelt it on the wind.

A policeman was quoted as saying 'In the light of these findings, we shall be broadening our enquiries.'

Yes, thought Carole, this is where I shall really have to be careful.

That day there was a memo going around the office which read:

> *'Due to the impending underground strike, it was thought sensible to put in place some*

contingency plans. As many of the people in this building have to come a long way to work, it was thought that perhaps some of those who live nearer might offer accommodation to associates. Below would you please put your name down either if in need of help or anyone who may be willing to offer accommodation.

<u>Out of town</u>   <u>Town Accommodation</u>:

Carole was relieved to think that her journey to work would be only one way and wondered who might house her for the night. There were many of the girls who worked in the building who lived just over the river in Southwark but she hoped that it was not a complete stranger with whom she was paired.

Downstairs Joe Southgate had seen the same notice and it occurred to him that, if his missus would agree, it might be a good idea to offer a bed for the night to Carole. His boys would probably be called to do overtime or nights as there were bound to be a lot of problems over the stoppage and so a spare bed could be made available. If either of the boys returned early, they could bunk up on the settee for half a night at least.

He had noticed that her sunny smile had completely disappeared since the murder and it was clear that something was worrying her. Surely, she could not be implicated? But he was a man of action and thought that if he could help, then this might be the moment to delve a little further into what was troubling her. At the very least he might be able to point her in the right direction, especially as Steve was not investigating the case but might be able to give some advice.

When he put it to her the next day, Carole was surprised but supposed it was better than a stranger. Anyway. she had established a link there as Peter knew Joe's younger son, Tom who was serving his time of National Service in Gravesend. They agreed that she would stay with them the next Tuesday night.

Arriving home that evening there was a complete stranger on Carole's doorstep who introduced himself as Detective Constable West. He had wanted to know more about their movements on the Sunday morning after the Ball.

"I can't tell you much officer," said Carole. "I am afraid I was taken ill just before we left. I was dizzy and feeling sick and my friend here, together with our partners, left as soon as we could. We were aware that Boris had fallen down. Fellow students who were with him had suggested that it was usual for him to get very drunk and thought that he was just in the same state. He had certainly drunk a lot that night. I don't remember much else as my own discomfort was beginning to be overwhelming."

"Erm, what do you think caused your attack?" He asked.

"I don't know as I drank very little but we had been dancing a lot and I thought at the time that was the cause of the dizziness but, well," she paused. "I've never had anything quite like it and I had no headache at that time. I mean," she added, "I've never been to an 'all night' party before and it had been pretty hectic."

"You were dancing quite a lot, you say. Who was your dancing partner?"

"Nicholas Baron."

"Did you stay with him all the evening?"

"Mostly," she said, "but towards the end of the evening, I went to the Ladies."

"What did you do then, do you remember?"

"Well, Janice and Alex had collected my coat and when we returned to the table Boris had bought us all a drink. We toasted an end to the Ball and gathered our things together. Shortly after this I began to feel ill and have a very hazy memory of leaving the building."

"Did you know that Boris was dead?"

"Of course, not! The girls from Le Lycée Francais had convinced us that, falling over dead drunk, was pretty much normal Saturday night behavior for Boris and the men unceremoniously dumped him on the bench, to sober up later. I am sure they would have called an ambulance if they had realised but, one way or another, they were not very 'switched on' by that time in the morning."

The detective continued to write in his black book. “That seems to be about all at the moment.”

“One other question I must ask. Do you know of any reason why someone would kill him?”

She held her breath and released it slowly. “No, officer. I can’t think of a single reason why he might be killed.”

Carole had tried to keep her words steady but was alarmed to hear, in her voice, a slight emphasis on the word ‘he’, and hoped that the detective had not noticed. At that moment, Janice appeared and the detective put the same questions to her. She gave more or less the same answers and remained calm but puzzled. “We really have no idea.”

CHAPTER SIX

The Old Sea Dogs – Plots

Mr. Harry Bailey was a dapper man who liked to sport his own brand of elegance. His well fitted suit of English tweed, hid most of his imperfections and increased his height imperceptibly and, to the trained eye, spoke of Savile Row tailoring. His double cuffs held monogrammed cuff links and he had a red bow tie. He sported the latest short, straight, double breasted waistcoat in mustard yellow to tone with his suit. Perhaps this was a mistake, he thought, as he had put on a few pounds recently and it was more difficult to keep the whole ensemble together. He had chosen a second higher button fastening but the button was threatening to escape from its buttonhole. He sighed as he thought of the penance he would have to endure to get back to his true self. Late lunches and fine wine were his downfall, but in the Arts world decisions were made slowly and all the finer points of the deal needed to be savoured over a long lunch.

However, today he was going to an altogether different lunch date. He was meeting an old acquaintance whose association went back a long way. In fact, they had been at school together at Harrow and Charles had been in the same House.

Some years later they had met in the Army when he had served in the Intelligence Corps. They were not natural family friends as his father had been a City Merchant who had prospered in the wake of WW1 and Charles was from an old established family of Bankers. Their work, interviewing prisoners during the last days of WW2, had forged a common bond in their love of Iconography. There were many soldiers who had stripped the churches of Eastern Europe of their religious treasures, who tried to smuggle them abroad when they endeavored to avoid capture. Inevitably most of them were caught and the resulting treasure trove found its way into British hands. Harry and Sir Charles were put in charge of cataloguing and estimating the value of these items, which were to be sold to help in war reparations or were bought by various museums in England.

This bond of brotherhood had remained over the years and Harry had articles to sell that occasionally came into his hands from ships in Port. Sir Charles became a collector of such items and bought many from Harry. They had also found other ways in which they could help each other.

As Harry saw the Cheshire Cheese pub, where they were to meet, he smiled in anticipation of the good meal to be had.

On the other side of London at Whitehall, Sir Charles Willingham Wright had donned his equally expensive jacket but was dressed in one of his less fine suits. He was going into the City to meet his longstanding friend and compatriot and did not want to draw special attention to himself. Their mutual interest in Russian Art had given Sir Charles a perfect reason for meeting his friend occasionally. He had acquired his collecting passion when he had been posted to Moscow to the Russian Embassy there and his present work with Harry's Import/Export business made a fine cover for other work of mutual interest. The constant flow of Imports and Exports to Northern Europe meant that Harry was perfectly placed to alert Sir Charles if there seemed anything 'fishy' about the boats trading to and from that part of the Continent.

"Hello Harry good to see you." Said Sir Charles, as he sat down in the booth that Harry had found for them. They would be nicely private.

"I hope you have something special to offer me but let's have some lunch first. Do you want your usual steak and I seem to remember they had a half tolerable 'Fleurie' to go with that, I believe?"

They conversed in easy manner about their golf

exploits, as both men found endless fascination to be had from the sport, and it was not until the food was brought to the table that Sir Charles broached the real reason for his invitation.

"I know that you must be concerned about the events at the Chelsea Arts Ball last week." said Sir Charles.

"Good Lord, that's a bit close to home isn't it." Exclaimed Harry. "How do you know anything about that? I didn't think that was your domain."

"It isn't," Sir Charles said carefully, "but my Secretary happened to be one of the same party as the victim. I would say that begins to be very much my concern, wouldn't you? Especially when it turns out that everyone else has Russian connections. Then it begins to look very much my area of special interest."

Harry sat back in his chair and looked with interest and consternation at his friend.

"My God Charles, you don't think my secretary has got herself mixed up with your kind of work?" He broke off and looked around the busy saloon but everyone seemed to be busy with their own affairs.

"The thing is Harry, I was hoping you might do a bit of quiet surveillance there for me. You know, be a bit of a 'Dutch uncle.' See if she might confide anything to you. For the moment, there doesn't seem to be a motive, and there's always a reason for murder."

"Charles, what do you want from me?"

"Well," he said, "The thing is, she may be implicated way above her head and may not know what to do about it. There is also something funny going on at her apartment block."

"We have a V.I.P. living next door to her. I can't say more, except that she also was a victim of some sort of attack and burglary but, as she is in a coma, we do not know any more. We hope she will regain consciousness soon and tell us something. If she dies, there will be hell to pay as she is at the heart of Emigrés politics and acts as a rallying point for a certain sector of the Russian Community."

Harry seemed to be dumbfounded by the turn of events. He had come to lunch thinking that he might tempt Sir Charles to buy a nice little triptych from him or, at least, bid up the price at auction against the Queen's Art Advisor, although it would certainly go in that direction if H.R.H. wanted it. They agreed to stay in touch and hastened back in opposite directions.

****

At work on Friday Carole had managed to put all her questions out of mind as she had a lot of work to do. As there was bound to be a lot of disruption the following week, Mr. Bailey was determined to get ahead with the catalogue for the auction. If it could go to the printers by that evening with photos of special items, they would find next week's stoppage having less effect on their schedule. By 12 o'clock Mr. Bailey had given Carole all his instructions and said he would be out to lunch and back later to sign her work off. The day sped past and she was surprised that her boss was not back as it was nearly time to leave. He arrived around 4.30pm. and asked if Carole could take them to the printers on her way home.

"I suppose you are glad to get this week over. It's been pretty difficult for you. Do you think there is anything else you might know about the evening? How well did you know your companions?"

"Well actually not very well at all. We were invited to go to the Ball when we met two of them at the Hammersmith Palais. Half the party was unknown to us until that evening, although the other two girls had been at the YWCA with us and seemed to know the boys from the Le Lycée Français, so they didn't seem like strangers. The extraordinary thing is that although they seemed very English and had been to public schools here, they are, in fact, of Russian parentage."

"Good Heavens," He exclaimed, "This does sound like some cloak and dagger affair. I hope you know what you are getting involved in. I shan't rest easy until the police have got to the bottom of it. Please let me know if things turn sticky. You might even need some sort of protection if whoever has done this thinks you know more than you are letting on to the police." They left it at that, but Carole had much to ponder as she rattled in and out of the Underground tunnels.

They had heard no more from Nicholas and Alex and she was surprised to see Nicholas waiting for her on the steps of her flat. Her heart leapt and she couldn't prevent a smile coming on to her face as she saw him. Carole forced herself to walk calmly towards him although she wanted to fly. "Hi," she waved at him and as he saw her, hurried to her side and put his arms around her.

"I missed you, my little English rose." Carole turned and kissed him as she could not disguise her feelings. "I thought it was time we spent a bit of time together without the others. There is a lot of explaining to do. Perhaps we could go out for a meal."

"Well, I had made some arrangements to go to the hospital again, but come up for coffee and perhaps we can arrange something for tomorrow."

She was hoping that Anna had recovered consciousness and could answer some of the questions about the pearls. Perhaps the assailant had been known to her. At least it might be possible to get an inkling of what purpose she had in giving them to Carole.

While the kettle was beginning to boil, Janice arrived and they chatted generally. The police had interviewed Nicholas again and all the others who had been in the party.

"Yes, they interviewed me Alex and as well and all the others too but I don't think they are any the wiser. We knew Boris, of course, but socially only, and were aware he was part of a different part of Russian Society. We knew him from school actually but he was much younger than me and was a year above Alex."

They had known Boris from the College as a friend of the other two girls but could shed no light on any reason for his murder.

Alex, Boris and Nicholas had been to Winchester School but had not known each other so well there. Boris and Georgiou were the sons of Naval Embassy Staff and Alex and Nicholas knew of each other's parents but were vague about their relationship. It had always been emphasized that they should keep their home life private, as there were so many different reasons why each one of them, had come to England, and they could have very different loyalties. They sipped their coffee and Carole arranged to meet Nicholas the next evening.

"Hey, is that the time? We need to hurry as we planned to visit Anna this evening." Said Janice.

Nicholas jumped up, "Sorry to have kept you girls but remember Carole, tomorrow at 7.00 p.m." He gave her a quick hug and joyfully clattered down the staircase.

The girls needed to hurry to be ready for visiting time at the hospital but were soon on their way. There was no sign of the thickset man and the nurse was a little more positive. Anna had regained consciousness but was very weak.

"I will allow you just five minutes with her as she

may respond better to you. All that has been said so far has not been in English." The girls were relieved that this time there was some improvement.

"Are you awake, Anna? This is Carole and Janice from the flat next door? Can you hear us?" There was a flicker of her eyelashes but nothing more. "Perhaps if we speak to you, you could move your eyelids for a yes."

"Do you know who did this?" She flickered her eyelids.

"Do you know why?" Again, her eyelids flickered. "Can we get you anything? We are so glad you are recovering." She began to cough and Janice jumped up to alert the nurse. Quickly Carole bent to speak into her ear. "I know about the pearls, and they are safe for the time being." She saw that Anna was trying to speak so she bent closer.

"Nicholai, Nicholai, please tell Ni…" Janice returned with a different nurse and Anna fell silent again. As the nurse leant down to give her a drink, Anna seemed not to want it as she pursed her lips firmly shut. Did Anna think that there was something in it which she distrusted? After her own experience, she could imagine that Anna was paranoid about anyone who was treating her. She began to wonder whether the bodyguard was one of the police or some other organisation. The police hadn't made any connections to the murder yet, had they?

The first nurse came bustling into the room. "Well

girls, I think that is quite enough for one day." At this, they looked around for the other nurse who had disappeared.

"We'll call again Anna when you feel better and can perhaps bring you anything you need." Carole felt Anna clutch her hand briefly.

****

Nicholas left the flat in a state of worried frustration. After all the events that had happened that week, he needed to get Carole on her own. He had been reassured that Janice was a sensible flat mate and that two of them together would be safe but the lack of progress by the police had left many unanswered questions and he was now caught between forces beyond his control.

Earlier that day a gentleman who appeared to be from the Intelligence Service had visited him. Nicholas was surprised at what he appeared to know about him. The fact that he had been educated at one of the best schools in England and had seemed to leave his past behind had been an illusion. He had thought that his life was an open book as far as the world was concerned but he supposed he could never leave his past behind as long as his father was alive.

If only he could find the pearls that he had been assigned to retrieve from Carole. Someone else obviously knew of their existence and had been closer to taking them than he could have imagined. He also was aware of how much was at stake and he wondered how he could juggle all the forces that were closing in around him.

Nicholas knew he must get Carole alone. Then perhaps might tell him more than she appeared to know. Had she discovered the authenticity of the pearls and, if so, where could she possibly have put them. He had managed to look in her handbag, when she had been taken ill, but couldn't imagine where else she might have put them.

It seemed to him that sublime ignorance of their value would have resulted in finding them in her evening bag, if she had put them there for any innocent reason. The fact that they were not there pointed to either; her being aware of their real value and not revealing this, or, he reasoned, that they had already been stolen by someone, and she had been too taken up by events to report, that some trifle of costume jewelry was missing.

But if she knew their value why was she not declaring that the pearls were gone. He grimaced at all the implications but knew he needed to find those pearls before Carole was in real danger again

CHAPTER SEVEN

The Truce – Trust

Carole was ready in good time for her evening out with Nicholas. The bright, frosty weather that had greeted her this morning had not dispersed, so that all the trees were beginning to glitter with fresh ice. She pulled her coat close and was glad that she had decided to put her Cossack fur hat on, as the weather was becoming very wintry. They strolled down Kings Road but quickened their steps as they neared the 'Good Earth.' Chinese restaurant. Nicholas had thought that this was an unlikely place to bump into their friends and it had been well recommended for its secluded atmosphere.

They arrived on the doorstep in a flurry of breathlessness and Carole stamped her new knee length boots on the mat. Nicholas looked down on her flushed face and laughed at her rosy cheeks. "Look, you have some frost on your face." He said, promptly kissing her upturned nose. "There, I shall have to keep you safe and warm, won't I?"

Carole forgot all her misgivings as she flashed a

cheeky grin at him from under her lashes. At least they had started the evening well, she thought.

They took their seats in a quiet part of the restaurant, although it was fairly full by the time they had arrived. It felt like they were alone in the middle of all the surrounding hubbub. They began to exchange stories about their lives, gradually feeling their way with each other. Carole told him about something of her life in Shakespeare country but did not mention the tragedy of her brother's death. It seemed idyllic to him and made him realise how different their lives had been.

He told her of his earliest memories of growing up in the Caucasus with wild horses to ride and woods and grassland to play in. They had lived there until he was eight whilst his father wrote a book, which had brought deep trouble to the family. The conditions in Russia that his father, Stefan, described in his book, openly criticized the Communist Regime. He had already come to their attention when being too free with his criticism whilst teaching in Moscow. and he had been forced to surrender his professorship. Deep in the country at the family farm, Stefan had continued reflections on life in the USSR. Finally, he had written the book, which had been published abroad and smuggled back into Russia. This had incensed the Politburo and Stalin. He had been sent to the very place he had protested about, Siberia. Their life had never been the same again and his mother, together with another 'Siberian Widow,' had left Russia and they had settled in France, in Montpelier, where many other Émigrés had fled, a quarter of a century before.

Carole was spellbound at his account of his childhood. “How did you come to England?”

“Well, my father had many admirers in the U.K. and his book had been really popular here it was even made into a play. So, there were good Royalties! He had friends in the University Community who tried to look after my mother, who sadly died very soon after we arrived in France. The Russian emigres in the South of France was very protective of us but eventually it was decided that England would be best for me. There were various letters that were smuggled out from my father and he said those were his wishes.”

“That must have been very difficult for you.”

“Well, in some ways yes, as I really missed my father greatly, but there was something about the part of England I came to that seemed a continuation of my old life. The Downs were always there for me to explore. Wide open land, to roam occasionally, and the wild horses in the New Forest reminded me of my first love.” For a second she had a flash of jealousy until she realized it was his pony. They had talked so long that the other diners had nearly all left.

Carole felt that she had left a magical land and the spell was broken. “We must go,” But there was reluctance in his voice and mutely she followed him out of the door. He held her hand and by mutual consent they began to walk towards the River Thames. The frost was even colder but they were enclosed in their own little bubble of sexual arousal. He put his arm around her shoulder and she leant towards him to feel the warmth of his body. They had stopped talking but were aware of everything around them. The lights along the embankment and across Chelsea Bridge made reflecting lights on every ripple of the tide and the smell of the river was in their nostrils at every breath. She was very wide-awake and felt a quickening of desire. She had thought of this moment many times and now she felt she could slip her mooring and go with the tide and see what the morning would bring. They clattered across the gangway and opened up the hatch. Soon Nicholas had stoked the fire and put on more fuel.

Now that Carole was inside, out of the cold, she began to shiver but she knew it was from anticipation. She had taken her hat off but before she had time to think further he had taken her hand and led her into the narrow bunk bedded room beyond the galley, leaving the curtain open to the re-ignited fire, fire on both sides of the curtain. He gently took her coat and touched his lips to each shoulder. He ran his fingers down her arms and, one by one, he kissed the inside of her wrists. She leant against him and reached behind to draw his head towards her, bending her head to one side to embrace him. He kissed her neck taking the pins from her hair, releasing her golden braids, which reflected a contrast of colour, dancing in the firelight.

He knelt to her boots and untied the laces and eased them onto the floor. Meanwhile, she had loosened her stockings and, as his fingers began to explore her inner thighs, she felt a swelling tide of longing.

Nicholas had started the evening fully intending to find out what had happened to the pearls and had expected to use all his charm to persuade Carole to confide in him. When they had started on their journey to Chelsea his head was clear and his natural charm and wit had been at the ready, confident that he would disarm her distrust. It had not been long before all was forgotten as her vitality and natural beauty had worked their magic and he was entranced by her loveliness.

They had sat over their meal and opened up about their childhood. It was a strange moment of intimacy as his life, before coming to England, had been buried with his mother and he found a strange sense of belonging in telling her. His reserve in giving any details of his past had been dictated by the fact that his father was still living his life of hell and was the reason why he had embarked upon his present course of action. By the time that they had left the restaurant, he was far from thinking of anything other than the smell of her perfume and the touch of her hand. Their steps had found their way to the river without any manoeuvering on his part. Their hands had entwined and her whole body had surrendered to his embrace.

The river had flowed deep and strong as they had turned towards the boat, as if they were already moving with the singing water. The rest that followed was a haze of glorious moments that left him completely enslaved, and he knew that whatever followed he was deeply in love for the first time in his life and that he would find it difficult to choose between the two most important people in his life.

He stood in the bows watching the dawn rising over the river and smoked his Sobranie. The wind was still and the hoar frost clung to every twig of every tree lining the bank and where the flow of the river was stilled, ice had formed. A skein of geese flew over the rising sun which shone gloriously over the mudflats which had appeared with the falling tide. He finished his cigarette and returned to the galley and put more wood on the stove. He worked quietly and when he returned to the fore cabin, Carole still slept, her golden hair spread over the pillow with the glow of sleep upon her cheek.

His heart leapt and the decisions he had tried to make blew away with the dawn. He must make a truce in his plans as the day stretched ahead of them. Beyond that, tomorrow could wait. He knelt awkwardly at her side and stroked her hair and she smiled in her sleep. He could see one knee outside the blanket and he bent to kiss it, pulling the blanket aside to expose the inner side of her thigh. She moaned gently, still only half-awake, but thrust the blanket aside with her other knee leaving her exposed and complaisant. He could feel every part of him awaken and he rolled onto the inviting cradle. He arched upwards to delay the moment of entry and touched her nipple, which hardened to his touch. He bent to kiss their pink fruitfulness and waited for her response. Her body arched upwards towards him and her hands reached up for him. She was fully awake now and throbbing with the same urgency as he.

Nicholas held off, feeling the rising tide of passion in her, waiting, wanting to give her pleasure also. He touched her secret place with his penis and it was warm, and wet, and he felt her hands reach up to him as he plunged into her inner sanctum. This time the gentle wooing of the previous evening gave way to a wild and hungry urgency and he was unable to tame the mad plunging and raw need that she had awakened in him and their wild cavorting left them spent and satiated with delight. That the world outside was a dark place meant nothing to them in that moment. Here they were secure in the knowledge that they had pledged something that night and there was no going back.

The sun was high in the sky when Carole woke and the sounds of activity were all around. There were sounds of motors on the river and a seagull calling raucously from somewhere astern. Lying on the narrow bunk bed, discomfort had set in, as she lay imprisoned happily in Nicholas's arms and he, trapped flaccidly inside her. She tightened her muscles provocatively but elicited no response from above her. She couldn't believe that she could have such a hunger but, as she lay there, she considered how the evening had proceeded. She had left the flat determined to remain on guard, as she must not give her trust until she knew more about him. That resolve had been broken the minute she saw him and responded to his charm and handsome body. There was a vibrancy in him that she had never encountered before and she found herself wanting to make him her slave. She wanted him to feel her power and began to unconsciously use all the wiles of womanhood to bring him to her side. It was a strange feeling that she must, in some way, exert her sexuality over him.

This was how it started that evening but by the time he had told her something of his family story, she was meltingly, hopelessly responding in the age-old manner of a mother wanting to protect and comfort a loved one and the step beyond tiger mother to earth mother was taken and she received him as only a real woman knows how, with complete abandon and unselfish pleasing. Now she knew that she had to trust him because there was no going back from this night's abandon.

Later when they had fed each other bacon and eggs for tea and reluctantly made preparations for taking Carole back to her flat, they agreed to meet again on Wednesday as the Strike was going to play havoc with everyone's lives. This would give them both time to think about the consequences of their changed relationship. He had to be out of town on Tuesday so it seemed that a little calm reflection was very apposite.

They arrived back at the flat just as Janice stepped out of a car. The girls' eyes met and a look passed between them. It was obvious to Janice where the weekend had taken Carole but Janice seemed embarrassed by something. She had received a call on the Saturday morning and had been very evasive about where she was going. She had said that she was going to visit friends out of town but did not explain further. Now to their surprise she had returned in a chauffeur driven black limousine.

Carole had been so wrapped up in her own world that on Saturday she did not press Janice about where she was going but something was clearly different about her although not in the same way that she had changed. Janice hurried into the flat leaving them to make their goodbyes, anxious to avoid any discussion of her weekend, which might prove awkward with Nicholas standing there. It might also have revealed just how involved she was in the life of their neighbour.

Although the two girls had talked about their work, Janice had not revealed exactly which department of the Foreign Service she really worked for. She had been approached in her final year at Edinburgh University when she was reading History and Politics and Russian and her special subject had been, the rise of the Post WW1 Ideologies, Cause and Effect.' Her present boss, Sir Charles Willingham-Wright, had been a guest lecturer at one of their seminars. She had asked a couple of searching questions and he had sought her out afterwards. This had led to a promise of interview, which had turned into a full day appraisal and an offer of a job in London. This had been non-specific but when she arrived she found that she would be part of MI5.

She had been accommodated in Kensington in one of the crumbling Victorian terraces off Cromwell Road. To begin with she had been asked to stay in the YWCA. in Onslow Gardens and was told to look for a suitable friend who might later join her in a flat.

Her task had been to observe the comings and goings of her opposite neighbour, Anna, in a casual but observant way. She had not been told the identity of the lady, but the office was very interested in any visitors she might have. The leap from observer to full participation in events had happened so suddenly that she was alarmed at her own immediate involvement. All her instincts had told her that there was some set-up here but couldn't imagine what this would lead to.

When a chauffeur-driven car arrived for her on Saturday, Janice was just as mystified but felt at least that some of the questions might be answered. She was taken, as instructed, with an overnight bag through the suburbs out westwards to the country. The City was far behind her when she arrived at some imposing large wrought iron gates. At the end of a sweeping drive, the car glided passed an immaculate lawn, surrounded by specimen trees. Now the whole garden was sprinkled with hoar frost, giving the scene a fairytale appearance. Ahead was a large Victorian House and she caught her breath. Outside the front entrance saw two attendants waiting to help her out of the car.

She entered the large hallway and was greeted by a Butler.

"Welcome Miss Murray, I will instruct the maid to show you to your room but would say that the party will gather for drinks at 6.00 pm in the Drawing Room."

She was shown up to her room, which overlooked a lake, and behind, a church spire could just be seen above the tree line. Not completely isolated then, she noted. She had little idea where they had come because the last few miles had been down twisting country lanes but she had seen a sign for Buckinghamshire some time back.

She had been glad of the warmth in the car on their way, as the air had turned to freezing and, out of the shelter of the tall buildings of London, there was a mist rising over the meadows. Thank goodness, she was used to Scottish weather and there was no anxiety about suitable winter country clothes.

There seemed to be quite a gathering and Janice had to summon all her poise to contemplate the evening ahead. Meantime, she had this lovely room with its ornate iron bath and fluffy towels beckoning to her to prepare for the evening ahead. She had supposed that they would change for dinner and she had brought with her a little black dress. The beauty of it was in the fabric which was of silk damask figured with fine silk braid which gave the surface a three dimensional quality. There was a wide boat shaped neckline with small cap sleeves, showing off her fine pink skin. She had the unruly curls of her Scottish ancestors and the fiery red colour to match. Freckles peppered her nose showing through her make-up but at this season these had faded to a hint.

Looking at herself in the mirror she wished that she could be wearing the lovely pearls that had been at the heart of their troubles. A touch more lipstick, a final inspection in her mirror, and Janice was ready to see what Sir Charles had in store for her.

To many in the office, her boss was a distinguished figure who held powerful sway in his Whitehall domain but for Janice, he reminded her of an uncle who was well known for irascibility in their family, but to her, he had shown a kind avuncular nature and she did not hold Sir Charles in awe either.

The Drawing Room was already occupied by three guests. One was a young man, Ian Duncan, whom she knew of from one of the departments and the other two were strangers to her.

"Am I too early?" She asked.

"Oh no, quite on form, it wouldn't do to be later than our principal guests."

"Allow me to introduce you Sir to Miss Janice Murray, Miss Murray this is Commander Tashaun Counter and his lovely wife Minka."

The Commander looked down on her from a rather lofty height but smiling said. "You met some of my countrymen recently at a Soirée. I believe?

She hesitated as she was taken aback at his outspokenness.

"I was also at the Soirée recently but was not fortunate enough to be introduced to such a lovely young lady." He said gallantly.

"There were two of you I remember, such fine

young Englishwomen, such a rarity at our gathering of what, I fear, is becoming the refuge for old men. Did you enjoy our little party?"

"Oh yes, very much, we felt very honoured to be invited."

"Ah yes, indeed, by my dear friend Anna Romaine, I believe?" He gently allowed her to open up an avenue of conversation but she did not think it wise to speak of the repercussions of that evening and turned the talk to less dangerous ground but was beginning to feel rather curious about this stranger who seemed very well informed about her.

He was a fine-looking gentleman with just a trace of an accent. but he had a fine bearing and his shock of wavy grey hair and curling moustache gave him a very continental air. She tried to show polite interest in his Russian connections and he happily began to tell her something of his background. He had been many years in England but seemed to be part of a world that was gone. He had served during the war in the Russian Navy and had grown to admire the English Officers he encountered.

"Have you lived in England a long time?" She said hesitantly and instantly felt foolish at her prying but he happily began to tell her more.

"Well, you should ask Minka about that. She might say, too long, but I now consider it my home since arriving here after the War. Of course, we take an interest in our Mother country but do not have any wish to return in its present state, too many sad memories".

"Oh, I'm sorry if I was rather impertinent."

"No, no," he said hastily. "please, it is just the ramblings of an old man. He said with a twinkle in his eye that was anything but 'old!' And, of course I now have my family who have been educated here and do not share my nostalgia."

Just then, the next to arrive were a very handsome looking couple in their late thirties. He was tall and carried himself with military bearing and the lady was also tall and handsome who swept into the room with utter assurance. Her face was a classic oval and her soft brown hair was piled high on her head in a French pleat. She seemed to know the affect she was having on the company and acknowledged their admiration.

"You know, of course, that she is more famous than her husband." Whispered Ian. Janice looked for enlightenment but before he could say more, the room was hushed as the Prime Minister and his wife were announced, followed by Sir Charles and a little lady of genial appearance who followed in their wake. Janice, by this time, was finding it difficult to keep her composure but the wife accompanying the Russian gentleman took her hand and introduced her to the rest of the party.

"This young lady has been doing a very special service for our dear countrywoman who sadly had a serious accident last week," Minka said to the Prime

Minister's wife.

"Ah, yes, I heard that she was in a coma. So many of your hopes and dreams are focused there, Minka. Be careful."

Janice was surprised that the Prime Minister's wife should be so well informed but Janice knew that she came from a very ancient family and was well aware of the repercussions of the Russian Regime. It was dawning on Janice that what had seemed like a fact of life to her was still a temporary Regime in the eyes of the Russian Royalists and that Soviet rule might topple in a glorious Second Revolution, as indeed had happened in France in a preceding century. Of course, there were always old men with old dreams but there were sons and daughters too who had been educated to take their place in any future upheaval.

The evening continued delightfully and each person had something to add to the entertainment but politics were never discussed openly. She was aware that this was a test of her discretion as there were many openings for her to reveal her knowledge of their country.

Later the men retired to the study for brandy and cigars and the ladies made themselves more comfortable. More intimate knowledge was exchanged and Janice was asked to give a good account of herself. She modestly refused to be drawn but the Russian lady spoke up for her. She repeated the news that they had been taken to the Russian Soirée by Anna and this seemed to impress them. The tall lady, with brown hair, laughed.

"Minka will be introducing you to her young men next. She has a soft spot for young people and is always trying to pair them off. Would she be right for your darling Alexandre or Nicholai perhaps?"

"No, no, don't tease her, I am sure she will find her own way in the world, but I do feel my responsibility to those young men." Defended Minka stoutly.

A cloud passed over her face but she said no more. Janice held her breath. Had she stumbled upon some other piece of the jigsaw?

Soon the gentlemen returned and the evening drew to a close but they had meantime challenged the party to a brisk walk in the morning, as the prospect of a round of golf seemed unlikely. "If you prefer there are stables nearby where you could procure a decent hack. They are livery stables to some fine horses."

"Oh, how I long to be out with the horses on a fine winters day, the cold weather doesn't deter me but my old bones are out of practice for such sport. Perhaps we could walk over to inspect the horses, if anyone is so inclined?" said Minka.

Janice thought of those Shetland ponies she was used to riding as a child and was glad that at least her knowledge of horses would give her a platform to talk more intimately with her new Russian friend. She was very interested to find out if those two 'young men' had indeed been their partners at the Arts Ball, but perhaps those two names were common amongst their compatriots. It certainly seemed a coincidence that she must explore, for Nicholai and Alexandre translated into the very names of their partners at the Arts Ball!

Carole followed Janice into the flat. It was hard to tear herself away from Nicholas as she realised it would be three whole days before she saw him again. A sense of calm had descended upon them both as they had put aside their mistrust. The whole event had hinged upon an explanation from Anna and she was not going anywhere yet.

Nicholas also had let the weekend take its own course. Content to live in their own sheltered world of a smoky cabin and lapping water. He still knew she held a secret to the killing but what it was must remain a mystery, for the moment. For the next three days, Carole would be involved in the daily grind and, as far as he could see, would be safe enough with the family she was to stay with. He had turned a fierce eye on her when he was told that this was a family of three grown bachelors. She had reassured him that they would probably be kept busy doing night duty whilst the emergency was on. He quickly realized that three Londoners would be her best protection in the Pool of London.

One more lingering kiss and he was gone as she watched him disappear into the night. Carole caught a whiff of tobacco as he stopped to light a cigarette. Something familiar nagged at her as before, only this time it was the red butt end that was all that she could now see of him, that alerted her senses to another time and place, but was unable to grasp the key She had better see what Janice had been up to but was reluctant to climb the stairs back into the real world.

She found her putting her clothes back into some sense of order and was surprised to find her with her evening dress on her bed.

"Wow, that looks like some weekend you have had?" She queried of her friend.

"Yes," said Janice slowly, "and I have something to tell you. By the looks of you, a good soak in the bath would do you good, but it can in no way compare to the one I was using on Saturday night," She boasted, laughing.

Carole looked at her in astonishment but was content to follow her suggestion until later, with a mug of cocoa, wrapped in her quilted housecoat, she listened to Janice's story. It was with astonishment that she learned more of the mystery of the pearls. Instead of worrying that Nicholas was in league with Boris, she should be relieved to find that he had been her guardian, or, at least, the guardian of the pearls. Perhaps Anna just needed to get them out of the house without alerting whoever was after them. So, Anna's accident looked less like one than ever and the stricken look she had given them meant she was aware of her danger. Anna had tried to tell them something but she had willfully blocked it from her mind. "Nicholai, Nicholai," was what she had whispered but Carole had been afraid that meant something sinister. Then she remembered Anna's last words. "Tell Ni".

Tell (Nicholas). Had the whole evening been devised by Anna to get the pearls away from the flat and with Nicholas to watch over them as well as her? That someone was aware that she had something of value was certain but who else but Boris had the same intent. This latest information sent her to bed with singing in her soul. If only she could believe what she was thinking. That Nicholas was innocent.

CHAPTER EIGHT

The Strike

Monday dawned grey and overcast. The frost of the weekend had given way to grey skies and the wind was blowing from the west. The Underground was particularly empty that morning, as commuters had arranged their day differently. For those who could manage their work on the telephone, it was a half holiday as they were spared the two-hour commute, and many others had staggered their working hours. But for the rest of London, it was a damned nuisance and had to be endured for the sake of all. Although they grumbled, they also knew that it might herald more pay for them so there was a collective resignation and general agreement that "It can't be worse than the 'Blitz."

She arrived at work to find Mr. Bailey already there. He was looking at the triptych that had come from the 'Ice Maiden' out of Helsinki, and was proving more unusually fascinating to him. He had been asked to keep an eye on Carole but had no idea what he was meant to do. In his line of work, he could follow clues to the identity of paintings and examine them for authenticity, but as for this muddle she seemed to have got herself into, he had no experience whatsoever.

While waiting for Carole to arrive, he had stared at the picture in front of him and the more he examined it, the more his instinct told him that something was wrong. He sensed that here was a picture with all the right ingredients for a triptych, but there was something too bright about the gilding and uniform in application and, as he looked harder, he was aware that he was not completely familiar with the subject matter. It was a picture of the Madonna at the feet of Jesus and all the traditional elements were there. The Cross, the hill of Golgotha, the waiting women and St. John at Christ's feet, with the caption, 'Jesus King of the Jews,' above His head. It was put in the catalogue under the title of 'Madonna of the Pearls of Sorrow, as around her neck was a string of pearls which mingled with tears coming from her eyes in sorrowing contemplation of her son.

This was a new subject matter, unfamiliar to him and he pointed it out to Carole as an example of when to have suspicions about a painting. She looked at the figure of Our Lady and gasped at the long string of pearls she saw there. It was so like the string of pearls she had been given that she could not disguise her astonishment. She sat down heavily and stared at the object in front of her. Harry looked at her and knew that he had stumbled upon a connecting link.

"What is it Carole, what have you seen?"

She shook her head, unwilling to say more but he

pressed her and the whole incident at the Ball, of recognising the value of the pearls, and hiding them after she had known of the murder, came tumbling out. "I didn't know what to do. I just knew that someone wanted them and had tried to kill for them."

He stared in amazement. "That puts a whole new slant on the situation, but why didn't you tell this to the police?" He asked?

"I was going to but first I was also taken ill and spent the night elsewhere. When I returned to the flat it was to find it ransacked and my neighbour, who had leant me the pearls, unconscious in a hospital bed."

He frowned, "This doesn't sound like a straightforward case but I certainly think you should have told the police about the pearls, after all someone might come after you."

"Don't I know that," she said miserably, "but I reckoned as long as I was the only one to know where I had put them, and Anna was unconscious, there was nothing else I could find out.

He shook his head, "You, young ones, you think too much, and you should have left it to the police." He repeated.

Whilst listening to her he had been staring down at the triptych and his eyes roved over the attractive frame. It had a carved edge of incisions cut at different angles and distance from each other and he realised he was staring at Cyrillic script.

"What on earth…" he mumbled, but quickly saw that this puzzle must be solved by more expert eyes than his and he was not about to say anything more. In haste, he quickly penned a message to Sir Charles and sent it, with the triptych, to Whitehall with a messenger.

***

When Sir Charles had finally got to work on Monday he was met by a messenger who handed him a parcel, saying he needed to look at it straight away. He tore the packaging and saw the triptych he had been offered by Harry last week and a letter explaining. He was cross with himself that he had not made arrangements to stay up in London.

Dear Charles,

Perhaps you would give this more than your usually close scrutiny. I was looking at this earlier and something was not quite right about it. As I searched the icon, I could see that the subject matter was familiar but of an unknown name for Mary "Madonna of the Pearls of Sorrow", I have never heard of such an appellation and began to look more closely. As you know, from my little knowledge of Russian, I devised that the carved surround was Cyrillic Script but did recognize the name of the ship mentioned 'The Ice Maiden' as we currently have a ship of that name docked in London, which has the name in both Roman and Cyrillic letters.

Perhaps you would cast an eye over the rest of the picture and see if you can make any connections to the present ship.

It seems a bit of a coincidence, don't you think?

Yours, Harry

***

Sir Charles took one look at the triptych and decided to change his plans and arranged to stay in town. It was going to be a long night.

Memorandum to Harry: *Good luck. My special interest is giving me pearls of wisdom and I have acted upon them. The Strike has proved a welcome interruption for furthering our interest but no breakthrough yet.*

Charles.

****

"We'll let that rest for the moment." Said Harry after he had sent the message. He asked Carole, "You are staying with Joe Southgate tonight, aren't you? You should be safe with them but think of anything else that might lead to the killer." She dropped her head and realised miserably that it could just lead the Police to her, and that it would be hard to prove her innocence.

At coffee break, Mary Currie came around as usual

and was pleased to see Carole take her usual doughnut from the trolley. "There Honeybunch, got your appetite back again I see. I hear you are going to stay at Joe's house tonight. His wife will love that, another woman in the house for a change. She moans something rotten to Joe about having a house full of boys with dirty boots and jackets and shirts in all states of condition. Someone has to do the mucky jobs but she has to clean and press four sets of menfolk's uniforms." She went on in that vein and Carole could only put in a word or two. Presently she continued on her way, having managed this conversation whilst pouring all the coffees.

Having worked hard on the Friday last to get ahead of the Strike, Carole found the day rather quiet. After typing up notes that Mr. Bailey had prepared, the day dragged on for he had gone out for an early lunch and had not returned. She found herself in a reverie about the weekend and she was glad that she could let her thoughts run free. Every time she thought about Mr. Bailey's words, about telling the police, she pushed it to the back of her mind and returned to re-living all her precious thoughts about the weekend.

Once started on her reflections, time flew and was brought back to reality by Joe putting his head round the door. "Have you got your things, the management have decided to close the building early, so if you have done here, we can go?" She grabbed her things and joined Joe and thousands of other workers streaming across London Bridge and pretty soon they came to a whole block of pre-fab bungalows that had sprung up on the building site shortly after the War.

There were billboards announcing new tower blocks to be built on the site. Joe pointed to the sign and said "We should have had those five years ago. It'll be another five before we get them, if we're lucky!" He walked up their tiny garden path and turned to the back door. "Welcome to our humble abode." Joe said proudly.

She stepped into the most amazing kitchen she had ever seen. Everything was streamline and cupboards lined the walls in one continuous flow. There seemed to be a space for everything and all the kitchen equipment was in miniature. He took her into the living quarters, which again had sofas attached to the walls, and carried her bags through into one of the tiny bedrooms which had beds attached to the walls with their own side drawer, and at the end of the bed, a wardrobe stretched from wall to wall. This was quite different to what she had expected but everything was spick and span. 'How did they get three healthy young men in here?' She thought.

At that moment, someone called from the door. "Hello, is that you Joe. Is the young lady with you?"

"Hello Doris. Yes, she is here exclaiming over your little doll's house." And he laughed Doris laughed back and into sight came this bird-like woman with her 'pinny' on, and curlers in her hair with a net over the top.

"Allow me to introduce you to this lovely young lady, Carole. She is the office pin-up and I am delighted to bring her home to meet you. Carole this is my darling Doris looking her very best I see," He joked but it was evident that she did not mind because she smiled.

"You're a bit early tonight. I'm afraid you have caught me at my worst but I was making myself beautiful for such a lovely visitor. Joe has told me all about you and I am only sorry that my boys are not here to appreciate such loveliness."

Carole blushed at such treatment but she knew that Doris's outspokenness was charged with sincerity and a lively interest in people. She understood this lively curiosity from her childhood where every new event was passed from person to person with no embarrassment at any embellishments along the village news channel.

"It's very kind of you to put me up. I really didn't fancy walking all that way twice in a day."

"Yes," said Doris. "It's a lovely walk out in the summer, along the river, but a cold winter's morning is a different thing. I hope you fare better on your way home in the evening tomorrow."

"Now then," said Joe. "What about putting the kettle on Ma", This young lady must be parched after that walk across London Bridge?"

"Oh dear, there's me not minding my manners but it's not often we have visitors. We usually meet our friends down the road at 'The Three Bells' and so we thought we would take you there tonight. If we are lucky one of the boys will be there, if they can get away for a little while between shifts. They have had their leave cancelled in anticipation of tomorrow's disruption. It is their job to keep the City going and reinforcements are bound to be needed."

Suitably braced by the strong tea, Carole unpacked her things and thought how kind they were being. A wave of homesickness washed over her as she thought of her own parents. Her own childhood had mirrored the warmth she now found here but it had been shattered when her brother had died in the car accident and her parent's grief was so overwhelming, that she had felt the need to distance herself, to find another life. Well here she was with that new life, but it seemed the ties to hearth and home were with her forever.

Later that evening they all went to 'The Three Bells'. The bar was crowded but the hum of the place was subdued. Joe had promised that they served lovely boiled beef and pease pudding. Carole wrinkled up her nose at this delight but Doris assured her they would not have got through the war without it. Carole was more used to Welsh mutton than beef as her home had been in sight of the Welsh mountains, but this kind couple were obviously trying to please. Soon this splendid dish came, piled high on their plates. Potatoes and carrots, boiled beef and pease pudding almost spilling over the edge of the plate and producing a chorus of approval from Doris and Joe.

"This looks lovely." Said Carole, but she protested, "But this is so much."

Doris laughed. "Sorry, I forgot I was not feeding men's appetites, but don't worry just enjoy what you can." Despite her protests, she managed to 'tuck away' most of it. She had been born during the War and had experienced rationing half her life, so was reluctant to waste food but finally it was too much.

"Well done." Said Doris, whose plate was empty. "I know you are a slip of a thing but you must make sure you eat enough."

At that moment, the door to the bar opened and a tall policeman took off his helmet and looked around. He spied their table and Carole's heart sank when she saw that it was the same young man who had come to the office to tell her about the murder. Joe got up and called him over, "Steve," and a smile touched the policeman's lips and he strode across the crowded room. "Hi Dad, I managed to get away for a bite to eat. Hello Ma, my you do look handsome tonight," And he took her in a bear hug. She blushed and giggled like a schoolgirl. "Well I never, it's nice to know that someone notices my efforts." as she glanced at Joe.

With a sharp change of expression Joe laughed, "Don't mind her Carole, one piece of flattery from those hulky sons of hers, is worth ten from me. I think you two may have met before." As he gestured to Carole.

"Ah yes." He said slowly. "Indeed, how are things progressing, I haven't heard of any arrests there yet?" She wished that the evening had not turned up this upholder of the law but she was non-committal.

Joe stood up and made sure that Carole and Steve sat so that they were forced to talk to each other and he turned away to speak to some old friends. There was an awkward pause. "Have they called you in again at all?" He began.

"No," Said Carole, trying desperately to think of something to change the subject but recalled what Mr. Bailey had said that morning. "What would happen Steve if some information was not given to the police because it might hurt someone else."

"What." He said in astonishment. Well, he said gravely, "The law takes a dim view of the withholding of evidence, especially in a murder case."

She held her breath then said, "But what if telling the police might result in another person being killed?"

"Carole, that seems a very serious situation, but I urge you to think very hard about it."

"Well, yes, but what if the information could be relayed without that person involved being known?"

Steve looked at her hard and said. "You mean like an informant?"

"Well yes," She said, but didn't really like the sound of it even to herself.

"Erm..., I have to be back on duty at twelve but perhaps you and I should finish the evening with a nice cup of cocoa and see what we can work out." Carole heaved a sigh of relief and flashed Steve a brilliant smile.

'Phew,' he thought. 'What a stunner. I better get to the bottom of this and no mistake.' Soon Steve was tucking into the same hearty fare and made very short work of it.

Back home, after dusting off their coats, Joe and Steve sat in their living room whilst Carole and Doris put on the kettle for their evening 'cuppa.' As they returned with the cocoa, Joe said, with a nod to Steve, "I reckon I'm all done in. I think I will have my cocoa in bed. Doris, shall we leave these two to chat whilst we turn in. Sit and relax a bit before you have to go back on duty. I expect you will have no difficulty entertaining a young lady for a while."

Carole smiled with relief at this piece of maneuvering but thought it was a piece of matchmaking and didn't protest it anyway. Minutes passed in silence while they drank their cocoa. "About the Arts Ball," she began. "there was a little more to the evening than anyone could have imagined. I was leant a long string of pearls by an elderly lady who lived next door to me. It was a 1920's evening and she had suggested I wore them with the dress she had leant me earlier and I felt unable to refuse as she had made it clear that it would make her happy."

She paused, unsure how to proceed. "Go on," Prompted Steve.

“Well, towards the end of the evening, I had need to go to the ladies. As I walked off the floor I idly ran the pearls through my teeth. As you may know I work for art dealers and part of my duty is to be well informed about the articles we sell. When I ran the pearls through my teeth, I couldn’t believe it. The pearls were real, not costume jewelry as I had automatically assumed. I knew that they must be very expensive and was appalled that I was responsible for such a precious necklace. I decided to take them off my neck, as already once or twice they had caught between my fingers whilst dancing the jive.”

“Aha.” Joe said.

“Yes, what a surprise, but I decided to hide them where they would be safe and not get broken.”

“Well, where was that?” Asked Steve.

“Where, for the moment, is not so important; what followed is?”

“When I returned to the table most of the group were still on the dance floor. Only Nicholas. Georgiou and Boris were at the table. Boris offered me a drink from a tray of drinks and turned to Nicholas with another, “A final toast for us to finish the evening.” He said. Whilst we waited for the others to return, I took a sip from my glass and tasted the very strong liquor. I don’t drink. I have seen the results of too much alcohol and I had been drinking tonic water. I quietly pushed the glass away from me and onto the tray, knowing I still had some of my previous drink left.” “It was the end of the evening and everyone was gathering their things up but when they had all returned Boris gave a final toast, taking my drink which was nearest to him."

"Schloss, cheers" And we all drank up in one. Boris had been drinking heavily, although always cheerful, and had been the life and soul of the party all evening. Two of the girls had been to other social events with him and were amused over something."

"When we got to the front door, with the cold air striking us, Boris collapsed and the two girls giggled that he was always in that state at the end of the evening and urged the others to put him to sleep on a handy bench in the hallway."

"Unfortunately, I was taken rather ill at that moment and my partner hurried me away, together with my flat mate and her partner, and I was almost carried to my friend's home, being dreadfully sick on the way."

"It was not until the next morning that we heard that Boris was dead and I knew that he had drunk my drink by mistake. I had killed him by switching the drink that was meant for me!"

"Good God, you mean that he had tried to kill you?"

"Well," she said slowly, "not necessarily. I cannot be certain that he had put something in the drink as any number of people might have done so from the waiter to one of our friends, but I knew it had been meant for me and realized that the real reason was the theft of the pearls."

"Well, well, well, but why didn't you tell the police about this?"

"Yes, I was going to but before that were possible, I arrived home to find that my flat had been burgled and my opposite neighbour, who had lent the pearls, had fallen down the stairs and had been taken to hospital and that her flat had also been broken into."

"I just needed to think things out as there seemed to be far more at stake than I had imagined and the less I said the better until I was able to speak to Anna."

"Anna?" "Anna Romaine?"

"Y… yes, how do you know…"

"Oh, that has been all over the Met.' She is a rather important lady so word got around about her but not in the press yet, thank God."

"Well, important or not, she seemed very frightened when we saw her in the hospital but was not able to say more than two words to us before we were ushered out of her room.

CHAPTER NINE

The Commander – Torn Loyalties

Whilst Carole was staying in Southwark, Nicholas was on his way to a meeting in Hampshire and had travelled by train through familiar countryside and he looked out of the window but his gaze took in nothing. The changing scenery usually held his interest, but not today. The grey streets of London gave way to countryside aglow with the morning sun giving a golden halo through the mist. The sun melted the early morning frost and give way to a brilliant sky and every branch of the trees display their own special colours. Nicholas was blind to all this artist's palette.

He didn't see the varieties of deer gaze unafraid at the train, as they grazed on the lawns beside the track, and his usual hunter's instinct was not being aroused at his passing. Nor the rooks circling the coppice on the skyline with his usual resolve to rid the world of these marauders of the farmland fields. Nor see, the seagulls that were already feeding on the treasures of the newly turned earth behind the plough, which had always reminded him of his earlier years racing in The Solent with Alex, in their summer holidays.

No, now he had such sombre thoughts that he was oblivious to such things.

He had come to this country when he was ten and had been welcomed into the community of schoolboys who were in the preparatory school in Sussex and had loved the life he had found himself part of, with its sense of security and brotherhood. That his father was no longer part of his life had grieved him, when he had first arrived from Russia. In the intervening years, his father had gradually become a sainted figure in Nicholas's mind. His father's bravery at standing up to the Politburo had become part of a legend that had been embellished over the years.

When his mother died shortly after fleeing to the South of France, he had been taken in by Tashaun and Minka Counter, to be a brother to their son Alexis and their generosity and kindness had been more than rewarded in the kindly young man sitting alone on that winter morning. The two young men, Alexis and Nicholas, then went to Winchester and fell in love with that great city and were always being told that it had been the heart of the Kingdom of Wessex. They had lively young men's interest in sport and took up cricket and rugby with skill and enthusiasm. Each boy excelling in the opposite season's sport. Alexis had loved cricket and Nicholas showed great promise at rugby. All these studies were overseen by Tasha and Minka but were only regarded as a prelude to their greater hopes.

Nicholas had managed to defer his National Service until gaining his Degree at Cambridge, where he studied Greek, Latin and Philosophy. He had eventually been sent to Cyprus to serve out his time of National Service in the Army and had returned that summer with all the advantages that a broad education could furnish.

Britain had nurtured his love of learning and fair play and a pride in nationhood and his foster parents kept alive his pride in his Russian heritage. That more would be required of him, had been a boyhood dream, but was not based on the reality of his existence. He knew and loved the country of his adoption and was very well aware of how different his life might have been if he had stayed a Soviet Citizen. He also knew that his father had paid the price of penal servitude for trying to change the direction of his country's politics.

Whilst Nicholas was pondering his future, he had been invited to a meeting of Russian Emigrés, called the Chevaliers de Russie, who all in some way, still held hopes of a return to more open government and perhaps a return to a political system based on monarchy. Of course, it was generally thought that all the family of Romanovs were assassinated on that dreadful day in 1917, when it was supposed that all the family were executed, but there had been a persistent rumour that the youngest girl had been saved.

Whether this was true or not, there was a party of Russians who wanted to believe it, as it gave focus to their aspirations of a return home and Anna Romaine was that lady. She certainly had many qualities, which could be made to look as if she was Anastasia but the reality was of less concern to the Chevaliers than what she represented. Her presence in England was an irritation to modern Soviet policymakers and her life was under constant surveillance. A guard had been formed to counteract any threat to her person and Nicholas was entrusted with certain duties. It was important that any encouragement or financial assistance that she gave to dissidents in Russia must be very carefully handled to prevent this knowledge being known by the Russian Embassy.

To further support Russian dissidents, including his father, a plan was devised. Nicholas was detailed to guard the pearls that were to be taken to Europe in exchange for finance for this cause. This had to be done without the Embassy knowing where the finance had come from, so a plot was hatched. He had taken to this mission with enthusiasm as he had thought that no harm would come to his choice of carrier. The resulting situation and his increasing emotional involvement, had not been a consideration. Now he acknowledged that he was feeling the pull of the greatest emotional force since leaving Russia. He also realised that his father's future might be at stake and his ultimate loyalty might be tested. This was now being stretched even further as he pondered Georgiou's revelation.

****

Georgiou had been in England for longer than he cared to remember. He had come from the Asian part of his country, and had the large, square head and flattened face that indicated his Mongolian forebears. As the son of a rising Diplomat for the USSR, he had been sent to one of the best schools in England, near Windsor, and had picked up the habits of an aristocratic Englishman. Unfortunately, with this had come a liking for all things expensive and exclusive, but he had not been provided with the wherewithal to satisfy his cravings.

He was a handsome young man of medium stature who carried his height to the best advantage as he had taken a liking to boxing, which he pursued with enthusiasm and he exuded physical strength. Although he liked to watch the sport, he also liked to bet on the results as well, and his streak of luck had run out. His creditors were chasing him for money and things were beginning to get ugly. He had met Boris at the gym, where he appeared for regular work-outs, and they had an obvious affinity.

Over the months, they had gradually got to know each other and were surprised how much they had in common. Both had parents in the Diplomatic Corp, although Boris was vague about anything else of his background, although they had both come from Eastern Europe. This was a bond indeed and when they realized that they were both to go to the Le Lyçee Français, it was a natural progression to share accommodation. There they met many nations but he became accepted as part of a Russian clique that were 'on the other side' of Russian politics and he did not care to enlighten them of his own affiliation.

His main interest at the gym took him away from

too much contact with the emigres Russians but was accepted as a flat mate of the party joker, Boris. During one of their drinking bouts, Boris had let on that money exchanged hands by other means than notes and, before long, Georgiou had extracted from Boris more details. Later, he had hatched a plan to get his hands on, what appeared to be a fortune.

Boris also was strapped for cash, more because of his lavish lifestyle and love of wine than any shortage of funds, but he could see the advantages of having more. Greed made him an easy conspirator. The night of the Ball was meant to be their opportunity. By drugging (not killing) Carole, whom they knew of, through friends at the YWCA, they hoped to switch the pearls at the latter part of the evening. That things had gone decidedly wrong, he put down to complete bungling on the part of Boris and, so far, his own involvement had not been detected. Unfortunately, this had not resolved his problem of debts and he was finally forced to think of approaching his 'Old Man.'

At the last moment, he began to think of another plan to solve his problems. When Boris died, Georgiou knew that his Sunday morning Guard Duty had not been covered. He thought it was an opportunity to see if there was anything of value in Miss Romaine's Apartment whilst she was away at church. This had gone badly wrong as he had been interrupted by Anna who had returned earlier than expected. When Georgiou saw her coming up the staircase, he panicked and in his haste, brushed passed her. In her fragile state of health, she had tottered and then fallen down the stairs.

When this plan had gone wrong, he decided to blackmail his friend Nicholas instead, by threatening to bring his connections to the Royalists to the attention of the KGB. He was blackmailing Nicholas into cutting him in with the money that would be raised by the sale of the pearls. He knew that Nicholas's father was in Siberia and, through that leverage, threatened to expose these activities to help get the pearls for himself.

To this end, Georgiou had cornered Nicholas and a plan was emerging that seemed to be agreeable to them both. He had co-opted another friend to help him in this endeavour, called Ronnie, who would be eager to get a bit of cash and a night's adventure. Everything seemed in place for his plan and he had only to wait for the high tide.

****

Nicholas's first duty had always seemed to be to his father's future and all that entailed. His second duty was to the country that had taken him in, which had educated him and turned him into the thoughtful and courageous young man that he now was. He had even served this country in foreign lands and vowed allegiance to its Queen. Was he now to turn his back on that generous host? After all he now held a British Passport. Didn't that have any meaning to him? He recalled the words that John F. Kennedy had spoken when he addressed U.S. troops in Berlin,

"Ask not what your country can do for you, ask what you can do for your country?" [sic]

Ah, but which country? That was the point. Was it the country of his birth, which was shrouded in the mythical 'Iron Curtain' or Great Britain, that had opened its doors to a young boy, who grew to hold the values, and love the life he now enjoyed as one of its citizens. That country whose people might be betrayed. One of whom he now saw, with a clarity that left him bereft, he loved ...Loved as though he had found the other half of himself, who had awakened a chivalry within him, that he could not deny. The sudden illness that had struck Carole down, whilst at the Ball, far from repulsing him, had brought home to him that she was in mortal danger. He had seen that Boris really was dead and was fully aware that the pearls might be the real reason for such an event. Carole, was now in danger and was probably the real target, especially as she had also been stricken ill.

In those few hours after the Ball his professional task had turned from a pleasurable but harmless deceit, into a dark and dangerous event and his need to protect her, had turned into something much more personal. Nicholas feared that she also might die and the thought horrified him. Now how could he prevent her from being harmed, yet still retrieve the pearls honourably?

Georgiou had him in a vice. If the KGB knew of his involvement, it would go badly for his father. If he defied Georgiou, would he harm Carole and betray the trust of the Chevaliers?

His thoughts were interrupted as he saw that the train had nearly reached his destination and put aside such thoughts for the moment. At last, he recognized the countryside as the Downs came into view and he prepared to leave, as the train turned South. He felt it slowing and saw that Winchester had been reached and his spirits lifted slightly. He jumped down from the train and looked towards the Railway Station building. Quickening his pace when he saw his old mentor waiting at the gate, he waved, and Nicholas grasped the hand extended to him.

"Good morning Sir, thank you for coming yourself to meet me."

"You're a welcome sight young man."

"I hope you are well Tasha, how is Mama Minka. Well, I hope?"

"Oh, yes indeed and Mama is looking forward to seeing you."

They left the station and climbed out of the town, passed the monument to King Alfred and turned along the river upstream, until they reached Kings Somerly, and into the drive of a large Lutyens style cottage and came to a halt at the coach house attached. The door opened and there stood a plump ample bosomed lady, Minka, his mother, or at least the only mother he was likely to have, who had shown him all the kindness of a mother since his own had died following their flight from Russia. She folded him into her bosom. His heart lifted as he embraced her.

Minka had taken him in to be a brother to her own son Alexis, and sent them to boarding school in England. Now they were grown men and were trying to repay their good fortune to the loyalties of old in their mother country.

"How lovely to see you Nico."

Minka tucked her arm into his bent arm and steered Nicholas towards lunch in the dining room overlooking the lovely garden, which had distant views of the downs.

"Now let me hear all your news."

For the next few hours, happy memories were exchanged whilst Minka gently prized bits of news from him about his studies and the shocking events of the past week. Nicholas was saying very little but his concern for the young woman who partnered him, was obvious. Her intuition told her that it was more than a passing concern that he was feeling.

She asked after Alexis and was pleased to hear that Janice was in evidence. She seemed like a thoroughly sensible girl who would not easily lose her head and who might keep Alexis out of trouble, whilst Nicholas was not around. But she didn't let them guess the extent of her knowledge about events. "It was best to let the menfolk think that they were bearing all the responsibilities, as it was a comfort to them to think they were in charge." She thought sagely.

After lunch Tasha and Nicholas went into the library and spent most of the afternoon closeted in the deep leather armchairs beside a roaring fire.

"Well, Nico, you have got into a scrape. I understand that you haven't got the pearls and that they are lost. There is a terrible uncertainty about these events. It is difficult to see where the treachery lies, but without those pearls to trade for roubles, we shall have nothing to buy your father's life with."

"I know, and I think I can still find them and take them to Europe. It is my deepest regret that Madame Anna was hurt. I had thought my instructions were to guard the pearls whilst on the neck of the young lady, but I was not there to guard the apartment of the Princess, so I am distraught that she has come to harm."

"Well, we are all worried there. but it was her wish that the pearls should be traded for your father's life. She knew how brave he had been in standing up for the injustices in our Motherland."

"I believe," Said Nicholas, "that the young lady has hidden the pearls and I am sure she will tell me, but we still do not know who is behind the killing of Boris and she is not saying anything to anyone for fear of also being killed."

"Well, we are running out of time and opportunity as your father, by all reports, is very weak and the ship will be ready to sail in two days. If we wait for the next suitable boat, who knows what we will find." Said the navel Commander.

"Somehow," he continued, "you must find those pearls by whatever means possible."

"In the meantime, we are trying every government channel we can. The last thing we need right now is a diplomatic incident. It seems that the Prime Minister is very jumpy about something afoot and Kruschev is being very secretive at the moment. Very little news is coming out by our diplomatic channels but the East/ West tension is definitely rising." He paused, "Let's keep to our purpose and hope you will succeed."

He stood up, "Now we must get you home." And Tasha walked Nicholas to the coach house door.

"God speed." Whispered Minka watching them as they disappeared down the driveway.

Nicholas returned to London with a heavy heart. He seemed to be caught in a web of others needs whichever way he turned, and his father was the pawn between them all. He could not reveal to his Godfather the pact he had made with Georgiou and yet, somehow, he must pursue his original purpose - to retrieve his father.

His heart was heavier still that his new love was also the unwitting pawn in the affair. How could he betray her? Yet she must confide her hiding place or else her life would be in more danger, for Georgiou and others, were prepared to kill again to gain the pearls for their own selfish ends, not the valorous deed, as he saw it.

Could he really choose between loyalty to his father, and the country that had nurtured him in good faith, and his new love? Could Georgiou blow them all away by his threats? He had to keep Georgiou quiet at least until he was out of the country, then nothing could be proved of his involvement.

The next day Carole awoke to strange sounds and remembered where she was. She felt much more rested in spirit and was relieved to have told Steve about the situation. At least she might get some protection from the police but where did that leave Nicholas? She could no longer believe that he had anything to do with the killing, but he certainly had something to do with the pearls, and she hoped that the police didn't put two and two together and make five.

As Joe walked back to work he was reassured that some confidences had been shared between Steve and Carole, as she was more cheerful this morning. When they arrived at work she thanked him and went up to her office. Harry Bailey came in later and straightaway told Carole that she needed to take a letter to a customer, that was particularly urgent. It seemed this was in Westminster and he suggested she take it straight away. In view of the stoppage, Harry suggested that she should see her errand as a day's work so that she could continue in the right direction back home. This seemed a happy solution to getting back to her flat.

She wondered whether the Rail Union would get anywhere in their fight for better pay and conditions. They have done their bit during the war, they were entitled to a share of prospects, weren't they? But as she trudged past Cannon Street Station and into Trafalgar Square, she questioned whether this was the right way to win the hearts of Londoners.

She was getting near to Whitehall and started to look for her destination. It was hard to find any number sequence and large Georgian buildings lined both sides with imposing grandeur, but no numbers. At last she recognised the Cenotaph and was able to find her way into a rather nondescript portal.

Inside she was ushered into an oak-paneled large office. Everywhere her feet sank gratefully into the plush carpet and all was hushed. On the outside of the door was a brass plate with the name, Sir Charles Willingham-Wright.

"Ah, good morning young lady, I was expecting you. Do sit down. Thank Mr. Bailey for the charming picture he sent to me yesterday. He set me quite a puzzle. I believe you have a letter for me."

She handed it over and waited whilst he read through what it contained.

"Well, well, you have led us quite a dance, haven't you?" And he looked her straight in the face. She stared back inwardly reeling at what he had said.

"I don't know what you mean." She managed, as straight-faced as she could muster.

With that, Sir Charles proceeded to outline pretty much everything of her movements during the last ten days.

"You have kept popping up amongst some very interesting people but I have been assured by my Secretary that you are above suspicion in this matter."

Carole gulped. So, this was Janice's Boss!

"Now, how about giving me your full story and we will see what we can do about it." There was an underlying sound of steel in his voice and she accepted that there would be no resort to subterfuge here.

She started her story and all was silent around her. He sat with his elbows on the arms of his chair, eyes closed and fingers touching each other almost in prayer. Her voice stopped and he leant forward sharply, "And the pearls? Where did you hide them?' He barked.

Carole jumped. "I can't say, I don't know." She whispered.

He continued to gaze at her, "I see," He said in a much gentler tone. "Divided loyalties here eh? But you see you will have to tell me and you will have to help me in this matter!"

In the next hour, she was in no doubt as to where her loyalties must lie, and left his office with her mind racing. She continued walking down Whitehall. She came to the Houses of Parliament and intended to continue along the embankment, past the Tate. Across the road, at St. Margaret's Church, there was a notice saying that there was a coffee and tea station for office workers to avail themselves of, on their weary trudge home during the Strike. She paused and decided to take up their offer, as she was overwhelmed with the task ahead and felt in need of a quiet moment in the church. She knelt down in this lovely church with its Tudor iconography. Echoes of other turbulent times were all around her, Henry VIII, Mary, Edward VI, Elizabeth I, all had been threatened by forces that they had to grapple with. Now here was she, having to prove her loyalty to Queen and Country.

Sir Charles had led her to believe that she had no choice and that she must do what he told her. What was surprising were his instructions, which ran contrary to what she would have expected. But did it mean that she would be leading Nicholas into a trap and that her ultimate loyalty would be tested? She could not decide and turned to the only certainty she had found in life, and closed her eyes in supplication.

After a while she felt comforted and continued her walk along the embankment. The weather was cold but sunny and the wind had turned to the east and was blowing her along with all the dried leaves from the trees. A false sense of euphoria began to grip her as the leaves of winter swirled around her. She remembered seeing horses toss their heads and gallop madly round their field in windy conditions, and this same sense of recklessness infused her.

****

Janice had left her office on Monday disturbed by the forces that were revolving about Carole's head but was glad that Sir Charles was in charge. By tomorrow, Carole would be back home and perhaps her involvement would be over.

Janice decided to go and see Anna. The hospital was not too far so the Underground stoppage did not concern her. She was used to tramping the hills around Edinburgh and walking the streets of London was easy for her, but the cold had a different quality here in the City. The constant change of temperature, from office block to windy streets, made it more difficult to keep warm but she was more sensibly dressed than most of her fellow walkers that night. A smiling nurse gave her a nod when she arrived.

"Oh, you will be glad to find our patient a little better today. She is still very frail but a bit of company will do her good. Fifteen minutes will be long enough, remember."

Janice entered the room to find Anna propped up in bed with a head bandage considerably smaller than the one she had been wearing. At the sound of the door, Anna opened her eyes and looked with dawning recognition at Janice and a small smile came to her face. "Oh," she whispered, "how kind of you to come."

"We were worried about you. Are you feeling better?" She didn't say more but took her cue from

Anna.

"Where is your flat mate. Is she with you?"

"No," said Janice, "She has had to stay in the City tonight but she came with me last time, don't you remember?"

"Oh yes, I remember. Is she alright?"

"Yes." Said Janice, not knowing whether Anna had been told anything else about why she was here, and what had been happening to her. Anna seemed to be tiring and Janice got up to leave.

Anna clutched her hand and whispered to her as she went to kiss her goodbye. "Trust Nicholas…trust…no… one…else" and released her grip on her. She had relapsed into sleep again and Janice tiptoed out.

****

After his visit to Hampshire, Nicholas was uncertain how to proceed. But when he returned to the boat there was a man in a Crombie coat and trilby hat waiting on the quayside. As he approached, the man moved towards him. He frowned, as this looked like trouble but he continued walking.

"Mr. Baron?"

"Yes, who wants to know?" The man showed him his credentials and asked,

"Would you come with me Sir? We would rather like a word with you."

"Damn." He cursed under his breath. "I don't need this right now." But he made no protest and fell into step beside the official. They had turned and were now walking downstream and Nicholas was surprised as he expected to be going to the Police Station, which was in the other direction. They continued along the embankment until the Houses of Parliament came into view. He was intrigued to know where this was leading but said nothing. They turned into Whitehall and were walking passed the Cenotaph when the officer directed him into a quiet wood-paneled hallway, up a wide staircase. The officer knocked on the door that had a brass plate on it with the name Sir Charles Willingham-Wright.

He entered and the gentleman, without rising from his chair, said, "Ah, Mr. Baron, do come in, we have been expecting you." The door closed silently behind him.

"Good afternoon," Said Nicholas. "I don't think we have met before, have we?" As a hand was outstretched to greet him.

"No, but we have several friends in common and certainly mutual interests." Said Sir Charles.

Nicholas looked blandly back at him waiting to hear more. He had already been subjected to this formula earlier in the last week and was not about to be disconcerted.

"Oh, really, and what could they be?"

Sir Charles chuckled. He could see that he was going to enjoy fencing with this cool customer.

"It seems your services are in high demand, at the moment. But it would be good to think that your best interests would be served if you listened carefully to me."

"Well." Said Nicholas bending forward. "I'm all ears."

Sir Charles leant forward and opened a wooden box on top of his desk.

"Forgive me, I haven't offered you a cigarette yet." And he passed the box, "Sobranie, Galoise, Camel, Dunhill?" He played with the box before meeting Nicholas eye to eye. Nicholas smiled and knew he had met his match. Of course, Sir Charles knew all about him and could chart his career by the cigarettes he had smoked.

"Well, I think, at the moment, it would be wise to stick by 'Dunhill'." He said.

"Aha," Said Sir Charles, "That would be wise. These others have great sentimental value but, although Sobranie has a pleasing aroma, you will find that there is more lasting satisfaction to be had by sticking to those."

Nicholas took one of the Dunhill cigarettes and lit it with the pre-offered cigarette lighter. He inhaled deeply and, leaning back in his chair, looking at the ceiling and, as though deep in thought, said nothing for a while. Sir Charles sat back and watched the young man's performance. He had to applaud his nonchalance and was content to play out this 'double entendre'

"Yes, there is much merit to sticking to the same brand but some habits are acquired in childhood and those are the hardest to break."

"Yes." Said Sir Charles. "Indeed, and some habits acquired in childhood are of lasting value and sometimes there is a mutual fusion of interests in introducing one to the other. That is how new blends are made and, more often than not, new habits are formed that make for lasting preference."

There was a silence in the room, which stretched to a lengthy few minutes, until a loud striking of the chimes of Big Ben broke their silence. With great deliberation, Nicholas bent forward and picked up one Sobranie cigarette. Without pausing he took another two Dunhill. Now all it required was for them to work out the details. His decision had been made.

****

When Nicholas had gone, Sir Charles arranged to meet the Chief Constable of Chelsea and Fulham, at his club in Pall Mall. "Good evening, Robert, scotch is it for you?" He turned to the waiter and ordered two large whisky and sodas. When they were ensconced in their large armchairs, and had checked the state of their rugby clubs' progress, Sir Charles broached the subject of their meeting.

"How are you getting on with your murder enquiries at the Chelsea Arts Ball? Has anything developed yet?"

"Well, apart from some inner circle vendetta, we have not yet found a motive. Indeed, we have found a very strange mixture of substances in his system so have no clues from the autopsy yet. Of course, all the partygoers are suspects, especially the group he was with. Most of them seem to have Russian connections." He paused as Sir Charles had not said anything. "Is that your interest?"

"As a matter of fact, it is. We're rather keen not to 'rock the boat' there, as things are rather delicate at the moment. There is a definite rise in tension in certain quarters and we are anxious not to create an incident of any kind."

"These émigrés have another agenda entirely and, although theoretically we sympathise, a cool distance must be seen to apply to our relations there."

"Aha," said Robert, sipping his scotch. "so, all our investigations are stirring the pot, are they?"

"Yes, indeed, you might say that you are spoiling the stew with your big wooden spoon."

The two men sat pondering the conundrum of serving the law and justice until Sir Charles said. "You may rest assured that justice will be done, but it is a bit awkward to let it be seen to be done. A little nudge to Fleet Street that there was 'death by misadventure' might help. After all, you did say that there was a confusion of substances found in the body."

Robert Pelham sat back, his eyes tracing the line of past members in their gilt frames looking down at him. What would they say to this accommodation?

"Some of these Fleet Street boys do like to jump the gun and make too many assumptions. Perhaps I should rein in their imaginations a bit until the Coroner's Court has all the medical facts. After all, these arty types do seem to get their hands on some dodgy chemicals these days. Don't know where such experimentation will lead."

With a smile, Sir Charles said. "Exactly so, Robert, I couldn't have put it better myself! Another scotch, old boy."

CHAPTER TEN

Commitment – Betrayal

Carole was tired now after her walk. The sense of euphoria had left her but she brightened when she saw Chelsea Bridge ahead of her. She had arranged to meet Nicholas at a pub on the river called 'The Eagle and Flagstaff' and they were to be joined by some of the other members of the party from the Arts Ball. Pushing open the door, she looked closely for a moment at a man seated just inside reading the **London Evening Recorder** with the headlines, ***New development in murder enquiry***. "*Was he murdered or was it misadventu*re?" She looked closely for a moment but could not see any further part of the news item. She stumbled across the room feeling suddenly faint and felt a steadying hand under her arm. "Carole, are you alright?" And there was Nicholas with his arm around her and her heart danced.

"Oh Nicholas." She smiled and there were stars in her eyes for him to see.

"I've missed you." He said huskily and buried his face in her hair. There was a sound in his voice that she had not heard before, a desperation that conveyed itself to her and which she recognized in her own feelings.

They joined the others and continued with the speculation that the newspaper had encouraged. "What, could it really be accidental after all? So, was there no murderer in their midst after all?" Laughed one of the girls with obvious relief in her voice.

"Well they don't have anything to go on yet, said someone else. after all we haven't had an inquest on the body." They all agreed that it was too soon to make any judgments and they busied themselves with drinks orders and steak pies to eat as well.

As the evening became jollier, so Nicholas and Carole withdrew themselves from the general chatter. Sometime later Janice came in and went to sit with them. They both, in different ways, looked rather more closely at her and were eager to hear how Anna was faring in the hospital.

"She is awake, but I kept my conversation with her fairly soothing as I did not want to agitate her about everything that has happened." She paused and looked at Carole and then Nicholas and then glanced at the others who were now out of earshot. "Anna did say something rather relevant though."

They both looked at her and waited, Janice again looked first at Carole and then at Nicholas, waiting for his reaction.

“She said ‘Trust Nicholas’.” And for a second his eyes locked with hers without any expression on his face, then turned to Carole with a wistful smile.

“It seems that someone at least thinks I am not the villain in the plot.” He said drily.

“Of course, I never thought that, how could I.” But Carole’s words sounded relieved rather than confident.

The party began to break up and Alex came over to Janice and said, “How do you feel about taking in a ‘movie?’ There’s that love story about London with Alan Bates and Joely Richardson, ‘Georgie Girl’, or there’s also ‘Breakfast at Tiffany’s,’ with Audrey Hepburn and George Peppard. Whatever you fancy?” They continued to debate this as Nicholas and Carole got up to leave.

“Well, we have to go but enjoy yourselves.”

Alex got up to shake hands with Nicholas who by now was looking rather strained. He drew Alex into a bear hug and kissed him in the Russian way.

“Well, goodbye brother.” and as he embraced him Nicholas whispered. “Trust Janice.” Turning away towards the door, his eyes were blinded by unshed tears. He stumbled out of the door and they turned towards the river but there was no discussion about how they would spend their evening.

They found themselves at the cruiser just as the moon was rising and it cast a blue radiance over the

River Thames. Tonight, there were a few clouds but the wind that had buffeted them both along the Embankment, had died down. The moon picked up every ripple and eddy. Looking to the opposite bank they saw the river water was returning to sea as the banks began to shine with glistening incandescence. They quietly watched all the magic of moonlight on water and seemed to drink in every detail of time and place until, feeling the cold penetrate even their warm embrace, they walked down the gangway to the boat. Several boats of assorted sizes had joined the flotilla since first she had come there but all seemed quiet around them.

They entered the galley and, once again, Nicholas tended the fire and the chill of the night was soon dispersed. They went into the cabin but were reluctant to go further. It was as if they wanted to catch hold of time and keep things just as they were. At last Nicholas bent down to unlace her boots but there was a slowness to his movement which belied the passion building inside him. He wished to delay every second of their union as he took off her stockings and looked into her eyes before kissing her gently on the mouth.

She seemed to understand his hesitation and she began to unbutton his jacket and, piece by piece, they undressed each other until they knelt naked and aroused. He looked into her eyes and he said, "It is time," and with a nod of her head he led her to the bed. This time he sat crossed legged and invited her to sit facing him. With her legs behind his back eyes gazing at each other, he gently lowered her onto his manhood and, rocking silently and slowly, their gentle thrusting became more urgent until she heard herself groan and shudder with delight and a triumphant cry came from Nicholas as his crescendo came and they finally were forced to part and lie exhausted, side by side, as they sucked in every breath that the other exhaled until a dizziness came and they slept.

Some hours later, when the lapping of the water was again noisy with the fresh breeze that had sprung up, Nicholas got up from the bunk and went into the galley. He put more logs in the stove and put water to boil in the kettle. He did not cover Carole, as he gazed down at her cream and perfect body, and he reluctantly went back to the galley. He began to prepare food and soon he was aware that Carole was watching him. He turned and covered her body with light kisses as he said, "come on lazy bones, I have prepared a feast for you," As he turned to open a can of beans to go with the sausages that began to sizzle in the pan. She grabbed his jumper and, putting it on, joined him in the galley, where they ate as if ravenous.

He began to talk of their evening and asked Carole if she knew why Anna had said to trust the pearls were hidden.

"Anna is a very important person to many of the Russians that live here and she is very generous to many who have difficulties in their new life. There are also Russians who would like to see her dead, or, at the very least, stop her giving help to the Royalist faction."

"I take my turn to guard her and, on the evening of the ball, I was detailed to be your escort and to guard the pearls she was to lend you. They were to be sold in Switzerland to help people to flee Russia specifically this time, including my father. There was quite an elaborate plan to get to know you which, God forgive me, I undertook without a thought of any consequences to you." He stopped and a harsh laugh was wrung from him.

"Then Boris died, and you too, nearly. This changed all the planning as the loss of the genuine pearls that Anna had lent you, meant that money they would have fetched in Switzerland, for all those waiting for relief, would go wanting. My own father was reported to be very weak and I was in despair. Everything had gone completely wrong and I no longer knew where to turn as I knew the enormity of what had just happened. Boris was dead and you, in all likelihood, had also been poisoned, and the pearls were nowhere to be seen. Added to this, in my concern for you, but later my shame, I realised that my guard duty hadn't been covered and Anna had been attacked."

Carole had listened to this with growing concern and, alarm at her part in all this. but knew that she had acted on instinct and couldn't think how it could have been otherwise. He had been silent for some minutes and she could see that he was deeply affected. She took a deep breath and said very slowly in a whisper, "Do you want to know where I hid them?" For a minute, he was still, with his head sunk between his knees, in a state of misery. He roused himself and looked straight at her, searching her face for some hint of the love he had known.

Her face was expressionless and her eyes were fixed firmly on the kettle, which had boiled dry. She got up as if sleepwalking and went through the cabin and beyond into the heads. Searching amongst the ropes and fenders she felt for the tissue paper. She hesitated slightly when her fingers felt the round hard balls hidden there. Taking the pearls out of the tissue, she placed them round her neck and, flinging the jumper aside, she walked through naked into the cabin and waited. "Is this what you want?" she said in a trance and Nicholas slowly opened the curtain and saw her lovely body bedecked with just the pearls, with her golden curls falling amongst them. To my dying day, I will remember this. he thought.

He crossed the threshold and gently took the pearls and placed them back into the tissue. He touched her hand and then her arms that by now were goose pimpled. He folded her in his arms and gently rocked her as he realized she knew he would betray her and that this was to be goodbye. Guiding her to the bunk, he gently pressed her down onto the mattress and, side by side, they lay. Then passion, when it came, was an elegy for what might have been. With the gentlest of expression, he gave his love to her and she clung to him and wept, knowing that soon he would leave her and together they floated into sleep.

Carole woke and reaching out beside her, felt that Nicholas was no longer by her side. She had heard the sound of a motor, somewhere on the river, and she felt the angle of the boat had changed. The river had reached the flood and was now rushing back to the sea carrying, as she had known it would, her lover. She did not know how long it would take to carry out his task, or that there was a ship waiting for him at Gravesend to take him further on his flight.

***

'The Ice Maiden' had slipped its moorings with the turn of the tide and was heading out with the rush of the receding tide. Somewhere, east of Gravesend, she would anchor up, awaiting a passenger to board, out of reach of the on-shore activities.

On the Thames, passing under Vauxhall Bridge, Nicholas looked back upstream and strained to see Chelsea Bridge and the point where his boat was moored. He turned away and set his face firmly towards the East and tried to concentrate on the job at hand. This might be his end. More than he could handle. But there was a lot at stake and he would strive to his last breath to bring his father away from the horrors that he was enduring.

He travelled for two hours downstream and had passed under the Tower and Pool of London. Round the next bend of the river, Woolwich was coming into view and he was on time for his rendezvous.

On his starboard side, flashing lights indicated his rendezvous points. He cut the engine to cruising and manoeuvred the motor launch towards the pins of light, which gradually became bigger, until the other motor launch was alongside, they facing upstream and Nicholas facing downstream in line, as they secured them together, and cut engines. He recognised the two occupants of the boat and was relieved to see that there was no one else with them and that he knew what he was dealing with.

He saw that coming up fast from Gravesend was a naval cutter. He fumbled with the painters but had secured them firmly before the two men realised that their meeting on the river at this early hour, was being investigated.

Georgiou called to make the exchange and Nicholas turned to the front cabin to retrieve the package.

"Hi, Georgiou, I have the pearls safe here in the fore-cabin." He called over the wind which fortunately was from the west and was muffling the sound of the approaching Police Cutter.

Nicholas slowly brought out the package but, by this time, the cutter was near and there was a shout from Georgiou, "Caste us off, caste us off." as they realized they might be caught.

He slipped the package inside his jacket and jumped to the port side of the boat, just as they heard a voice from a loudhailer.

"Hold fast there, we are coming alongside." A shot

was fired and a flare passed over their heads. Before Nicholas could release the boats, the cutter was alongside Georgiou's boat and several armed officers trained their guns on the men.

Without waiting for more, Nicholas rolled backwards over the side of the boat, having secured two of the loose fenders lying in the scuppers, around his wrists, and surfaced several yards downstream in icy water.

There had been a shout, and a round of gunfire, all missing their target, and he managed to pull the ripcord of his inflatable jacket. He held onto the two neon coloured fenders, which acted as extra buoyancy and which gave out a strange glow bobbing in the water. His ability to control the situation was rapidly disappearing as the icy current carried him downstream and seeped into his very core. Nicholas was gradually losing consciousness but the buoys were firmly fixed around his wrists now and they acted like beacons, bobbing up and down with their neon colour, shining in the early morning light. The current was swift and carried, his now, almost lifeless body downstream, but within a minute he was spotted by a Customs launch that was waiting in the main stream and seconds later he was fished out of the water.

"He's still alive, Sir," Said Peter Swayne, the crewman and the man on the bridge grunted in approval. Sir Charles was beginning to regret taking part in this escapade as he was by now feeling rather seasick but was satisfied with the subterfuge.

Back at the interlocked boats, the other two men were roughly bundled into the police patrol boat. They brought the two men to the cabin in front of the Captain. "Well, and what might you be doing on a cold winter's night in the middle of the Thames Estuary? No good, I'll be bound."

"Have they caught the other man yet?" He said to his companion, Steve Southgate.

"I'm afraid not, Sir, but I don't think he will last long in that icy water, but we are still looking."

Turning to the two men they had just hauled on board, he said "Now tell the Captain, what's your game?"

The two men remained dumb. Georgiou silently cursed Nicholas for being so slow with the exchange. They would have been away, no trouble, if only he had been quicker about it. Well Nicholas deserved whatever was coming to him in that icy water. But his anger gathered as he thought about the loss of the pearls. The only good thing was that the police could not pin anything on them, as the exchange had not been made, and the pearls were lost in the Thames mud.

"Take them away." Said the Captain. "I am not satisfied that this was an innocent night's tryst. We'll find the truth of it soon enough."

On board the Police launch, the lifeless man was quickly wrapped in warm blankets and was force-fed a slug of brandy.

“Get that down you.” Said Peter, the crew member, and he stripped the man of his wet clothes briskly and replaced them with warm dry ones, and sensation began to return to Nicholas’ body.

Peter bent over him to inspect his condition and said, “You’ll do.”

Nicholas opened his eyes and attempted to smile but something was happening to his cheeks as he thawed out unevenly. Ten minutes later Sir Charles came down into the cabin and looked at Nicholas.

“How do you feel now? We are fast approaching ‘The Ice Maiden’ and you will need all your strength for the climb onto their deck.

Nicholas nodded, saving all his remaining strength for the trial ahead. He felt across his chest and realised that the pearls were gone.

“Oh, by the way,” said Sir Charles. “we retrieved your personal effects from your wet clothes. Here they are.” He passed over the oilskin package and their eyes met. “I think you will find everything in order Mr. Baronski.”

Sir Charles turned to the Captain and said, “Shall we get on with it before they miss the tide?”

“Yes Sir.” Said the young man.

As they came close to the ship, Sir Charles spoke again to Nicholas.

"Well, this is where we part so it really is goodbye. I wish you a safe journey and success in your quest." They shook hands and Nicholas caught the rope ladder that was thrown down the side of the ship, making sure of his precious cargo.

He took one look back at London in the distance, the morning sun reflecting on the tallest buildings, with the Tower of London just visible in the distance. Once again, he was leaving behind all that he valued in his own world, for a cause that he now doubted, as he had seen how they had all manipulated him. "Goodbye England." He whispered, as he watched the river below him as he hung onto the swaying ladder. "I'll be back one day."

***

Dawn broke with a wintry sunrise, full of flaming promise. But the morning had also brought desolation.

Carole rose and went into the heads and leant her aching head on the close timbers and sobbed at the realisation that her last gamble had failed. The gamble that many women before her had taken when their husbands went off to war, that somehow, they could have something left to remember their men by. Failed, as she felt, her courses start to trickle involuntarily from her.

A while later she was roused by a transistor radio across the water playing a haunting melody 'Moon River.'. She recognised the tune and the mellow tones of Johnnie Mathis, 'Moon River, wider than a mile, I'm crossing you in style, someday… wherever you're going I'm going your way' and she smiled Yes, somehow that Moon River would carry her lover back to her. She remembered the moon rising last evening and hung onto her faith in Nicholas that he would return. She rose and went into the galley and there, next to the kettle, was a key and a note which said, FEED THE CAT.

ARCHIPELAGO
PART II

CHAPTER ONE

Baltic Passage

Nicholai had been plucked, half drowned and frozen, from the lower reaches of the Thames. After warmth and whisky, senses returned to him. But all this was as nothing to the task ahead. With new clothes and new identity, he was taken to the trading ship 'Ice Maiden', anchored up awaiting his arrival. Nicholai had to scale a slippery, icy, swinging rope ladder to gain the safety of the ship, and was not sure he was capable of it. Rung by rung, every step a lung-gasping triumph, slowly and painfully he climbed, until sturdy hands reached for him and, in a tumbling heap, landed on deck. The hands that grasped him were the hands of seamen who handled him with rough efficiency but he knew they were hands he could trust as he sank into unconsciousness.

The plan had seemed so simple, when it was devised and put to him; to take the pearls and to sell them on the European market to raise funds for the enterprise ahead. To sell them in England would have resulted in too many questions being asked as the pearls were of exceptional quality and had historic connections and would have aroused a lot of attention. Also, to exchange pounds into roubles was not an easy task in these Post War years. Better that the bankers of Zurich deal with them, with their usual discretion.

So, the plot had been hatched and the single idea of using an innocent young woman as a decoy to transport them publicly to the point of theft seemed a reasonably harmless thing to do. Well it had not turned out like that and he must make good on his ability to deliver them to the European money market.

Stealing the pearls from the young lady decoy had resulted in many more complications than he could have imagined. First, one of their friends Boris had probably been murdered, and the girl, Carole, had been put in danger. He had also found his behaviour towards her very questionable as he had fallen in love and he was forced to examine his duplicitous dealings and where his loyalties really lay.

Nicholai had been tossed around in a millpond of opposing forces as each faction sought to manipulate him. But here he was, having done their bidding; But the climb onto the deck, had tested his strength almost beyond endurance.

He slept, and he slept, until the natural vigour of youth returned to him. He was aware of the motion of the sea on the hull of the boat, and was helpless in his surrender to the motion of the North Sea. He marked the days and night by the rolling and pitching of the ship increasing and the light from the porthole steering him northwards.

Water was left by his bedside, but no food passed his lips, as the gut-wrenching seasickness left him helpless. When finally, he had felt able to leave his cabin, several days of stubble was on his chin, transforming him into a hairy roughneck. He no longer knew the face staring back in the mirror.

Dawn was breaking to the East and the watery sun reflected a grey sea and curling crests of waves. Large sea birds surrounded the ship, squawking and flapping around the stern, waiting for any scraps to be tossed from the galley.

Nicholai noted the lessening of the seas and knew that the storm was almost over. He made his way to the bridge and climbed the gangway. The officer on watch glanced up as he entered the bridge, and said in English.

"Good morning Mr. Baronski, shall I tell Captain Aaronovich that you will join him for breakfast?" He said with a grin, noting his passenger's dishevelled appearance.

"I think that would be the polite thing to do, but I am short of a razor at the moment and would be glad of some assistance in the matter."

"I'll send down all that you may require, Sir. Have you need of any cold weather clothes as we shall be in arctic waters soon?"

"That would be much appreciated as I came aboard rather in need of such things." He said in masterly understatement, and the officer looked at him with respect, having been on watch when the 'transfer' was accomplished.

"My name is Lieutenant Leibviev. Happy to have you on board," he said, extending his hand which the passenger took in a firm grip.

"Thank you for all your assistance, my name is Nicholai," He said in perfect Russian and the two men smiled at each other. He turned to his rating and said, also in Russian. "Please go with Mr. Baronski and furnish him with anything he might need, then escort him to the Captain's day cabin at 7.55 am sharp." The Rating saluted and gestured to return to the deck which, Nicholai reflected, was infinitely easier than climbing up to it in the early dawn on a swinging rope ladder!

Refreshed and clean-shaven, Nicholai reported to the Captain, after finally washing the Thames water from his stale body, and felt more the man he had been. A stout fisherman's breakfast was all he needed to set him up and he was looking forward to a fine Finnan haddock or a pair of kippers. His companion, named Anton, knocked on the Captain's cabin door.

"Come in." Said a commanding voice from inside. "Ah, Mr. Baronski, I think," Said the bearded figure at the table. "Just in time for breakfast I see. Do sit down."

Nicholas bent his head to enter and took the seat indicated. "We have just opened a new barrel of pickled herrings, or perhaps some smoked reindeer. I can recommend them both highly."

Nicholas hesitated only slightly before expressing his preference. He thought ruefully of his obvious misconception and saw he was in the hands of foreign sailors, with foreign customs.

His host chuckled, "I see you hesitate. Perhaps you have lost track of the time?" "Happy Christmas Mr. Baronski, welcome to our Christmas feasting. We shall not make harbour for another 48 hours, so I hope you enjoy sharing this special feast with us."

He was allowed time to devour his food in front of Captain Aaronovich who smiled to see the hearty enthusiasm of his guest.

"These northerly trips always end in large breakfasts." He remarked conversationally. "You have not eaten your passage yet as it is three days that we have missed your company. Some vodka?" Gestured his host, already pouring a large measure into a glass. On a small brazier on a galleried sideboard, a canteen of coffee was brewing on a samovar. He nodded and the Captain raised his glass, tossing the vodka down. Nicholas saluted him with his own glass and drank it in like manner.

Hunger assuaged, he turned to Captain Aaronovich and said.

“I must apologise for my tardy thanks. Indeed, I have much to thank you for. I didn’t realise quite what a task I had agreed to, but I am fully recovered now.”

“Enough for you to have room for bacon and eggs as well?” The Captain suggested and he flicked his fingers at the waiting steward. “We shall not celebrate until this evening so you have some catching up to do.” And Nicholas discovered that his hunger had returned, as the vodka spread slowly to warm every part of him.

Captain Aaronovich had sailed these northern seas all his life and it was a life he would never want to change. He had served his war, ferrying food cargoes to and from his native Baltic ports to Copenhagen and the ports of Western Europe and there was a wealth of seafaring knowledge stored in that bear-like exterior. He had friends in many ports and made best use of them as the trader he had become.

At first glance, he appeared to trade in timber but, if there was also a chance to pick up a more lucrative cargo than lumber, he was very happy. He was aware of the needs of individuals taking passage without official sanction.

Europe might be at peace but there were many reasons for this human cargo. He didn’t care. He didn’t think it was his business to enquire and he didn’t like nosey Customs Officials anywhere. He had been trading backwards and forwards to London for many years. He had first made good contacts with English city merchants when he had been on the Baltic convoys, bringing food to the Russians during the Siege of Stalingrad, and he had not regretted his trading partners.

There were many goods that were needed, after that time of famine for his people, and he respected the reciprocation that had been forged. Captain Aaronovich was sad that their two countries were now enemies but, like traders everywhere, he kept his mouth shut and continued to serve the purposes of both countries.

His good friend, Harry Bailey, had been pleased with the latest artefacts that he had brought to London, as, being a trader in Fine Arts, was more than happy to buy any interesting pieces that might come into the Port of London, via the captain, when bargaining for passage with human cargo. His prize piece, last time he was engaged in such a way, had been a triptych of a 'Madonna with Pearls of Sorrow,' and he had been paid handsomely by his passengers, as well.

Now, he was being asked by others along the chain, to transport this 'piece of flotsam' to Copenhagen, in a reverse exchange. He was a man of humanity but knew that he must also be a man of his word as his trade depended on it. He had certainly taken a liking to this young man, when he had seen his courage in scaling the ship, and knew that if he had any opinion in the matter he would do his best for him.

****

Harry Bailey had been visited by his wartime compatriot Sir Charles Willingham-Wright. They had first been thrust together in World War II, when they were in Army Intelligence, and had been called to interview prisoners after cessation of hostilities, mainly Naval personnel, but also returning at this time, Prisoners of War. Their combined abilities had been honed to extract meaning from pierces of obscure information and make sense of them. The also had to register many examples of contraband Works of Art and their love of Russian art was ignited by this 'hands on education.' With the War over, Harry had returned to his peace time occupation as an Auctioneer of Fine Arts. Since then, there had been many useful sales, as Harry had found suitable items to offer Sir Charles, who had become a collector of Russian Art.

Harry had recently made a purchase from the Captain of the 'Ice Maiden' and, between them, Harry and Sir Charles had deciphered the message on a triptych he had received from Captain Aaronovich. In order to further Sir Charles's Foreign Office machinations, Harry had been instructed to arrange the transfer of a certain Mr. Baronski on to the Finnish ship, "Ice Maiden,' without the benefit of border control or customs clearance in a highly irregular use of Customs & Excise personnel.

His close association with Captain Aaronovich ensured that the 'Ice Maiden' would anchor up mid channel close to Chatham to await the arrival of the individual to be transferred, and to ensure his safe arrival in Copenhagen.

Harry had been troubled by the turn of events, especially as his secretary Carole was somehow mixed up with them. This did not interfere with his loyalty to Sir Charles, but it seemed that his suspicions, in connection with the Soirée that Carole had attended at the Russian Embassy, had involved more of his staff as well. It had even involved one of his employee's sons in the River Police. He was discovering that Sir Charles had great influence and could command formidable resources.

****

Sir Charles sat in his wood panelled office and thawed out after his trip on the river. He was relieved that the operation was over and that he had left the choppy waters of the lower Thames. He realised now just what a 'close run' task it had been and how his recent plans would have been in vain if Nicholas had failed to scale the rope ladder, remembering how he had hung there, twisting in the wind. Sir Charles blamed himself for not calculating the recovery time the young man would need to scale the ship, but Nicholai had hung on until the sailors could grab him.

He fervently hoped that his future plans would not sail so 'close to the wind!'

****

Another 48hrs. in Captain Aaronovich's company, had cemented an instinctive bond of friendship between the two men. He saw in Nicholai, the son he had lost at the same age, to the ravages of war, torpedoed whilst serving on the convoys.

'Plague on all their houses,' He had vowed and continued the next part of his life in paralyzed emotion and concentrated on his boat, the only thing he loved and trusted.

He had not been told the purpose of his passenger's journey but speculated that it was to be hazardous, and his new regard for the young man left him surprised at his anxiety for Nicholai.

The Captain was to take him to Copenhagen and to assist him onwards, and was to receive news of his re-embarkation point later, when on another turnaround.

Nicholas had a rather more formal entry into the Port of Copenhagen, as his new papers were in order. and, in fine crisp winter weather, he disembarked formally, after waiting on the deck, as the statue of 'Little Mermaid' seemed to welcome him into that fair City, in the distance.

He had been assured of a bed at a boys' boarding school near the centre, within easy distance of Parliament Square and the Tivoli Gardens, and he was soon on his way into the city. His exertions in the waters of the Thames had left him very stiff but otherwise none the worse and he looked forward to a fine adventure, in the way of youth, with hope and excitement.

He followed his instructions to the school and asked for Fr. Ignatious, a lean spare man of ascetic appearance. The friar's firm handshake and steady gaze belied his scholarly appearance and reminded Nicholas of some teachers he had known. Many of them, as young men, had been forged by their time in the Services in World War II, and they had a breadth of experience that was not commonly seen in the post-war Masters. Nicholas instinctively knew this man could be trusted to guide him on his way.

The bars, around the school, were mostly frequented by sailors and he thought that a visit to one of them might prove useful and he wanted to get a more comprehensive idea of the city layout. Bar staff were a fraternity in themselves, and could be relied upon to supply valuable information on the locality. They were also a good source of hospitality if he should need another base.

Nicholas was 6 ft. tall and of slender build but his fine shoulders, strengthened by many hours of swimming and years of playing rugby, had developed power that was not immediately obvious. His fine physique was complimented by a handsome face, dark haired, with a fine nose and startling blue eyes, which were guaranteed to hold the attention of any barmaid he might meet.

This combination of charms had their usual affect and there was soon a welcoming response from a long limbed Nordic beauty behind the bar. She was more than willing to give him any information he required and provided pleasant company for his evening of entertainment.

He slipped away before the bar closed but showed sufficient interest in the barmaid to ensure a welcome return should he so need it.

He was to meet a contact tomorrow to further his journey and was happy to sleep in a bed on dry land again.

Tomorrow he was to take a train south to his first destination, Geneva.

He walked slowly along Stroget and crossed the river, turning right at the next crossroads.

He went down into the Underground and bought a ticket to the Town Hall Square. Journey quickly over, he entered the northern end of the wide space in front of the Town Hall. He looked around. To the right the gay awnings of stalls at the entrance to the Tivoli Gardens, and to his left, the building with its red brick exterior and cupola shaped tower complete with a model of a ship.

A few stalls had been set up on the far side of the square but this was forlornly empty and only the pre-Christmas detritus remained to be cleared.

In the centre of the square was a huge Norwegian Spruce tree bedecked with Christmas lights, the only cheerful remains of the newly celebrated feast.

Nicholas looked at the empty stalls and he remembered the welcome he had been given on board the 'Ice Maiden.' He saw that the decoratons for the Christmas festivities were gone and he felt bereft of human contact, especially the young woman, Carole, he had left behind in London, whom he had betrayed by his disappearance. The trust she had given him, not only with the pearls, but with her love, was now in pieces.

He vainly thought of his final act. He had left the key and instructions about the cat. He held on to the hope that she would see, in that single gesture, a hope for the future, if ever he could return to her.

The task ahead of him was full of perils and his loyalties must stay with the older ties of family and principles and his gratitude and inclination must lie deeply buried with his conscience until he had brought his father out of the Gulag.

****

Sir Charles was sitting at his club in St. James awaiting a guest. A tall gentleman with rimless spectacles came through the door. He was wearing a broad shouldered lightweight worsted tweed suit with long lapels and a coat, single buttoned, and below hip length. A large 'kipper' tie, fashioned in a double knot, was brightly advertising his transatlantic credentials. He strode towards him and after shaking hands, unbuttoned his coat and sat down.

Sir Charles said, “It is good to see you Buzz, Scotch, is it?”

“Oh, hell no.” Buzz said heartily and in rather a loud voice for the hallowed traditions of this London club. “Bourbon is my ruin,” and Sir Charles recognised the futility of restraining the manners of this Texan, who knew more about the open prairie than the enclosed world of Whitehall, and ‘who bowed to no man’ in his assertion of American supremacy.

“Well I guess you want our help, huh?” And laughed again at his not so subtle reference to American aid both during and after the War.

“Actually, ‘Old Man’,” Sir Charles drawled, “I rather thought we could help each other in this matter. Mutual interests you might say.” Outlining Nicholas’s dilemma.

“We need to facilitate an exchange of currency into roubles from the sale of some rather valuable pearls without the usual bill of sale, etc.”

“It is to facilitate the ‘extraction’ of a certain ‘item’ from a very cold and unfriendly place. I rather thought that you might have an interest in our success.”

“Erm.” Said Buzz, all sign of southern brashness erased

“Well we sure have interests there as things seem to be ‘hotting up’ on our Cuban doorstep. I guess any bit of knowledge on that Front might be very useful to us as any news from," he paused, 'very cold and lonely places,' are hard to come by. How fruitful might this alliance prove?" He said in an altogether softer voice.

Sir Charles sat back in satisfaction and reeled in his line.

"Well," he said slowly and quietly, "potentially, very fruitful."

"We understand that we have a 'toiler in the field' in our sights, so to speak, who has been 'reluctantly engaged in production,' for many years. He is highly intelligent and certainly able to put two and two together. We want him out."

They both sat back smoking their respective countries brand of cigarettes and drinking their respective whiskies. The moments lengthened and, to the rest of the members, of this venerable Gentlemens' Club the two men could have been asleep. Only the occasional puffs on their cigarettes, and the slugs of whisky, indicating their active state. The men no longer fenced but in their minds, they were working out the level of co-operation that would be necessary.

****

In South Kensington, Carole was astonished at the news that her friend Janice had to tell. They had fenced with each other about the outcome of the events at the Arts Ball, both reluctant to tell the other of their real involvement, but Carole's flight back to her parents' home for Christmas had been partly enough to cover her distress at Nicholas's departure.

Janice had been fully aware of the part that Sir Charles had played in the subterfuge but was concerned that her friend had suffered because of it. "I should have known, that such a damned handsome man would wreak more havoc than I care to contemplate. Well what's done can't be undone." She reflected, and dismissed it from her analytical mind. That she had never experienced such an emotional attachment gave her sympathy, a perfunctory edge to it.

"I've been posted to Geneva." Said Janice when Carole returned to London after the Christmas break, "and I have to be there straight away."

"Oh, just what you have been waiting for. Carole exclaimed, then asked. What am I to do about the flat?"

"Well," said Janice, "we have paid up to the end of January so there is no hurry. I shall be allowed relocation assistance and I am sure that will cover it until then. Perhaps you could find another girl to come from the YWCA. It worked well for us." Janice gave Carole a hug for there was a definite droop to her shoulders.

"Yes," said Carole forlornly, "I guess we went through rather a lot together."

"Keep in touch with Anna who should be back in her flat soon as she seems to have partially recovered from the ordeal. I heard from the caretaker that she was to have a nurse in place upon her return. said Janice before continuing.

"Carole, does she know that the pearls have gone?"

"Well, she hasn't said anything outright to me but she does seem to know a lot more about events than I would have originally thought possible. So far, she has not asked about the pearls, but seemed restrained from saying much whilst in hospital."

"Yes, that's what I thought." Agreed Janice.

After a pause, Carole said cheerily, "Well, does that mean I have a place to stay if I ever come to Switzerland?" Looking enquiringly at her friend and forcing a smile.

"Of course, said Janice, better still, what about helping me to move and spend a few days looking around. I believe it is a beautiful City, right there on the lake. I shall have a flat provided so there will be no problem of initial flat hunting. You could spend New Year with me?"

Janice was pleased at her new posting but if Carole agreed to join her for the New Year it would ease her first few days in a new city.

****

Joe Southgate and his missus had enjoyed their Christmas. For once, their 'boys' were off duty from the River Police for much of their Christmas and the break seemed to mark the end of his worries over Carole. His fatherly concern over the young woman in his office had reached some conclusion. He had heard from his 'boy' that there had been some covert River Police operation on the river but was not privy to any more information than that. He had tried to protect her from any involvement in the 'Arts Ball murder' and, in the end, the Police had decided that it was 'death by misadventure' but he did not like to think that she had been dragged into something unsavoury.

When he heard that she was to leave the office at the end of the month for a place in Whitehall, he was surprised but glad, that her reputation was still intact, but saddened that he would not see her smiling face every morning. Not that he had seen any evidence of that since she had returned from her holidays and he sighed. He had known that the 'London Effect" would descend upon her and the face she presented to the world was as close shuttered as the rest of the workers. He supposed, as was the way of things, that he would lose contact with this ray of sunshine.

****

On Parliament Square, Copenhagen, Nicholai was looking for 'Café Tricolour.' He was to meet a man in a Burberry raincoat and, so far, he could see no sign of him.

Although there were tables laid out in the street, most of the customers were crowded into the busy interior of the establishment. Customers of all kinds were huddled into the café and the smell of coffee assailed his nostrils. He was tempted by the coffee with alcohol shots to keep out the biting cold but rejected this idea, thinking to keep his wits about him.

He fought his way to a corner of the room, to a table that overlooked the square, and sipped his coffee and ostensibly read his newspaper. The conversation flowed around him but most of it was lost in the general hubbub Five minutes elapsed before he spotted a short, stocky man come into the café with a briefcase, a short mackintosh buttoned up, and muffler around his neck. Nicholai looked again, yes, it was a Burberry and he did look slightly official in his office suit. The man queued for his coffee and casually looked towards where Nicholas was sitting and their eyes met.

With a slight incline of his head, the man had acknowledged him and waited for him to join his table.

The man crossed the room and, without further acknowledgment. He sat down next to Nicholai and turned towards the window onto the square. They sat in silence, drinking their coffee, with the briefcase by his side. The man finished his coffee in a hurry, and left the table without the briefcase, having pushed it towards Nicholai so that it was beside his right leg.

Two minutes later Nicholai left the café with the briefcase in his hand and headed towards the Tivoli gardens. He turned left, across a bridge, and headed south. Within minutes, he found himself beside a church and slipped inside to examine the contents of the briefcase.

On top, there was an envelope and inside was a ticket, marked Geneva, and he was now on his way to his second destination. His fingers felt for the round beads in his chest pocket and was reassured that all was in place.

****

Buckland Berkeley Redfern was pleased at the outcome of his conversation with Sir Charles and felt that they had come to a satisfactory conclusion. Any information that could be gained about Russian relations with Cuba would be desirable. There appeared to be many Soviet ships coming in and out of Havana. It was very uncomfortable having a Communist state on their doorstep and they needed to keep a close eye on the new Castro regime. He knew that somehow the C.I.A. had missed some piece of information about Russian intent and that tension was rising in their relations with them. President Khruschev was doing everything to aid such an ally in America's back yard. It made a perfect jumping off spot for any military action they might dream up. It was certain that they were supplying arms to President Castro, but how far Russian intentions might go, they had only the briefest of information about.

It might be very useful to know more about the manufacture of arms and war materials, currently being produced, and the proposed rescue of a dissident might provide proof of any such connection to the Cuban situation. It was certainly worth a few thousand dollars to get this information and he was willing to speculate in this venture.

He had returned to his office to brief one of his European operatives and felt he had invested wisely. Their information out of the USSR. had been woefully sparse of late and already he had lost two operatives. Any operation that had the dual purpose of providing knowledge and the propaganda engendered by the rescue of a dissident, made this a very attractive investment and Buzz was quick to realize its potential. It also meant that he did not have to train up any possible field worker, which was notoriously difficult to do.

There had also been a disconcerting number of leaks recently and he was in need of a coup to help the 'Firm' regain some credibility.

****

Nicholai took the night sleeper to Strasburg to change for Geneva. There he was to meet his English contact J.M. to hand over the pearls. From there he was to go to Zurich where funds would be available and cashable, in either francs or roubles, and a Swiss bank account set up in the name of the Chevaliers de Russie.

He knew it seemed a simple transaction but experience had recently taught him that simple plans could go wrong and did not, again, underestimate the dangers of the task. He had arrived at the station, after perusing his instructions, in good time for the overnight sleeper and to replenish his meagre wardrobe and pick up books and newspapers for his journey.

He understood that the levels of comfort would rival the English Pullman and his thoughts turned to food, as he had not eaten since that morning in Parliament Square. His good appetite had been strangely diminished when he recalled his last hours before this adventure had started, and, in quiet moments, found it hard to concentrate on anything else. Nicholai was haunted by the suspicion that Carole had known of the game all along. But she had trusted him, hadn't she, and given him the pearls of her own free will?

He would never forget the sight of her naked body walking towards him with the pearls around her neck. She had appeared to be in a trance but she had clearly expected him to take them from her.

It was at that moment that he had felt the full sense of his betrayal and he needed to express his love for her even more eloquently, but no words came. They had lain in each other's arms more gently than in all their passionate exchanges but here they were, already saying goodbye, and their lovemaking, when it came again, was as gentle as a kiss until those final shuddering moments. Somehow, he had tried to communicate his farewell and had left her lying there to fulfil this obligation to his father.

Nicholai was brought out of his reverie as the train pulled into the station. One hour's wait e.t.a. 6.00 pm. He had a couchette already booked in his name and he picked up the holdall he had purchased and climbed up into the train and along the corridor to his sleeping accommodation.

Compartment found and baggage safely stowed, he had not seen the man, in another grey but crumpled overcoat board the train, and sit in the next carriage. In haste to start his journey, Nicholai had not followed the basic procedure of checking whether anyone was following him.

He awoke to a sunny landscape and watched the peaceful fields unfold in front of him and was in no hurry to go into the Breakfast Car. With all this time to kill, he did not need to rush.

He had briefly met his partner for the couchettes in the dining car last night and who seemed a pleasant fellow. They had shared a 'dram' together before turning in, to save disturbing each other's slumber. Now he was alone and clearly his travelling companion was an earlier riser.

The Steward knocked on the door and proffered a bowl with hot water and was able to accomplish his shave to a reasonable standard.

Spruced up and relaxing into the rhythm of train travel, he went down the corridor until he reached the dining carriage, carrying his briefcase.

He felt in his jacket pocket to check the pearls and was reassured. This was the most difficult part of his journey as money had yet to be traded for the package.

He saw that his companion of the night was already on coffee and cigarettes and noted the American brand, recalling his conversation with Sir Charles, and idly tried to pin his neighbour to one particular country, but failed. That he was well travelled, Nicholai already knew from their conversation last evening, but had not yet decided upon the man's country of origin. There were many nationalities on the train and it was clear that many of the businessmen were bi-lingual or multi-lingual and he was drawn to the international flavour of his fellow travellers.

Nicholai had initially been spoken to in Danish but when it was clear that he was not a Dane, they had settled on French as the 'lingua franca,' as both seemed fluent in this language, though neither seemed to be speaking their native tongue.

The time passed pleasantly enough, but soon it would be time to change trains, to take a train with two engines, front and rear, as they anticipated the climb into the Alps and over into Italy.

He had been conscious, when they had passed over the Ruhr, how much devastation was still to be seen, and the pockmarked houses of machine gun fire were testament to their recent history. Great barns were open to the sky and churches stood half crumpled. The bridges also showed evidence of fighting and one or two still had rusty relics of the conflict on their banksides.

He thought of the history of his people and remembered the stories of Stalingrad that Tasha had spoken of and of the awful loss of life. Tasha was always full of gratitude for the Allied effort to bring food to his country at that vital moment and he wondered where his own efforts would lead.

He knew that he wanted to rescue his father but was unsure about the motives of his fellow Russian Emigrés. Did they just want to retake their own country by reinstating a monarch in some vainglorious scheme or were they also wanting to help their adopted country resist Communism?

Nothing was clear to him anymore, but his long train journey gave him plenty of time for introspection.

They arrived in Strasburg in the evening and, since his second train would not be leaving till midnight, he decided to look around the City. It had many fine buildings of mediaeval importance which were to be dwarfed by the newer buildings going up for the New European Parliament, and old and new jostled for attention in this cosmopolitan city.

Nicholai found a small bar near the station and ordered a beer. Once again, his appetite had deserted him as he thought of Carole. The tavern got noisier, as the time passed, and he flirted outrageously with the barmaids, drowning his sorrows. He endeavoured to put

Carole out of mind, and an evening of harmless banter suited his mood. He wanted to restore his life to the easy-going one he had lived, and this was balm to his aching heart. But it didn't change anything. He was no longer the light-hearted Sir Galahad of his youth and he knew it.

As he left the tavern and started to walk towards the station again, he was hailed by his couchette partner.

"Oh, hello, are you getting on the train for Geneva?" He asked.

"Well, yes I am, I have been tasting the beers of this part of the world." Said Nicholai.

"The best in the world," Asserted his travel companion, and, hearing the pride in the man's voice, thought he'd guessed his nationality. They walked together, amicably discussing the merits of top and bottom feeding yeast and the flavour they imparted. Just as the enthusiasm for German beer betrayed this man's nationality, so Nicholai's knowledge of bottom feeding yeast betrayed his English connection. They strolled back companionably to the station, not seeing the man in the shabby raincoat following behind.

They climbed into the train once more but, on this occasion, had separate cabins. However, they were not averse to sharing a nightcap, as before, and fell into easy conversation.

Nicholai was visiting family, as his cover, and his new friend was a salesman in anything he could barter as an agent for several western companies trying to trade in Europe. A facilitator is what he had called himself and Nicholas appreciated that here was a useful man to know.

He checked into his room at La Grande Hotel, Geneva, and was pleased at the cosmopolitan nature of his accommodation. Most of the guests were businessmen and nobody bothered you unless you wished it. There was a smart American bar and a quiet lounge so, happily chose the bar. They had eaten breakfast on the train and his new-found friend, had given him a business card with a flourish. "Happy to be of service, anytime." And Nicholas saw that he was based in Geneva.

His journey had left him feeling travel stained and weary, despite the comfortable couchette, so he decided to go up to his room and use the shower before a bit of exploration. Nicholai had several contacts on his list but first he was to present himself to the English Embassy. His contact had the initials 'JM' and Nicholai hoped that he would be accommodating. Not everyone in political circles liked the idea of foreign meddling and he might be just such a person who was a stickler for the rules.

CHAPTER TWO

Shadows and Illusions

He checked out at 12 noon, went to explore his surroundings, and turned towards the lake to the right of the hotel. One minute later a young woman, with blonde hair and a svelte figure, came up the steps of the lobby and asked for a coffee and menu to be brought to her in the lounge bar, as she flopped down on a sofa chair.

This sightseeing is rather exhausting. This is a City for businessmen not so much for tourists. She decided, feeling rather exposed at sightseeing alone.

At Janice Murray' suggestion, Carole Semele had come for a week to help her settle into her new Posting at the English Embassy. But it had been spoilt by days of urgent work for Janice, and they had been temporarily housed in this hotel nearby. It had been lovely to think of getting away for a while but the reality had been less than exciting.

Her sense of loss after Nicholas disappeared, had not lessened, and she did not feel like mixing with any of the hotel guests. It was used mainly for businessmen and she certainly wasn't in the mood for casual male company. All her natural sparkle had drained away and she had ignored any overtures of friendliness from all these, away from home salesmen. She took out her book and sat in the corner, away from the sounds of laughter in the bar.

***

Janice was thrilled to be taking up her second assignment since coming to the Foreign Office. To be posted to Geneva for six months was a' feather in her cap' and she intended to make the most of it.

Now she appeared to have arrived in the middle of a crisis brewing, over some visitor new to town. She had been detailed to entertain him, when he arrived, and had just ordered a discreet dinner at a nearby hotel for them.

She fleetingly wondered whether she should invite Carole along too. It would certainly make for a very happy evening for any gentlemen to be accompanied by two young ladies, but decided, rather shrewdly, that Carole would outshine her and Geneva was to be her patch.

She tidied her desk and went down to meet this Mr. Baronski who had breezed into town. She had yet to read her brief but thought, at least, she could meet the fellow and make him welcome to this fair City.

She took the steps to the lobby of the Embassy and saw a tall, dark haired, young man with his back to her, reading a magazine. At the sound of footsteps clattering across the polished floor, he rose and turned to greet her. With her arm outstretched, and a warm smile on her face, she was confronted by Nicholas Baron. In equal surprise, his jaw dropped when he recognized Janice. Recovering first, Nicholas smiled uncertainly.

"Why Janice, what a surprise to see you here. Of course, J.M. that's you. Is'n't it?" He said, vainly trying to keep some composure.

Janice took in two facts: That he was discomforted and glad to see her in equal measure.

"Hello Nicholas. May I call you that, Mr. Baronski?"

He looked her straight in the face and said. "Actually, that is my name but I never use it in England. Now, is it right that you are taking me to dinner?" And gallantly he said. "I shall look forward to that. More earnestly he continued, and we can catch up on old friends. Carole is well I hope?"

"Actually," she drawled, repeating his word. I was posted here straight after Christmas but she was rather 'down in the dumps' when I saw her last. Can't imagine why?" She said maliciously, as the face looking back at her that had been full of expectation, clouded over.

"Yes, I rather think that I may have contributed to that. Look I can't talk now as I have to see someone here but perhaps we can talk later, I shall look forward to it." and he smiled uncertainly at her now.

She ushered him in to the Ambassador's Office and left him.

She could not decide what had affronted her most. The brazen double dealings with the Embassy or his double dealings with Carole. She had seen, first hand, during these past days, what his disappearance had meant to Carole and Janice's fiery nature was ready to defend her friend from this natural charmer. What could he be up to and was he to dash her flatmate once again. During this time, she had seen how low Carole had sunk and she feared that meeting Nicholas, in these circumstances, would not be good for her and all Janice's instincts were to protect her from a meeting. Janice decided that she would not tell her of Nicholas' appearance here, and leave it to chance that they might meet.

During the afternoon, Janice had time to read the dossier on Nicholas and began to realise the importance of his mission both to MI5 and, more importantly, to the CIA. Rumour had been circulating wildly about Cuba but, so far, nothing positive really added up. Clear evidence of an increase in uranium mining and nuclear heavy water would indicate that their fears were justified and assistance in gaining this knowledge was desperately needed.

It was clear that Nicholas did not need any distractions from his purpose and would need 'a following wind' to succeed.

She also saw that it could not be left entirely to chance that the two lovers might meet, and was left to ponder how she could prevent that.

Carole received a note from Janice to say that she had been given two tickets for the theatre that evening but would not be able to go. Would she mind if Janice found her an escort, as the opera was highly recommended and it would be a shame to miss the opportunity. She was cheered by the thought of a night out. At least it is a chance to dress up. One more evening in the hotel, with those odious men in the Bar, was a dreary prospect. She was sorry that Janice again had to work late. Such a bother. Janice had hardly had time to unpack her bags, but supposed that it was all part of the life she has agreed to.

She set about preparing for the evening ahead and lazed in the enormous marble bath that was provided. She washed and brushed her lovely blonde hair and stared into the mirror at her own green eyes. She looked critically at her appearance, acknowledging that she was looking decidedly peaky. Her lovely eyes were dark rimmed and strained and she had definitely lost weight.

She needed to pay special attention to her make-up if she was to disguise her haunted look, and she admitted to herself that she had lost her smile. Well there was very little to smile about at this point in her life, she reflected woefully.

Nicholas entered the Ambassador's office in rather an unsettled frame of mind and it was some seconds before he was aware that the Ambassador had greeted him. He extended his arm and the two men shook hands.

Mr. Ponsonby Brown was intrigued to meet this young man. His profile briefing had been curious and, on first sight, he was impressed. That he was handsome was undeniable, but this job now certainly didn't require charm. His accent was perfectly modulated Public School English, but he would not require that either. His physical fitness and strength had been demonstrated already by his swim in the icy waters of the Thames and his rescue climb into the 'Ice Maiden', and he would need all of that strength where he was going.

What he had not yet demonstrated, was whether he had the cunning and intelligence to carry out the task that was required of him. He was almost certainly fluent in Russian, from his first few years in that country, but whether that would be sufficient to avoid suspicion was yet to be tested.

"Hmm, he thought, 'this is an interesting character." And he was ready to do what he was briefed to do.

"Good morning, Mr. Baronski." He said.

"Do sit down, have you had coffee yet?" He turned to Janice and indicated the need for some more. "Do you care for a cigarette." As he opened the box in front of him containing Du Maurier cigarettes. "I recommend them," Said the health conscious Ponsonby, they have filter tips, so much healthier for you, don't you know?"

All polite form over, they began the serious negotiations.

"Well Nicholai, may I call you Nicholai?" He queried in fluent Russian.

"Of course, Ponsonby." He drawled in perfect mimicry of his host in English, but with a Russian accent.

They both laughed at the impudence of it "Then let us get down to business." He continued in Russian and the two men started negotiations.

There were many details yet to be finalised and Nicholas agreed to return for another meeting the following day, when Ponsonby Brown wished to introduce him to a possible contact. Indeed, the whole essence of the plan had first to be financed and the pearls, that Nicholas laid on the table, had to be valued. They had chosen a reputable jeweller, called Choshadi, to value them, but Ponsonby Brown could see the depth of the lustre and little doubted their quality.

The meeting tomorrow was to be of an altogether different kind. As he said "Dos vidaniya, God be with you" to Nicholas, he reflected that, maybe here, they had the makings of a perfect spy, but for whom, he had yet to decide.

Janice showed Nicholas to the door. He seemed inclined to detain her but, in very businesslike manner she said, "I've booked a table for two at Hotel du Lac. I shall send a taxi to pick you up at 7.30 pm sharp. I hope that it will be to your liking, Mr. Baronski; the food and wine there is excellent."

As they had reached the swing door of the lobby, he had to content himself with a murmured thank you, and surrender to the dictates of this official emissary. Well, he thought, Janice does have an air of efficiency and has a certain Scottish charm." But, at this moment, he didn't need any distractions, and his heart lurched when he thought of what he might learn from her.

Carole was ready for her evening's entertainment and was standing in the lobby. She was early for her escort and had asked the Reception to page her, when he had arrived, to where she was waiting in the lounge.

William Wardour was one of the Attachés at the Embassy and was pleased to be of service. He had often had to entertain visitors to the Embassy but this seemed like a duty that promised to be more of a pleasure. He was to take her to the Grand Théatre to see 'Madame Butterfly' and he was 'awfully pleased' at the prospect. He was also pleased to further his knowledge of Grande Opera. He had begun to enjoy such music at his mother's knee as she was an opera singer of local repute, but certainly not more than amateur, and he was delighted, in London, to go to the Royal National Covent Garden Opera House to see some wonderful productions. Now he was to hear Maria Callas and he knew how lucky he was.

When he met Carole, his joy became ecstasy, to be escorting such a 'stunner.' He was an earnest man of medium build and mediocre features, none of which made him stand out for any particular reason, but this was compensated for by his good manners and cheerful disposition. On occasions, those who knew him well, would even say he could be humorous, but that was not an attribute that would be evident on this particular evening.

He arrived just as Nicholas passed him, going to the reception desk to ask for his key. As he took the steps two at a time, he was just out of earshot of the reception desk when William made known his arrival and Carole walked into the lobby, looking pale and interesting. She smiled uncertainly but William immediately came over to introduce himself. She looked at him and smiled sweetly and he was her slave instantly.

"Hello William, so kind of you to escort a lady this evening. Janice has once again been delayed and it was fortunate that you could take her place. I am afraid I know little of High Opera, as I have only been a City dweller for a short while, but I am familiar with much of the music."

"Well don't you worry, there are always English translations, although much of the story is easy to follow. I'm afraid it is all too obviously a tragic love story. The special thing this evening is that you will be listening and watching the finest opera singer of the age, Maria Callas."

"Oh really, then I shall enjoy it as I have heard her once before at Covent Garden," and away they went already at ease in each other's company.

He swept her out into the waiting car and they were well on their way before Nicholas descended the stairs again. He looked at his Rolex watch and, being rather early, he decided to have a drink. Entering the American Bar, he overheard three men talking rather loudly about a young lady.

"Did you see the 'Ice Maiden' go past?" "She didn't have eyes for us boys." "Did you see her escort?"

"Rather ordinary, I would say." said another.

"Yes, but probably very well heeled." "Only the best for that sassy blonde." said the third man.

"Well that rules you out Bill, neither looks nor brains to make big bucks," and they all laughed at his joke.

Nicholas had been half listening to the men but was jerked into awareness at the description 'Ice Maiden.' He thought about Carole and rejected the description. No. She was no Ice Maiden, for her fire had held him in thrall ever since they had met.

He drank his vodka in one toss and left the 'bar flies' to their idle chatter and returned to his own thoughts and soon the taxi arrived. Janice was already seated in the cavernous interior of the Rolls Royce and he did not immediately see her sitting there, but they were soon on their way, with only small talk between them.

Both parties enjoyed their evenings out in their various ways. William was a perfect host and had no difficulty in imparting his knowledge to Carole, without sounding stuffy, and she, for her part, was enthralled by the drama and was quickly in tears at the fate of the crossed lovers. It was all too easy to relate to her own abandonment, but William sympathetically appreciated it too.

Nicholas was pleased at the venue that Janice had chosen, which looked over the lake, and his naturally refined taste had taken in the exclusivity of the setting. Janice also appreciated his good manners and attentiveness and decided to call a truce. After all, there was no spark here but she could, like any woman, enjoy being in the company of such a handsome escort.

So far, she could relax, as her organising skills had worked and she might as well enjoy his company.

He had arrived in rather absent mood and there was a hesitancy about his answers to her questions, but soon he was his usual, charming self and his good manners and enjoyment of the moment were soon re-asserted.

He asked her about her home in Scotland, and her family, and appeared to have put any introspection behind him. She told him about her father and mother, her one brother and two sisters, all younger, still at home.

He laughed out loud.

“Ah there I have it Janice,” he exclaimed. “You have had the perfect training for keeping your menfolk in order,” and he shook his finger at her in mock disapproval.

She looked at him and laughed herself. “Och, that ma’be troo, she admitted with a Scottish brogue, but I kenna keep yoursell doon, ken I?” and he laughed heartily again.

They continued their evening in the same vein, with mocking candour, and he was able to enjoy the evening more than he could have imagined, by which time he knew that Janice would be a good friend for anyone who appreciated her humour.

As the evening was drawing to a close, he saw Janice look at her watch and remembered, with a start, that this was a professional entertainment for her.

Nicholas allowed a pause to develop and said, hesitantly. “You promised to tell me more about Carole. You hinted that she was … not … well?” He said, trying to draw her out.

Janice looked at him seriously for a moment and said, slowly. “She is fine at this moment, and I hope she will be fine from here onwards, but it is no good you thinking about her now.” And she lightly touched his fingers.

“You have a job to do and you don’t need to be thinking about what you left behind.”

“I know,” he said sadly. “I always thought it would be on one big adventure but reality is different, isn’t it?”

She nodded and tried to keep a strict tone in her voice. “It is indeed, but keep your mind on the job at hand if you want to make it home. You are not working for or against lovely people and you must be able to recognise who is your friend or your enemy because, believe me, you are just a pawn on their chessboard, and you are only safe if you keep your eye on the other pieces.”

He looked at her with respect and knew that here was someone who had lots of good sense. He was glad that she was Carole’s friend and he dared to ask.

“Thank you, Janice, for that warning. It is easy to be flattered by all this attention.” and he gestured to the room. “But promise me this, if you will?”

“Ask,” she said, and he looked earnestly into her eyes and, briefly closing them, said, “I can see why Carole likes you so much as a friend, and … as my friend too, I hope." "Please be her friend while I am away."

She shot him a startled look then gravely murmured. "I am her friend and will continue to be her friend, if possible, from here in Geneva, and I am already your friend, Nicholas, believe me." With that he had to be satisfied. They shook hands on it and walked out of the restaurant.

He didn't see the crowds spilling out of the theatre as he was looking out at the lights reflected in the lake and the castle underneath the Alps.

But Janice saw and held her breath as she caught a glimpse of the distinctive blonde hair. She leant over to Nicholas, pointed out the castle and gave him the history of its placement until she was certain they were safely past.

She toyed with suggesting an evening sightseeing but guessed that they would arrive in good time at the hotel. This was a game of hide and seek, but she was determined to maintain the initiative.

Carole had enjoyed her evening. William had been a relaxed host for her entrancing evening of Opera. She had loved all the drama and musicality of the performance and was aware that she was seeing a wonderful event. He had not been at all patronising in imparting knowledge but subtly gave her amusing snippets of 'opera speak.' She would remember the evening for a long time to come it had set her on a course for a lifetime enjoyment.

He had taken her to a small Bar near the theatre where many of the cast came after the show. It had been fun to celebrity spot but they didn't see the Diva of the opera. Nevertheless, Carole was content and vowed she would come to this fine City again.

By the time, they returned to the hotel, it was midnight and Carole was still excited by her evening and reluctant to go up to her room but could not see Janice in the lounge. She saw, by the absence of the key, that Janice had already gone to their room and she began to climb the stairs.

Nicholas had gone into the bar on his return, for a nightcap. The same group of drinkers were in the bar and he avoided their company and found a seat at the back of the room. He wanted to think about what Janice had said of his enterprise. He heard the same comments coming from the bar as before and caught, 'Oh, Oh, the 'Ice Maiden' has lost her cool tonight. Why she even has a smile for us! Hello darling, do you want to join us?" and he looked up to see a retreating back walk up the stairs.

His heart turned over as he thought he had seen that back before. He started from his chair but caught his jacket on one of the arms, impeding his progress. By the time, he reached the hallway, she was gone. Where was she? He shook his head.

What was he doing, chasing shadows? Was he just drunk? He ruefully conceded that he probably was and decided to call it a day.

Janice had phoned and left a message at the office to say that she would not be in before 12.00 pm. She had to make sure that Nicholas had left the hotel before they went downstairs.

She knew that Carole would probably wake late, so, she had ordered breakfast in their room to avoid a possible chance meeting.

Nicholas had an appointment with a Mr. Ponsonby Brown and a representative from the C.I.A., Otto Strauss, a Pennsylvanian second generation German, who knew his way around Europe in his role as general trader and he had been guarding his country's future investment.

Nicholas was ushered into the Embassador's office and, to his surprise, there sat his train journey acquaintance.

"Allow me to introduce you Nicholas to our American compatriot, Mr. Otto Strauss."

"Well, Mr. Baronski," he said in perfect Russian. "I hope you are pleased to be here all in one piece. You might think that you arrived without incident but, take it from me 'buddy', you should be glad that I was watching your back."

Nicholas looked surprised. "Hello again, what do you mean?"

"Well, someone knew you were travelling on that train. He has been watching you since Copenhagen."

"Well that is true of you, Sir." protested Nicholas.

"Yes, indeed, but I have watched you openly, and openly I have been your protector. This person made every effort to conceal himself but he dogged us all the way through Europe. Someone else knew that you were coming."

"I don't understand, someone that knew I was carrying the pearls?"

"Well actually that might not be the reason they were following you but they might know where you are headed."

"That rather changes things doesn't it," Mr. Ponsonby Brown interrupted them.

"This is straying from the point of our meeting." "First, we must set up the method of payment during your journey, as you will need a variety of currencies." "Also, you will need to plan staging posts along your return route."

"If possible it would be wise to build in a variety of transports to break up any possible pursuit."

For the next two hours, they were deep into plans for his forward journey.

None of them spoke of the other possible reason for a watcher. Someone in the Chevaliers des Russie, those vain glory architects of this whole plan, might also not trust the money into Nicholas's hands and might have been guarding their investment. After all, was his arrangement with Georgiou a double bluff, or had he indeed had a hand in the death of the young fool, Boris? Their own plans had been thrown to the wind, or so they had initially thought, when the young Russian, Boris, had been murdered at the Chelsea Arts Ball and they were relieved that Nicholas had been successful in retrieving the pearls and making it to Geneva.

But could they trust him with the money?

****

"Wake up, Sleeping Beauty." Said Janice to Carole when 9 o'clock arrived She rolled over and saw Janice at the foot of her bed.

"Morning," she said sleepily, closing her eyes again to the bright sunshine streaming onto her pillow.

"I've been given the day off today so I thought we could go up into the mountains by ski lift."

One blink more and Carole rolled off the bed and over to the window. Light was dappling her counterpane and she saw the magic of the pink sun-covered Alps.

This was the first clear day she had seen in her few days here and she was transfixed by their beauty.

"Oh, Janice that would be lovely." Carole said in gratitude. "You really are spoiling me, especially after the wonderful evening you gave me last night. The opera was…"

"Yes, yes," interrupted Janice. "You can tell me all about that when we are on the tram car but for now sleepy-head, have some breakfast and put on your warmest most casual clothes because we are going to join the skiers up the mountain."

Without more ado, Carole drank the coffee provided and ate the delicious pastries that accompanied the drink. She was bursting to tell Janice all about her evening but saw that they had time, all day!

It was clear to Janice that Carole had a return of good spirits and was glad that her strategy of the last 48 hrs had held fast. There might be a shock ahead of her, but for now, she could relax and give Carole some happy memories of her time here.

Knowing that they were so busy in the Embassy, Janice was surprised when she telephoned the office, to be offered the whole day off with strict instructions to be in the lounge with Carole at 5.30pm. The rest of their instructions seemed pleasurable enough. She was much relieved that her guardianship was almost over.

Carole and Janice arrived at the ski station like any other tourist. They took the tram car and joined the weekend crowds going to the Alps. Some were skiers but most were the townsfolk taking a winter hike from the City to breathe the mountain air. The sunshine had blown the winter blues away and everyone was chatting and laughing on their way around the lake and up the valley. As they climbed slowly upwards, the full majesty of the Alps opened before them and they were content to look at the scenery.

They skirted the lake on the south side and eventually came to Evian. There they disembarked and decided to stop for coffee. The town was bright with flags and decorations from Christmas. It gave a westerly view of the lake, accessed along a beautiful lakeside boulevard with outside tables along the shoreline. Although it was mid-winter there were many people sitting outside in the sunshine dressed snugly in quilted jackets in bright colours.

Janice said she wanted to find the times of the ski lift or train to the top of the mountainside so Carole stayed to order the hot chocolate covered in cream that seemed the alternative most popular choice. She watched speedboats skimming across the lake and a ferryboat full of people still plied its trade.

On the north side of the lake vineyards covered the hillside. The weather of the last few days, rather warmer than usual but dull, had given way to this glorious sunshine but now the air was much colder and temperatures would drop to freezing by dusk.

Janice said, "Now Carole, you must tell me about your evening. I imagine I missed a good opportunity there to hear the finest soprano of our day."

"Oh yes, you can't imagine how beautiful it all was. From the first to the last, I loved every minute of it. Thank you for arranging it for me. I seem to have been a bit of a nuisance to you."

Janice laughed and said, "Well I need to keep you out of trouble, don't I?" And Carole was unaware of the irony of her words.

****

Nicholas was pleased with his second meeting with Mr. James Ponsonby Brown and the American, Otto Strauss. He thought ruefully of his naïve journey with that gentleman and realized that his assumptions as to the origins of his fellow traveller were wide of the mark and served as a warning in future. He was pleased with the successful mechanics of the sale of the pearls and the valuation.

He knew that it would go a long way towards helping many of his father's fellow sufferers.

What he was both pleased and doubtful about, was the proposition they had also put to him. To spy for the Americans

Any young man is happy to be offered such a lucrative deal but he had mixed feelings about it. So far, he had been motivated by the thought that he was acting honourably, in a good cause, but he held no particular affection for the Americans and his instinctive loyalties lay elsewhere. He pushed his misgivings to the back of his mind and tried to concentrate on the job at hand.

****

Karl Daneshoff was satisfied that he had Nicholas in his sights. He had been remarkably easy to follow as Nicholas seemed unaware of his presence and he meant to keep it that way. The only problem he could see was that dratted fellow trying, with his usual sales patter, to engage Nicholas's attention.

He had not found any opportunity to check Nicholas's baggage but he had been travelling in the right direction to Geneva and all the other indicators told the story as he would expect it to play out.

He was given the unexpected perk of sitting out his spare time looking at a lovely young lady occasionally and that was a treat.

He had only to hang on until Zurich to scupper the deal. If he gained the pearls before then, all the plans of the Chevaliers de Russie, to finance a rescue attempt of a well-known dissident writer, would come to nothing and he could simply disappear. How foolish of Georgiou to be such a braggart about his plans to steal the pearls himself, and how easy it had been to convince the Chevaliers to send a watchdog to follow Nicholas. After all he had been closely implicated in the death of Boris at the Arts Ball and it was easy to sow the seeds of mistrust amongst them.

He had been along to some of their meetings with his fellow Russians although had not expressed any particular allegiance but had enjoyed being with other emigres in a foreign land. Now he saw a chance to lead his own life, free of any particular loyalties he just needed to get his hands on those pearls and leave Nicholas to take the blame.

He might also have found gratitude from the Communist Regime, if he had known the extent of Nicholas's task. But he did not, and his plan was based on the value of the pearls and was unaware of the bonus he could make, if he could reveal any dealings that Nicholas had with the CIA.

Plans for lifting the pearls were foolproof, but he first had to sit out the waiting game. There was also the prospect of watching such a lovely young woman while he did so

****

Nicholas arrived back at the hotel just as evening was falling and went to his room to pack. He had been given precise instructions to the minute of what he was to do and he checked out at the reception and stood waiting in the lobby.

He could be seen by anyone at the bar and made sure that the man described to him was in full view. He stood there for one minute, looked at the doorman and asked him to watch his case, giving him a tip to put the case in the taxi in his name and page him of its arrival all done in a clear voice.

He came into the bar and ordered a coffee, taking it to the inner recess of the room, and looked for the door he had been told about. He sat down and had a full view of the bar and the glass fronted wall of the lounge into the lobby. He counted the minutes and was ready for flight.

"Oh boy, here she comes again, ooh, ah, shala shala ding dong," chanted one of the bar crowd and all eyes turned towards the lobby. Through the swinging doors came Janice with Carole behind her and the doorman taking Nicholas's cases to the door.

For a fraction of a second he hesitated as he saw, through the glass window, Janice come with Carole following behind. But, like an automaton, he followed his instructions to the letter. Out of the back door, along the corridor and out of the kitchen side door, without pausing, meeting no-one on the way. In the side street, a Mini was drawn up, he got in and they drove up to the last bus going up the valley.

He had taken his grey Crombie coat off and put on a black quilted hooded jacket and was able to change into heavy walking shoes and sling a large rucksack on his back. All this was accomplished in ten minutes, out of sight of the hotel.

Karl Daneshoff couldn't believe his eyes. The man had disappeared. He had seen the cases waiting in the lobby and then they were gone and no-one was in the bar.

Why, he had only taken his eyes off Nicholas for seconds, hadn't he? He acknowledged that perhaps it was longer than that, as the bar mates had enjoyed their early evening treat of 'babe-watching' and he had been as eager as the rest. Could he really have missed Nicholas in the process? He thought not and cursed when he saw that there was a door at the back of the lounge bar.

He jumped off his stool and ran to the back exit but was far too late to see anything of him. He reached for the kitchen door but it was locked. He turned around and barked at a kitchen boy, "did you see anyone coming through here?" He shook his head and Karl ran back into the bar to look through the front of the hotel. He saw a limousine pull away with a businessman seated in the back and called a taxi to follow him.

It drove carefully in the direction of the station just as the train for Zurich was about to leave. With case in hand, a Crombie coated man, with a hat, jumped out of the limousine and on to the train. Karl scrambled to keep up with him and, with a leap into the final compartment, heard the whistle blow for departure.

He found a seat and sat down breathless, feeling triumphant. He wasn't to be outdone; he had been quick witted enough to make good his mistake, and here he was back on the trail on the non-stop sleeper train to Zurich.

****

Nicholas was distraught. "Ticket please, said the conductor to deaf ears. "Ticket please, Sir." He said again as Nicholas roused himself to produce the ticket.

What, oh what had he seen? This time he knew he had not been drinking and she had been proceeded by Janice. This time he knew that she had been part of an elaborate plan and he was desperate to make sense of it.

Janice was the key to all this. He thought about the conversations he had had with her and snatches returned to tease him. "She's fine at <u>this</u> moment…Keep your mind on the job if you want to make it home…Just a pawn … keep your eye on all the pieces." He closed his eyes. And accepted what a fool he had been. Indeed, she had warned him. But he had not taken in what she was really saying.

What had she assured him. "I am her friend. I am already your friend, believe me." But how could she be, when she had obviously kept them apart?

He sat there staring unseeing out of the window of the bus. Gradually he calmed down and realised the truth of her assertion. Yes, she was his friend, for she had understood his turmoil. "Keep your mind on the job at hand if you want to make it home."

She had known the difficulties he might face and it was up to him to heed her warning, as he remembered his depth of feeling, at one glance at the most precious thing in the world.

****

Otto Strauss was enjoying a fine wine in the Pullman dining car. He felt it was worth using this train for no better reason than their wines but he was also happy to enjoy the fine dining too.

He lamented the fact that he was not going to be joined by his young companion of last week. Such a shame, there was a fine man in the making.

He was enjoying the reflections of the day as well as the fine wine. What perfect planning, what perfect timing, what perfect discipline they had all shown and he was in perfect accord in his estimation of the MI5 machine. Mr. James Ponsonby Brown was a fine example of the British system but, and here he thought he knew better, so predictable. He was glad that they were on the same side as they could be relied upon to do his bidding.

****

Nicholas finally arrived at his alpine hotel at 8.00 p.m. He had taken the bus to Evian and had used the ticket that had been purchased for him earlier in the day and from there took a taxi to the ski resort of Chamonix. He arrived at his hotel and went straight to his room.

He thought it wise to have some food brought straight up as the less people that remembered him the better. He tested the bed and fell fast asleep only to be woken soon after by the waiter at the door.

With a quick shower and hunger satisfied, he sat in a chair and reviewed his plans.

He hoped they had covered all the options when discussing his itinerary and he wanted to check that it best served his final destination. He knew that he could contact his Russian family by going this way. They had chosen to try a southerly entry into Russia and this would take him close to his birthplace near Samara. He hoped that he could call upon his uncle and aunt for assistance but had no idea what situation he would find in his town.

He also knew that his familiarity with boats would be useful for camouflage. There were constant boats plying the river Volga and the Don and a useful crew was always valuable. It should give him deep cover for part of his journey but left a very vulnerable piece in between.

Once he was over the border from West to East, his papers would be constantly checked for authenticity if he took the train. The alternative route through Germany and Poland was so guarded that he felt it was too fraught with problems to be an option. This all seemed fairly straightforward provided he watched his back and he hoped Otto had been able to throw his tail off the scent.

****

Through the front of the dining car Otto saw a man with a worried look on his face. He had seen him several minutes before going the other way and Otto's face was a picture of bland satiation as he eyed the stranger. It was obvious he was looking for something and Otto hailed him jovially. "There's room at my table if you want some company, most of the other tables are full." with a gesture for the man to join him.

The man sat down and thanked him dismissively. Otto waited. They had plenty of time before they reached Zurich and he was in no hurry.

He offered his dinner partner a glass of wine which he took and after two minutes reached into his breast pocket and brought out an Havana cigar. "Do you mind? he queried before lighting up. I got this custom, when I had a spell in the States. It's a filthy habit, I know, but once you have acquired the taste, it is hard to break." He said in a friendly manner.

"Unfortunately," he continued, "I don't often have the opportunity to buy them. Fortunately, as it happens, I came across a batch of 2000, from a trader fresh out of the States, in Geneva, so I can indulge myself for a while, and of course, a special price for a friend." He laughed

"Otto Strauss your man," And extended his outstretched hand to the astonished Karl Daneshoff, who half-heartedly shook it, at the same time taking the proffered business card in bemusement.

CHAPTER THREE

Goodbye to the West

Janice was saying goodbye to Carole at the airport. They hugged and promised to keep in touch and Carole walked over the tarmac.

Welcomed on board by a smart BEA air-hostess, before long her plane was cruising down the runway. She felt much better for the change in scenery but was sorry that they had not been able to see much of each other. Their last day, up in the mountains, had been so invigorating, and she resolved to return one day. After all, the interesting things in the City would not change.

She reflected on their return to the hotel, the men at the bar who had been such a nuisance. and the strange events as she arrived in the lobby. Carole could not believe what she had seen, and thought that it was a trick of similarity. When you long to see someone, you see them on every street corner, but she still held the picture of Nicholas looking straight at her, thunderstruck, then turning to leave the lounge through a back door.

Surely it was her imagination but couldn't shake off her conviction that it was him. She had spoken to Janice, who seemed evasive in her answers, brushing off her conviction as fantasy; but Carole was left with the impression that Janice knew more than she admitted to. For the latter part of the day she had been looking at her watch rather a lot and seemed anxious to arrive back at the hotel at a certain time. One of the men at the bar had become most agitated at the disappearance of the man she was certain was Nicholas and rushed round like someone demented before jumping in a taxi in great haste. Suddenly Janice seemed her usual self and Carole could not shake off her conviction that she was watching a play.

She sighed. There was no logical reason for the whole moment, so must forget about it she decided.

****

Sir Charles was pleased to hear news from Geneva. So far so good. The exchange of the pearls for currency had been quietly conducted with the Banque Suisse and everything was progressing.

He was struck by the report from James Ponsonby Brown that the friend staying with Janice had been a very useful diversion and he realised that it was the young lady who had been used to get the pearls and Nicholas out of England.

James had said that they had used her as a 'honeypot' and realised that she would have this affect with such ease with her very beautiful presence acting as a magnet for the men. It gave impetus to his own thinking that he would like to recruit her. There was a knock on the door and Carole was shown into the room.

He greeted her with a smile. “Hello Miss Semele, do sit down. We must congratulate you on your efforts on our behalf. I can assure you that everything had a satisfactory conclusion. We were impressed that you showed a cool head and recognize the loyalty you showed to your country. With this in mind we are very keen for you to join us here.”

“It would mean completing a course of instructions, but I assure you that I feel certain you would be up for the challenge. Of course, you would bump into your friends again.”

Commander Tashenka (Tasha to his friends) was worried he had lost Nicholas. There had been no communication from him since Geneva, when he had confirmed that the pearls had been exchanged and that he would shortly be on his way and then, silence.

It was now a week since any contact had been made and then the trail had been lost at Zurich. They had provided Nicholas with several contacts on his way but none so far had been accessed. He was worried on two levels. His deepest concern was for Nicholas. He was his godson after all and he had a deep affection and concern for his safety. He had brought up his godson since his father had been sent to Siberia for speaking out against the Regimé in power in the USSR, particularly Stalin, 14 years before, and he had taken in and educated him as a brother for his own son, Alexandre.

He had turned into a fine, intelligent and thoughtful young man with all the dash and handsome attractiveness to draw both men and women to be his friend.

Tasha prayed that his own affection for the 'boy' had not blinded him to a character fault of opportunism and greed. Others had suspected that he was double dealing in the affair of the pearls and feared that they would never see them again, nor the money either and they had set in place a minder to keep tracks on him.

Tasha's instincts rebelled against any such suggestion, but he had to admit that there were things about the plan that didn't add up. Although stoutly defending Nicholas, he was secretly fearful of the evidence stacking up against him.

At the first confirmation that Nicholas had made it to Copenhagen, they had instigated a double check on him to guard their interests. Unfortunately, they had chosen a man who was more in sympathy with the existing Regimé and did not share their aspirations for a return to the Monarchy.

The frustration that the Chevaliers now felt at having lost touch with Nicholas was clouding their judgment as to the difficulties of carrying out his task. First, he had needed to use all his strength to reach the ship. Next, he had to negotiate and set up the bank account in Switzerland for the sale of the pearls. Then he had to reach his home country without suspicion. Once there, he had to create a situation that would allow him to retrieve his father without detection. Were they asking too much? He hoped not but he felt they must allow him room to manoeuvre.

****

Nicholai had woken the next morning and heard the early morning church bells sounding and saw the sun rising on the peaks and, once again, he admired the pink dawn washing over the mountainside. He dressed in all the hiking gear he had been given and checked that all his papers were in order.

He remembered that it was New Year's Eve, for there were stalls in the market square with all their festive specialities on display. There were mountain sausages, hams hanging from the awnings and chickens and geese hanging ready for plucking.

Housewives bustled amongst the goods and filled their baskets, ready for the next day. Great loaves of bread were piled high and their yeasty freshness could be smelt in the crisp mountain air. Brightly wrapped bonbons were displayed in decorated boxes and fresh biscuits were eagerly sought to satisfy the children for a while.

They laughed excitedly around their mothers and snowball fights were indulged by busy parents. All these festive purchases were piled onto sleds, which the children were directed to pull, and winter kindling was added to the rest. Nicholai watched all this preparation and wondered how he had arrived here alone at such a special feast day. He hesitated in his preparations to leave the hotel, eventually deciding to head for Mont Blanc and the road into Italy. He made his way up to the mountain tunnel and looked at the cars full of returning skiers with their festive purchases, and was drawn to their cheerful appearance and excitement at the coming feast.

He hoped he could thumb a lift to Aosta and spend his holiday feast in the company of mountain folk and skiers who knew how to enjoy the festival and après-ski.

He arrived in Aosta amidst all the returning shoppers with their special New Year delicacies.

Skiers mingled with housewives and young children and all were chatting excitedly. Some of the skiers broke into song and he recognised one of them from his youth.

'Il est né le divin enfant.

Jouez hautbois, résonnez musettes!

Il est né le divin enfant.

Chansons tous son avènement.

The couple, who had given him a lift, directed him to a walkers' hostel and recommended a place for good food and soon he was testing out the most enormous feather bed. Without allowing himself the pleasure of such a soft landing, he headed out to join the New Year's Eve revellers.

The next morning, much cheered by his night of carousing with the skiers of the town, he headed for the railway and set off for Milan and then onto Vienna. There was a brilliance to the atmosphere and he felt that there was a different spirit abroad on this side of the mountain's more southerly slopes. The light from the snow sparkled and shone reflectively on the chalets in these Italian valleys.

But it was a timely moment for Nicholai to regain his sense of purpose and look to the rest of his journey. Ahead lay a far more difficult part of his plans when he crossed into Czechoslovakia. This was to be a far more problematical part of his journey as the border between

East and West was near and checks would be more thorough at every border post.

He would soon have to be speaking in Russian and he wondered how his Moscow accent would fare in the Southern States. He hoped to use a train to Constanza on the Black Sea, and from there to work his passage to the mouth of the Volga/Don. It had been pointed out to him, that a similar return journey would not be wise, as the checks and cross-checks would be much more thorough on the return journey. A more northerly circular route towards Russia, would attract less attention. In theory, this made good sense but he knew that his father's strength was questionable. An easy boatride down the river seemed preferable to an uncertain journey by sled or cart.

Nicholai fretted over his plans as the miles to Vienna were eaten up. All around was a snowy landscape and he calculated that he must also take account of the weather conditions later in the season. "Damn it, why had they embarked upon this venture in the middle of winter!" So, it went on, all his plans churning around in his head as the train went slowly north again.

So far, he had been surprised at the efficiency of the continental railway All the trains ran on time and the stations were clearly marked. He had been able to travel 1st Class, with an excellent Dining Car to break up the monotony of his journey, but later, he would be travelling 'Ordinaire' and that would be a different matter as he would have to sleep in his carriage, as and when he could. He was young and the young could sleep anywhere, or so he hoped.

Mile after mile he had leisure to think his own thoughts and to remember life back when he was ten and they had fled Russia. It seemed to Nicholai that he was seeing it through a prism of golden moments, each picture held in glorious isolation. He remembered his mother (something he rarely did now) and saw his Aunt Babeta, kneading bread on a rustic wooden table, her face all pink and shining. He saw his uncle, with bearded chin, seeing to the horses after a day in the fields exercising and training them. His father and mother were the faces he could least recall, as they figured less in his life than his uncle and aunt.

Samara was a centre of horse breeding and his father, Stefan, had been born and bred to it himself. The changing face of politics and WW2 had changed his father's life and he had been educated away from his native roots. He had left the farm and joined the Navy as an apprentice engineer. He had always enjoyed the mechanics of farming and his brother had a natural affinity with the horses. War over, he had managed to gain a professorship in Engineering at Moscow University.

His clear mind and incisive analysis was meant to be put to the use of the Party, when teaching younger students in Marine Engineering, but his transition from Party Activist to Party Dissident had been the natural consequence of opening his mind to everything around him. That he thought he could influence the young, to modify the system, was his arrogance, and his hubris was his downfall. While Stalin was alive, any different ideas of Russia than his own were unthinkable, and his father was stripped of his post.

The following two years were spent back in his own village where he went back to his family, those that were left after the devastation of the war, and started to help breed horses again. But anger was still burning inside him and he had written a book, that he was able to get published by friends, ex-patriots in France. It had been a sensation. Amongst Émigrés, his views were well received, but the hand of the state acted quickly to silence him, by sending him to work in Siberia.

This sober fact had ended Nicholai's childhood. He and his mother had managed to leave Russia through their contacts in the West and had ended up in Montpelier, where there was a small circle of Russian Émigrés who had fled the Revolution.

His journey to England had been organized by his godfather. He had taken Nicholai under his wing after his mother's early death of a broken heart. Since that time, he had been living as a second son to Commander Tashenka, a Russian Sea Captain, who had served on the Russian Convoys, as interpreter to the English fleet, bringing grain to Murmansk.

His admiration for the British had determined his choice of post-war home and he had settled with his family in Hampshire and had treated Nicholai as his own son; as Alex's brother.

There was a judder of brakes and clouds of steam and Nicholai was jolted out of his reflections, as the train stopped to take on water.

****

Karl Danesoff was very cross. He had managed to lose his quarry and now this irritating man was chuntering on about cigars. He tried to take in what he was saying but his mind was elsewhere.

What had happened to Nicholas? Where was he? He had searched the whole train from back to front and back again, with no sign of him... Had he got off? But there had been no stop to take on water or any time that would have made it possible for him to leave the train?

Karl needed to take another look at the passengers as he thought that it was possible that Nicholas had affected a disguise. He relaxed slightly and focused on more of the man's monologue.

He had thought this man irritating on the journey from Copenhagen and, here he was again, between him and his business. He was like a nanny, not allowing him near to Nicholas. He stopped listening to this bore in front of him and held on to his last thought. Almost like a nanny. Yes. He was. he was as he remembered how he had popped up even in Strasburg, from the tavern. His brain began to change gear, as all the gear changes took him from 0 to 5. Karl gave Otto a considered stare and felt his hackles rise in a primaeval dislike of the man.

He forced a smile and a look of interest onto his face and engaged the man in polite conversation.

There was plenty of time to have a good dinner. There was no stop between Geneva and Zurich so, as they say, the night was young. After all, he had nowhere else to go; and sooner or later this oaf would rejoin his quarry. Karl thought as he sat and enjoyed the Cuban cigar.

****

Nicholai arrived in Vienna as the evening began. He had watched the sun sink into a fiery red ball over the mountains but was glad to be finished with the train for the time being. The station was another astonishing sight of steel and glass and he looked forward to exploring the city.

They had come to the end of the safe zone and tomorrow he would be behind the Iron Curtain, setting out to his native land. His soul longed for the happiness of youth but attachment to the land of his father's birthplace had yet to reawaken in him.

He was to take the more local train through Czechoslovakia to Constanza, which would take much longer, but he needed to feel nearer to the people of the soil to acclimatise to the change of cultures and more earth-bound peoples. He did not wish to appear a naïve westerner, (which he was), and hoped that being thrown together with country folk would re-tie the strings to his youthful life for he wished to <u>feel</u> Russian.

He checked into the Hotel Orient and asked at reception for messages in his name. There was a cryptic one from Otto about a local bar but it did not arrange any meeting. He had left him in Geneva and hoped to meet him here in Vienna. He had supposed that Otto had dodged the tail that had been following Nicholai but perhaps not. For the moment, glad to be on firm ground, he ran the bath and proceeded to enjoy the luxury, the last this side of the Iron Curtain.

Freshly laundered, he decided to explore the City, but first he must send a telegram to Tasha, who by now, he thought ruefully, "must surely think that he had absconded with the money."

He crossed the road and headed for the Central Post Office and sent a message to Tasha and then looked about him. There were several Coffee Houses and Bars, all full of people. By now the office workers had given way to evening strollers. Checking the Bar mentioned by Otto, he looked for a suitable place to sit.

He ordered his meal and sat looking out onto the street.

The lights were twinkling over the river and he was impressed by the grandeur of the elegant buildings. Darkened by smoke, battered by neglect, these Baroque monuments were testament to the impressive past of the Austrian Empire. To think it had all come crashing down with the murder of King Ferdinand. So small a ripple, can create such a tidal wave of destruction, and the fate of Europe had been changed forever but not if his

Chevaliers had anything to do with it, as they hoped for a return to their former Dynasty. It had happened for the Greek Monarchy, so why not for theirs, and so they dreamed.

Nicholai knew these dreams from talking to Tasha, but he somehow couldn't share them. He didn't even know whether he wanted too. All his loyalties now centred on England and this adventure had its roots in family love and duty. So many complex currents were swirling around him and he felt impatience take hold of him. With the energy and impetuosity of youth, this waiting was very hard to take. He ate with intent but no real appetite. Eating alone did not suit him as he enjoyed company too much to choose solitary ways. Was he to do this all the way to Russia? He thought.

****

Otto Strauss was feeling uncomfortable. He was beginning to think that his cat and mouse game with the watcher was being turned on its head. When they had arrived at Zurich, he was aware that the man, who had introduced himself as Karl Danesoff, had begun to stick to him like glue and he had been unable to shake him off.

He had been to his Bank to make a first payment to Nicholai's second account, set up at a different Bank to the one he had opened in Geneva, and all was above board. This first payment was to show goodwill and intent and to help finance certain items to be ready for collection later in his journey. He had also purchased a

Russian Malakov pistol for Nicholai whom he knew was familiar with firearms, from his mention of hunting deer, but his prowess with a modern pistol of such velocity had perhaps, not been tested.

He thought that needed to be remedied before being let loose on this lethal item. Arrangements had been made for them to spend some time in a shooting range in Vienna but he was having the devil of a job shaking off his shadow.

He had finally picked some trade goods to sell on his way eastwards and to give Nicholai a lesson in the art of selling. He should be an able pupil, if he was any judge of character, as his natural love of people would be the best starting point.

Otto had to teach Nicholai how to woo them into needing the thing he was selling and he also needed to know what to buy to tempt them. These were the universal simplicities of trading but he doubted whether Nicholas had ever really needed to practice these arts.

He collected several thousand cigarettes of assorted western brands and, that old favourite, stockings or rather the latest innovation – tights, that required no suspender belt and had no gaps between toe and waist. Perfect with the latest fashion in short skirts.

He sighed, he supposed that he couldn't have it both ways, a touch of knee to see or an erotic touch of thigh above the stocking. Oh my, he could not have both but the thought was having a powerful effect on him.

When he had gathered his sales goods together he had returned to his hotel and noticed a message in his pigeon-hole. They had agreed a code and he checked it for authenticity.

"Uncle May has departed for Ventnor and he will meet you at Osborne House on Sunday for a drink and gossip. Seems ages since we met."

He was satisfied that Nicholai was now in Vienna and he had time to enjoy a little New Year spirit. He left Zurich two days later, full of New Year cheer from that cosmopolitan city.

Otto had asked the staff to make out his bill and bring all his documentation to his room and said that he wished to see the Manager, giving the Receptionist a large tip.

He had the bellboy take several large packages to the hallway and asked for a taxi to take him to the station. He went into the bar and ordered a coffee and sat at the back of the room looking out. As in Geneva, he created a diversion with the bellboy being chastised by the doorman. Quietly he used the door to the back of the room into the kitchen and took the service lift up to the first floor.

The watcher, knowing the trick that had been played on him, followed Otto into the kitchen where the door was open to the backyard. Without stopping to check the lobby, he stepped out into the alley and knocked over an ill-placed bin, which sent him sprawling, while Otto stepped out of the ground floor lift and into the taxi that had already been piled with all his packages.

Karl was not going to be fooled twice and, when he saw the same trick being played on him, knew that he should stick to his decision to follow Otto through the back door. He was convinced that the same ruse had been used and looked around to see if Otto was anywhere in sight. He cursed that he had been fooled but thought he knew which way he was heading.

He arrived at the station to find that the last train to depart was the night train to Munich and the next train to depart was the night train to Prague, also going via Munich. He paused for breath and decided to take the train for Munich. One of those two would surely take him to the same destination and he could catch up with Otto there. Five minutes to wait and a ticket to buy gave him no time to think further and Karl was on the train and departing when Otto finally arrived at a leisurely pace to catch the train for Vienna.

****

Eight hours later Otto stepped off the night train. He had gone straight to his couchette and slept soundly. He had been travelling these trains for 20 years and was not to be fooled by anyone. In his younger years, it had been a matter of necessity to know how to make a quick exit and his repertoire was polished by long practice.

It was one of the joys of his job to play such tricks to keep boredom at bay.

Despite his jocular manner, he spent many hours alone travelling, and diversions of this kind made a pleasant change to the monotony.

****

Nicholai had found some Sobranie cigarettes at the kiosk on the station precinct and was having an early morning smoke with his coffee. He had come several times to the square to look for Otto during the past 24 hours, especially when trains from Zurich arrived, and was in no hurry to finish such an excellent smoke. He remembered the time he had fenced with Sir Charles over the box of cigarettes and thought carefully about his choice. So far so good, but he was a long way from achieving his objective and his next journey was to be the moment of no return.

He had checked that his visa was in order to enter Soviet influenced territory and everything was ready for him to travel as an agricultural salesman to that part of the world.

Across the quadrangle outside the station, came a struggling figure, with many bags and boxes piled high on a station trolley. He watched a rotund gentleman, fuss over their safe arrival on the street. Nicholai finished his cigarette and waited as Otto Strauss looked around him. He hesitated, to see if anyone was following, but Otto appeared to be alone.

Nicholai crossed the street and hailed his new friend heartily.

“Hi there, old comrade, were you detained?” And slapped him on the back before giving him a Russian greeting on both cheeks.

“Ah hello Nicholai, am I glad to see you. Had a bit of bother with a leech, just seemed not to be able to prise it away, but old Otto knows a thing or two,” and he gently stuck his forefinger against the side of his nose.

He laughed, “What have you got there, Otto?”

“Nicholai, I have here, your future education.” He announced grandly, and Nicholas stared at him in mystification.

“Yes.” He went on, “Your education and perhaps, he looked earnestly at him, your lifesaver If you have something to sell, and you can sell it, you will have something to eat, my comrade!”

Nicholas was still puzzled by all the boxes but was content to wait for the explanation until Otto was ready to tell him more. “Where can we put them all, Otto. Don’t you need to eat?”

“Indeed, but first I must deliver these to Meidley Street to store before our journey.”

“Our journey?” Queried Nicholas.

“Yes, I have permission to trade in Czechoslovakia, to the Black Sea, so we shall see how attentive you are to your lessons.”

“Now I will take these to Meidley Street station and purchase our tickets for tonight and you will bring your cases there also and then we have one more thing to do. I have brought you something you might need but I have booked some instructions and practise before I give it to you.”

“If we finish our business before 4.00pm. we can while away some time catching up in a delicious Viennese coffee house that I know. Vienna is most famous for its cakes and you should sample them at least once in your life.”

Orders given, Nicholai was bemused but glad to have a friend along for this part of the journey, which promised to be tedious otherwise.

Again, they took the night sleeper but this time there was no comfortable couchette, just the benches of the rail carriages, and comfort largely depended on the number of passengers in the compartment.

At each stop along the way different kinds of people came onto the train. At first it was full of returning commuters from the city of Vienna in their city suits and briefcases.

As they went further into the country they took on more local traffic, with women and children predominant at school times. There were late skiers, with all their equipment, who were returning from the slopes, many in their twenties with jolly smiles and sunburnt faces. As they went over the Austrian border into Czecholovakia, the sunny atmosphere of the carriage became more sombre and the men had a more shuttered look.

Here Otto tried out his sales technique on them and soon many of his packets of cigarettes and lighters were exchanged for the local currency. Later Nicholai tried his luck on an exchange of a jacket. His quilted ski jacket for a Tyrolean style woollen one but Otto shook his head at him, he had not made enough profit out of the exchange.

Otto continued to show Nicholai what a master trader he was and gradually he began to approve of Nicholai's technique. He had the most luck with the ladies, of course, and his trade in tights was always successful.

Otto concentrated on the men, as there were always takers for his Bourbon and razors. Also, there was a steady trade in Swiss penknives, which he traded to all ages of men.

Sometimes they exchanged their goods for the food and drink that was brought into their carriage, on its way to market, so that they ate very well. The beers of half a continent were sampled and many illicit spirits were tried. These were always opened and handed round to all of the passengers in the carriage, to increase the bonhomie and between them they began to become a formidable team.

Many of the women flashed their eyes at Nicholai and he was not beyond flirting with them, but his taste in opportunism failed him and most of the conquests were achieved by Otto, who quite ruthlessly pressed home the desires that Nicholas had stimulated. There was a steady stream of corridor encounters but Nicholas had no wish to join them.

By the time, they had reached Bucharest, Otto was pleased with the progress Nicholai had made and the way he adapted to the rhythms of language and customs. These surly men of the Slav nations were putty in his hand as he was able to divine their avarice and withhold his price on the deal with cool aplomb.

That man will never starve. Otto thought to himself, and that was the highest praise he could give.

He knew that their time to part was approaching and it was necessary to set up some code to pass messages and hoped fervently that Nicholai would succeed in his venture.

The young man had the optimism of youth on his side, and his cause was noble, but Otto was under no illusion that it was nigh on impossible .to help him from hereon in. Otto had done what he could on this side of Russia itself, but now Nicholai would be on his own.

CHAPTER FOUR

Working the Waterways

Nicholai had said goodbye to Otto with regret, as he had enjoyed his company. His irrepressible way of selling had been enlightening, as he had said it would be. His way with the ladies was priceless and he encouraged Nicholai to join in and try his luck. They had enjoyed the fat of the land, all for cigarettes or tights in exchange, and had managed to be on top by a few bottles of schnapps and wine, a long sausage, 3 lbs. of apples and a dozen eggs. The Slavic people were natural traders and the journey had been a bazaar of colourful purchases.

Nicholai had also exchanged his quilted ski jacket for a Tyrolean one, a pair of leather trousers, a thick woollen scarf and fur hat, and still he had tights and cigarettes, etc., to spare, so was ready to carry on trading all the way to his Russian home and beyond. He said goodbye to Otto at Bucharest, who then headed south. Nicholai stayed on board for the short journey to the Black Sea. Black in many ways as they had passed near to the oil refineries with the black gold being poured into awaiting tanker freight cars heading to the coast.

When they reached Constanza, he lifted his rucksack onto his back and, with his dufflebag over one shoulder, left the Railway Station and walked to the quayside. The harbour was full of ships of all kinds and, even at this early hour, there were people loading and unloading the cargoes. Huge derricks lined the quay and stevedores were scuttling from ship to shore bringing in and taking off goods from all over the Black Sea. There were spices and saffron intermingling their smells of the Orient with homely fare of fruit and vegetables

Far to the north, the oil refineries could be seen and the smell of bitumen filled the air, seeking to blot out the more exotic smell of spices.

Beside the railway tracks were stacked the freight tankers ready to discharge their black pitch into huge oceangoing ships to take their foul-smelling cargo to all the countries of the eastern Mediterranean and beyond.

On the dockside were huge grain silos storing the bounty of Europe's grain harvest to be shipped to the world. Along the quayside, at the far side of the cargo docks, ferries were taking people to work all along the coastline. They were full of locals taking their baskets of goods to more distant communities but were sparsely filled in their content. Eggs, chickens, and vegetables jostled with embroideries and household goods. Men with tin pans and tools to sell, sat alongside workers with their tools of trade upon their person, hoping for a labouring job somewhere around the bowl of the Black Sea.

Nicholas watched the frenzied activity and strolled over to where the smaller sea going sailing ships were docked. Most of these were essentially dual purpose, with the lines and restrictions of a sailing vessel but with engines powerful enough to ply their trade more efficiently. They belonged to the breed of sailing ships, which had plied the waters of the Black Sea for centuries, using wind power to get them there, but with the adaptation to engine power. But their lateen sails provided extra security and speed, and helped them keep down the costs of trading these waters.

Their sailors were traditional and did not change their ways in a hurry. They did not trust themselves entirely to engine power on this mighty sea. Marine engines were seen as unreliable and would only be used in an ancillary way, when entering and leaving port. Local sailors were independent and instinctively distrusted new ways. Their work along the whole shore of the Black Sea took them to other countries, other peoples, and they needed to make their own judgments of the worth of any new way of doing things.

Nicholai knew something of boats and seamen and knew he had to build up his credit. He carefully looked at the boats lying at anchor and assessed their worth. He was looking for a coastal vessel out of Yalta and one that was well managed and seaworthy. There were not many of these as prosperity had come slowly to this part of the sailing fleet. Modern ways had deprived these sea captains of their traditional ways of doing things.

But one of the boats looked very smart and, more importantly, very shipshape. Its ropes were in good condition and coiled neatly and its brass fittings were not corroded or loose. Its decks were well varnished, despite their obviously aged timbers, and he felt, here was a boat he could trust and a captain who kept a tight ship. Discipline and pride in their work, were the hallmarks of a good sailor, as the unexpected had to be dealt with in smart order when a storm brewed.

He casually enquired of a seaman lounging there, of the name of the Captain and where he might be found.

"Do you know the name of the Captain of this vessel?"

"Who wants to know." He asked suspiciously.

"That's for the Captain to find out." Nicholai said mildly, handing the seaman a cigarette as they stood there, smoking in silence. Then the sailor said.

"His name is Captain Malakof, and you will find him at the Tavern over there after 6.00 pm" Gesturing behind him. "But you had best be quick for he will sail with the morning tide."

Nicholai thanked the man and found a café to sit and watch the scene in front of him. Most of the trade he saw was local, but there were many ships of a more distant, ocean going kind. He also spotted many military ships, mostly frigates and police launches, but there was a massive aircraft carrier later in the day, steaming south to the Bosphorous.

This caused quite a stir with the sailors watching from the quayside Café but there was little conversation for him to pick up on. Most of the people looked furtively at their neighbours and seemed reluctant to make comment. Their side glances seemed to be directed at a table where Police were drinking, so he knew that he would get no more enlightenment here. He also needed to lose himself in the crowds; he didn't want to draw attention to himself and his fancy sailing jacket was enough for that.

He wandered into the body of the town and soon found the market. A bright bustling place where, what goods they had to trade, were to be found. Objectively it was not quite a market as he was used to, with stallholders and manufactured goods, but individual traders, mostly women, sitting on the cold ground with their goods around them on the floor. He realised that he would have no difficulty trading his goods here but continued to watch the ebb and flow of customers.

Overseeing all this would be a Marketeer and he needed to know how the pecking order went. Hours went by and, piece by piece, he was building a picture of their commerce.

Mostly the lives of these people seemed drab and dreary but their ability to laugh and joke was not diminished and he revelled in at last listening to his native tongue occasionally, interspersed with Slav, in their daily exchange of greetings.

He wandered around the docks and surrounding promontories, to get a feel for the military presence, but anywhere too close was clearly guarded by military personnel. He needed to commit his findings to memory as it was too dangerous to put pen to paper.

He had checked into a small tavern on the harbour waterside where he hoped to take a ship to Rostov.

He hoped to work his passage but, if necessary, would hope to board as a guest.

He bought his beer and sat talking to the barman mentioning his sailing experience, but not where it had been gained, and expressed his eagerness to join a crew and, particularly 'The Northern Crane,' lying nearby. He had asked where they were bound and on hearing its destination, Rostov on Don, knew that was his best choice. It looked a sturdy ship, with clean lines but full bellied, and would take a large cargo. It was engine driven but it also had a lateen sail to give it extra speed in the right conditions.

Nicholas loved the sea and hoped that his experience in the Solent would be enough to get him a crewing job.

The Black Sea was a very different place to sail but he was willing to try it. He wanted to be accepted as Russian and hoped to establish his usefulness in order to get another job, going up the Don and Volga, on the barges that plied their trade up the waterway to Samara.

Captain Aaron Malakoff was happy that he had exchanged his cargo for a good price. It had been a particularly harsh winter and his furs from Siberia had sold well. The prices they would sell for in Europe far exceeded those in the Ukraine and his fox and beaver were very popular. It was a steady commodity but was getting harder to sell. The fierce winter had created a mini boom and, regretfully thought, he had sold them too cheaply. But a profit was a profit and he was ready to look for more goods to return to Yalta.

He entered the tavern with only one problem. His winchman had decided to go inland to visit his family and he was short of a crew. Here was the place to find one but it was late in the day and he wanted to make an early start.

He approached the counter and asked the barman whether there were any seamen looking for a passage and was directed to Nicholai, who sat with a bottle of Schnapps and two glasses. Nicholai held out his hand.

The Captain shook it and immediately noted. "Soft hands, but a firm grip. No regular here."

"I am wanting passage to Russia and want to feel the wind on my face again," He smiled disarmingly. "I have been visiting family but I am more used to the sea than trains and wondered whether you could use a crew. I am wanting to get to Rostov."

He assessed the young man. He was young and had plenty of muscle to be put to use. Was he agile? Well, he no longer appeared to have either puppy fat or corpulence about him. "What makes you think you would be suitable?"

"Well, I have sailed racing craft for most of my life and am familiar with wind and tide. I haven't worked this size of boat so would need to familiarise myself on that, but if you need a winchman or a steersman I don't fear failure on that score."

He poured the captain a second dram, taking care to limit his own intake.

"Erm." Said the captain, "What about rigging. Can you dance?" He shot at him.

For a minute, Nicholai didn't understand the question. "Well. he laughed, I can certainly entertain the ladies on the dance floor but I imagine you want to know how I would be, up the rigging changing sails in a gale force wind?"

The captain grunted.

"Well, I have done plenty of climbing and I certainly know how to 'shift my arse.' I've done my share of that" He said, again not specifying where.

He looked at the captain, challenging him to disbelieve his boast. For a long moment, the captain looked back at him.

“You’ll do.” He said and they downed another glass of schnapps to seal the bargain.

“Six am. Sharp.” He said, “The Northern Crane.”

****

Tasha was relieved to receive the telegram from Nicholas. It had been many days since his last message but this confirmed his faith in the boy. His only query was, how he getting to his destination. He already seemed to have taken a long time to get to Vienna, but where would he go from there?

Commander Counter remembered the way he had fled Russia and that certainly hadn’t been orthodox, but he had no way of knowing which route Nicholas would take to return there.

He had managed to reassure the Chevaliers that their plans were still in place and, more importantly, that their money had not been misappropriated but there had been an edge of pique to their relief at being proved wrong in their doubting.

Minka, his wife, was also able to sleep more easily in her bed that night knowing that at least he was still alive. She had taken him in as a lonely boy and had grown to love him as her own. He had been a wonderful companion to her own child, Alexandre, and they had done everything together. Now was the time when they must both seek their fortunes, and she must not fuss, but she knew that Tasha had been worried.

He had a more realistic view of the success of this venture and his only reason for consenting to their part in it was his consideration of the debt he owed Stefan Baronski, Nicholas's father.

They had both served on the Baltic Convoys, he as an Interpreter/Commander and Stefan as an Engineering officer. They had served together on Russian warships and on minesweeper duty and they had been torpedoed by a German U-boat.

In the Arctic Convoys, you don't last long in those icy waters, but Stefan had hauled him onto a large piece of flotsam and kept him conscious, until being rescued, and he had no doubt that he owed Stefan his life.

The choice of Nicholas as bearer of the pearls and of bringing his father to Britain, was one of expediency and purpose.

The Chevaliers wished to use Stefan for anti-Soviet propaganda and knew that Nicholas had more reason than anyone to be successful. What they hadn't bargained for, was the disruption to their plans by outside forces possibly stealing the pearls, and there had already been one suspicious death.

That Nicholas had been implicated in a plot was certain, but his guilt was not. The Chevalier de Russie sat in critical judgment of the outcome, in comfortable chairs and warm clothes, and refused to contemplate the difficulties of the venture.

****

Nicholai woke before dawn and made sure everything was well stowed in his kit bags. From now on, he needed to make sure that everything was in order. He already felt more comfortable with his new persona, a sailor, home after education in eastern Europe and he wished to appear as ordinary as possible. His appearance, now that his chin had a beard of several days' growth, was less obviously European and his hair fell untidily around his face and had more the look of a poet than a ruffian.

He presented to the world a half-finished product. Neither boy, nor man, still lithe and lean of body and broad of shoulder, but with no obvious strength and solidness of gait. But his face, which to most women showed laughter, now had a steadiness of gaze and hardness of jaw that demonstrated how far he had come in the weeks since he had left England.

He sniffed the sea air, (the sunshine had little warmth in it) and his natural spirits rose as he saw the 'Northern Crane' crew already about their business. The seaman on watch nodded his head to the rear fo'c'sle and he found a berth which appeared empty of anything and stepped up to the main deck, reporting his presence to the captain

"Reporting for duty, Sir." He said, in military parlance.

The captain nodded. “Take the cross-springs and keep her steady until I have her about, then look sharp and pass them out and stow them. You’ll need to be quick, as she turns smartly.” With that Nicholai was left to handle the guy ropes and painter and, as the ship turned into the stream, let go the springs from the bollards and stowed them swiftly aboard. Without stopping he jumped onto the foredeck and retrieved the ropes, coiling them smartly and securing them on the deck. He checked that all were on board and safely in place and stood at the main mast.

“All stowed, Sir.” He reported and another grunt of assent was forthcoming from the captain.

There appeared to be five of them in the boat, each with their own task to perform, and soon they were away from the other boats and heading to the harbour entrance. They were sailing on engines alone but Nicholai knew that he would be called upon to hoist the sail as soon as they cleared the retaining wall and lighthouse.

By this time the sun was rising from the East and the boat headed straight towards it, silver shooting rays of light, shafting through a haze of clouds. All set fair.

“Break out the sail Nico.” Shouted the Captain at Nicholai and he responded by hauling away at the halyards. It was backbreaking work, even with a winch to help him, but he knew that once it was halfway he would find it easier and the wind was light on the sail.

“Halyard secured.” He shouted back to the crew, “Look to your mainsheet and bear away.” And soon all the madness of the last moments died away and they were firmly on their way, the sea gentle in the dawn.

“Bosun, I think it’s time for breakfast now. Are you all done? Coffee at least. We have a new man on board?” “Nico, this is Maro, Bosun and the best chef on the Black Sea. and here are the rest of the crew, Nagi, Ahab and me, Captain Malakoff.”

Nicholai looked at the crew and realised their assorted pedigree. This was a meeting of East and West, all chosen for their ability to do a job not by their nationality and was glad to be counted amongst them as he had already witnessed their prowess in the last few minutes.

He took the proffered coffee and grinned like a schoolboy. This was the life. he thought, the only place he felt truly at home.

****

Carole knew that what Sir Charles had asked her to do had ripped her heart apart. She had done it, as she supposed, for the good of her country and she already knew what that had cost her.

She had finally given the pearls to Nicholas when she had revealed their whereabouts,

She realised that he was implicated in something she did not understand, when Boris had died at the Arts Ball, but the intervention of Sir Charles Willingham Wright into the situation had made her understand that there was more at stake than a theft and possible murder. Here was espionage as well and she had been enlisted to aid her country's interests.

But this had resulted in the disappearance of her lover Nicholas, and she was left with the knowledge that he had betrayed her when he had disappeared with the pearls.

Now she was left to pick up the pieces and Sir Charles's offer had astounded her.

He had asked her to join his undercover team. Here was a way to put all that behind her and lead a life that she had never imagined.

He had not minimised the difficulties she might face but he had said she would be well trained for the tasks ahead. He had indicated that she would be under strict military discipline and would have to complete a six-month course of physical training before any firm decision could be taken on her future deployment. She was thrilled at the challenge being presented with. Her schooling had been most ladylike, having been educated at Cheltenham Ladies College, but childhood, (with her deceased brother David), had been robust enough. Swimming, sailing, canoeing, riding, walking and hockey had all been enjoyed by her over the years and saw that, here was a chance to use those skills, and she jumped at it.

After her initial six weeks of training she had passed out with adequate results. Her unfitness had told, after her six months of sedentary life in London but stamina improved over this period. She was sent away each weekend on specialist courses and found them both stimulating and surprising as her knowledge increased.

She had left Messrs.Bailey, Bailey & Whigstaff at the end of January and had not returned to London until mid-March. She had thought hard about the decision to live on the boat and, now that the winter had lost its grip, had determined to use the key which Nicholas had left, and had been kept safe, she fervently hoped, until his return to her. She had been amazed at how quickly the time had passed and how much she had enjoyed the challenges she had been set, but they didn't take the ache from her heart.

****

Sir Charles was having lunch in his club with 'Buzz" Berkeley Redfern and wanted to express his thanks for the co-operation he had received from the Americans. The monetary transaction had been conducted with the utmost secrecy and it had been confirmed that Nicholas was now in the Black Sea, heading for Yalta.

With luck, some very useful observations could be made there, as it was the Southern Sea Port for military hardware out of Southern Russia. If there was any increased activity in the area, Nicholas should be able to turn up some evidence.

"Do come and sit down." Said Sir Charles to 'Buzz' as he escorted him into the dining room. They recommend a rather special salmon today, down on the night train from Scotland." Buzz refrained from expressing any preference, although he personally thought New England salmon equal to anything 'the Brits' could catch.

They sat down and Sir Charles poured his guest a light white wine. "Hell no, Charles old boy," moving to put his hand over the wine glass. "Its Bourbon for me, I can't say I care for all this French tradition. I am happy to drink their reds but all this pale stuff is like dishwater to my taste." He expostulated.

"How like a Texan." Sir Charles smiled thinly, waiting for his annoyance to subside. He was here to thank the man so let him have whatever he liked. They talked of the weather and what the golf was doing in Atlanta, and nothing was said of their real purpose.

They had finished the salmon and were onto the steak when Buzz reached for his cigarettes, Marlboro's. He offered Sir Charles one but he declined. It was far too soon for him. He couldn't get over the practice the Americans had of smoking through every course and he didn't need to emulate this.

He kept his calm and went on to the business in hand "We seem to be at a critical stage and I hope that we will soon hear some good news."

"Yes." Said Buzz. "He's certainly 'flying solo' now but I reckon he has passed most of his tests with flying colours." Using the usual jargon of the times.

"Our man gave us a good report of his progress and they seemed to be firm friends by the time they parted. He gave him some very useful training in sales, I hear. He certainly might need to use those skills if he has to hunker down at some point. What's your e.t.a. on this?"

"Can't say with any reasonable estimate. It all depends on the weather. It is a very fragile parcel he has to bring back, so we can't use rough tracks to deliver it." Said Sir Charles.

"Indeed." Agreed Buzz, trying to think of a way to get over this dilemma. He concluded. "Well, we'll just have to see how that pans out. No good crossing bridges till we come to them," and they sat contentedly finally smoking their cigarettes together Marlboro and Dunhill.

****

The sea crossing to Yalta had done Nicholas a lot of good. He had finally been able to stretch his limbs with some honest exercise. The passage had been uneventful but the comradeship was real. They had worked the ship in fine professional style, each responding with an extra notch of efficiency and the captain was very pleased with his new crew. He was only sorry that he had to lose him here at Rostov to return - to his family – he said, although Captain Malakoff doubted that. He had paid him a bonus for his hard work and Nico had given him the last of his schnapps. They had also exchanged jackets, the captain's old worn pea jacket for his state of the art, inflatable jacket, that he had admired on Nico's arrival.

The Customs Officers were very particular about their cargo, poking around in the hold. When they came to Nicholai he explained that he had returned to visit his family and he openly showed them some cigarettes and, more embarrassingly, the tights and condoms. He explained to them that he wanted to impress the local girls with his purchases and urged some on them as a gift for their girlfriends and, man to man, they laughed at the young man's tale of opportunism and they relented, stuffing their share inside their uniforms. He pressed some of the cigarettes on the officials and they looked no further.

The captain watched this exchange between the corrupt officials and Nicholai. "What a shame I am losing him here. Now that's an art I could use in these parts," He thought regretfully.

Captain Malakoff had promised Nicholai he would recommend him to one of the barge captains he traded with, to help him on his way, and he made sure of another job for him on the barges going North. He promised to meet Nicholai later in the day at a quayside Tavern, and went to find a cargo for the return journey.

He often traded with barges bringing farm tools and machinery parts but today he could not see any barges with this cargo.

Many more than usual seemed to be bringing fertilizer and chemicals and he wondered why these were not being used for their own farmers. Surely the winter had been harsh. They would need these commodities to re-invigorate their fields. Perhaps the snow still lingered and they were overstocked with such items but there did seem to be a great amount.

Captain Malakoff's usual cargo was in seed corn and potatoes and seasonal vegetables and variation on vegetables, all packaged neatly for transportation. These could then be disembarked quickly, and was the secret of his smart operation. He allowed himself minimum turn around time unloading and loading cargo and, in so doing, maximized his profit. He was not a greedy man but he liked to employ efficient methods and had built up a reputation for fair trading.

He struck his deal and had his cargo discharged into a huge barge in one section of the hold. Most of the other compartments were already filled and the bargeman was in a hurry. Captain Malakoff suggested that he might need more crew to man the barges and recommended Nicholai as a steady worker, wanting to go up river, and so the onwards travel was secured and he shook hands with the Captain.

"Goodbye Captain Malakoff, Thanks for the passage."

“My pleasure Nico, you have served me well. I’d take you on tomorrow if you were not going north.” He shook his head, what a waste of a good man to be going in that God forsaken direction and he turned towards the sea.

****

Sir Charles was pondering his conversation with Buzz. He was definitely jumpy about something because he was not usually such a bore over lunch. His chain-smoking and drinking seemed much more pronounced and it was only lunchtime. He seemed to have definitely got wind of something. Sir Charles had assumed that their American contact would leave Nicholas in Vienna, but he had gone all the way to Bucharest before leaving him and had contacted Buzz from Istanbul. He seemed to have picked up a trail to follow to their southern allies and wondered whether Nicholas was aware of it.

He pondered what else he could do to help Nicholas but, for the moment, it was wait and see.

He decided to bring his assistant Ian Duncan in on this at a minor level and sent some of the dossier to his desk. He wanted to use his analytical brain to come up with positive feedback on the present indicators. He felt that here was a brain that got down to the kernel of the project, without thinking too deeply about personalities, as Sir Charles understood that he needed to distance himself from his operatives.

****

Nicholai joined the barge 'Ivan,' with a crew of four, and saw how large the barge was. It was quite unlike anything he had ever seen before. In fact, it dwarfed any barge plying its trade on any British canal system. Not only was the barge large, but so were the waterways of the Volga and the Don and the barges were passing every 10 minutes, one after the next. Each had their own special characteristics but each was loaded completely and travelling at a great speed. It was a miracle they did not collide but each barge had a cox-like figure in the bows with flags to keep them on course. It was a simple method but it worked and the boats kept up their speed. Those moving south were able to go at twice the speed of those going northwards, for the flow at the lower stretches of the river was huge.

The crew took turns to steer the boat, one hour on and one hour off, as the task was very arduous and this was considered the maximum time for safety.

At the end of their first day Nicholai was exhausted by the level of concentration needed. They anchored up at dusk and brewed up another huge pot of coffee, black and strong.

The captain, Ismail Zetrov, was a burly, taciturn man with little conversation but who was a fair task master and nodded in approval at Nicholai's first day. It was a lonely and hard life that the crew worked and he could not imagine how they did it day in day out.

The river had its own charm, and the open skies had such a changing panorama of clouds and light. In the early morning, he woke to the sounds of the river and saw great skeins of duck and geese flying to and from their roost and they came again at night. They flew against a sky filled with colour and drama, sometimes grey and threatening, but often gold and purple and pink with unbroken views over the flat plains. This was the land of the Tartars and they were mostly open grasslands and cornfields with occasional hills in the distance.

To the west of them acres of land were covered with 'nodding donkeys,' sucking the lifeblood of 20th century existence out of the veins of mother earth, and all the detritus of the oil industry was there to behold. Rusting carcasses of pumps and barrels and tools all found their way to the surface landscape and pipelines stretched away into the distance. It seemed they had travelled for miles through this despoilation of the land and there were huge numbers of barges which carried cargo up and down the river.

To the east, great marshlands stretched to the horizon but even here the glisten of oil could be seen in the irrigation ditches. They were full of bird life and water creatures but every now and again a carcass could be seen covered with oil, where it had ventured too near the industrial activity. Nicholai was shocked by this contrast of desecration and desolation, which he had never encountered before, but the rhythm of barge life gave him little time for reflection.

He tried to draw his master out about the life on this mighty river but his overtures were met with little response, Other members of the crew, were not much better. They seemed content to eat, sleep and work their shift up the river, and he fell into the same pattern, content to know that the faster they went, the faster he would be at his destination.

They reached the city of Volgagrad as nightfall approached. The sky was full of the fiery red of portending snowfall. The light from the dying sun shone rays onto the brutal tower blocks newly arisen from the ashes of wartime carnage. It seemed to Nicholas that the city looked like one gigantic flower with the corollary of jagged bombed out buildings holding a crown of concrete stamens thrusting their newly aroused tips to the sky. Everywhere, was to be seen, the dichotomy of old and new, with life and energy emerging from the shattered form of the old city.

It was remarkable to see such renewal from a city battered by yesterday's quarrels. The sun's dying rays had laid a mantle of fiery red, pink, purple and bright yellow over all the buildings, and had created beauty where all had been destruction and brittle newness. He gazed at the sight in wonder, until the blackness of the night enfolded them, before docking in the ugliness of the busy canal basin.

He awoke at dawn to a brilliant blue sky and the world covered in snow. Everything sparkled and glistened with new icy blossom on the trees and over the marshland wastes. Reeds stood in serried rows, stiff to the sky and all was a monochrome world. The icy water was the most brilliant of all, pitching the sun's rays to a state of blinding reflection. The crew stamped their feet and flapped their hands to goad their bodies into the day's progress.

Nicholai was glad he had seen the City in such brilliance as even this snowy morning could not hide the reality of the ruined parts of the centre. Pockmarked buildings gave way to half standing skeletons of factories and warehouses, their empty ribs rusting to a bloody red.

Everywhere there were wide open spaces where buildings had been, with the barest signs of latter-day civilization. Electric pylons, both old and new, traced the city streets and bus shelters, hastily erected, showed the signs of a functioning city. Some of the lights of the night still shone onto the winter landscape and people began to appear.

What had looked like a dead city began to hum with renewed activity as the workers scurried to and fro.

On the waterside, the noise of hammering and hailing enlivened the landscape and the sleepy city awoke, its petals opening to the returning daylight. It was several hours later that they had left the city behind and headed due north.

They worked the mighty locks, which gave way to the great reservoirs on their way ever northwards. The ice on the reservoirs was thinning now and was easily broken to maintain their passage. Miles and miles of marshland stretched eastwards and were teeming with awakening life after the harsh winter.

Different members of crew came and went at each staging place. Some of the cargoes were discharged on the way north and other cargoes replaced them but throughout. Nicholai saw that some of the barges seemed to be on the river day and night and he asked the captain about them. "We don't have anything to do with them, they are government barges. They are taken straight to the military base." He said no more and Nicholai let the subject drop.

Each evening they sat down to borscht soup and black bread, which tasted good after a whole day working the locks and steering the ship and they drank vodka to deaden the pain of their exertions. Nicholai had never felt so exhausted before but he settled for the hardship on board as barge life brought him closer to understanding his father's life.

He was left with a grudging respect for the endurance and tenacity of these men and with their punishing existence. Nicholai realised that his father was experiencing these tough conditions right up on the Arctic Circle and couldn't imagine how he had survived. These were the men who had carved Russia out of this forbidding landscape and way of life, to make it the mighty country it now was.

They came to a great bend in the river, turning westward towards Moscow, and ahead was the City of Samara, with his old home nearby. Nicholai prepared to leave and questioned the skipper as to when he might next be returning. He told him he might have a cargo for him to carry and arranged a meeting point on his return from further up river. In this way, he hoped to divert any questions that were asked of the skipper, wishing to give the impression that he would be returning the same way.

Ahead lay the City of Samara, a megalithic assortment of chimneys, tower blocks of industrial activity and even taller apartment blocks. It bore little resemblance to the city of his memory and the romantic nostalgic ramblings of his godparents. City of culture, home of Chopin and Shostakovich. He had imagined it to be full of Baroque public buildings and refined culture but from the barge it looked very forbidding. The chimneystacks belched steam and soot and the noise of its activities came to him. Even the noise of the barges engines could not drown out the hum.

"Watch for me on your return run. I hope to have a cargo for you next time you pass. I am buying horses and hope to transport them to Yalta. I should need one or two sections of your hold, if they are free, but my timing is uncertain, so if I am not waiting for you, do not keep the space just for them."

Nichalai shouldered the pack and headed east looking for traffic going towards the family's village.

There were many vehicles and carts streaming into the city and he followed them towards the rough direction of his destination, but it was unlikely that he would arrive before darkness fell, so began to look for a tavern. Sometime later he had reached the tram system and presented a coin in payment and, with surly looks, was given most of the change in the driver's bag of money. He noted that he must learn the values of the money he was using or he would attract attention.

He had been shown how to barter and had not needed to use any paper money from the Bank. Fresh notes were going to be a source of suspicion but he needed to buy some staple food with them to add to his coinage. Local commerce would not welcome suspiciously new notes and any goods Nicholai bought, should help to feed him at his family's farm for a few days.

He found a hostelry near the town centre and shed the packs. Tomorrow he would go and register with the Secretariat for Agricultural Foreign Trade. He checked the Papers he had been given by his Copenhagen contact but for now all he needed was a bed and food for he knew that sleep would overtake him quickly tonight.

CHAPTER FIVE

Home in the Steppes

A man of about 60 in cotton smock and baggy trousers and boots was combing the back of a fine carthorse and had been too engrossed in his work to hear the man cross the yard. He heard a knock on the stable door and a man in his 20's, with wild dark hair, weather beaten and whiskered, with deep blue eyes, came into the stable.

"Hello, may I come in?" He said and the other man stared at him as though he had seen a ghost.

"Stefan?" He said uncertainly, realizing that was impossible.

The young man extended his hand, "No not Stefan but Stefan's son. I am Nicholai."

"Good God." The farmer said in astonishment. "I thought I was looking at my brother but, of course I am not, as he would not look like you now. But you are so like him at the same age Nicholai." And his uncle,

Dimitri, took the young man in his arms and hugged him.

"What in God's name are you doing here? By all that's wonderful. Come into the house and see your aunt. She will not believe it."

He took the pack off Nicholai's back and, with arms over the young man's shoulders, he ushered him towards the neat thatched farmhouse and called. "Babeta, Babeta, you won't believe who I have here to meet you."

They crossed the yard as his wife came out of the kitchen. She put both her hands to her cheeks and ran to them.

"You haven't seen this young man since he was a child, who do you think it is?"

Nicholai ran forward and put his arms around the fat little lady in front of him, twirled her round and said, "Beta, Beta, don't you remember me?"

As she shrieked with merriment at his treatment. "Put me down, put me down. It can't be you, it can't be you…Nico, Nico, is it you?" And he put her down with great gusts of laughter and joy in his voice.

"It is indeed, Beta. Let me see you, why you don't look a day older, still as pink and rosy cheeked as ever you were."

She blushed and coloured, "Oh, what a flatterer, just like your father. You must break the hearts of all the ladies." And the laughter drained from his face.

"No, just one." He said bleakly.

"Beta, don't stand there, bring that young man inside and welcome him home."

They entered the low wooden door to the kitchen and he breathed in the smell that he remembered from so long ago. If he had closed his eyes anywhere and sniffed that yeasty herb laden air, he would be here in this long unseen kitchen. His Uncle Dimitri strode to the cellar and brought up a bottle of vodka. He poured a dram for Nicholai and himself, while Beta put bread and coffee on the table.

Dimitri raised his glass to the returning member of family and said, "Welcome home Nicholai." And tossed the vodka down and Nicholai did likewise.

At that moment, a young man came through the door and saw this unusual scene in front of him. It was a tableau he would have burned on his mind forever. His father was a man of habit and to see him, in the middle of the morning, drinking a toast and his mother blushingly fussing over a young man, that he saw was almost his mirror image, left him dumbstruck until his father cried,

"Mikhail, Mikhail, come and welcome your cousin home. It is Nicholai returned to us by some miracle."

And the man came slowly into the kitchen and took the glass he was given. He did not smile, he did not embrace his cousin like his father had, and he stared at this apparition from the past. Nicholai stared back at him and extended his hand in greeting but some long-forgotten antagonism arose unbidden in him, as his cousin refused his hand. Mikhail put his tools down on the kitchen table and chided his parents.

"Why father, at only 11.00 a.m., to be drinking? I would have thought the occasion didn't warrant that. What has my cousin come for, I wonder?"

His father turned to him angrily. "Why Mikhail there is time enough for that but for now just be glad that Nicholai is here and welcome him to his own home."

"Ah, that's the truth of it, isn't it? His home. Have you come to reclaim your inheritance after all this time, after we have worked and nurtured it for you?" He challenged Nicholai, openly hostile.

"No, no, don't imagine that at all, but I hoped for a welcome from my Russian family." Said Nicholai with eyebrows raised.

"Indeed, you should, indeed we do. Mikhail, welcome your cousin and let us hear no more of this." Said Beta in distress and she took Nicholai by the hand and led him up the stairs to a room that had all the treasures of his childhood still there for him to see. He sighed and leant against the doorpost. He could look through the small window at the Steppes behind the house and horses grazing. It was as if all his pent-up longings for house and family and home had not been scattered to the four winds. That he was not part of a new life and his father would come home from the fields.

Nicholai closed his eyes to the sudden sting and Beta, looking across at this stranger that was no stranger because he was so like his beloved father, was glad that she could welcome him home. All the passion was spent but she knew that she loved this boy for the sake of the father that she had loved so long ago. Stefan, poor Stefan, who cared so much for his principles that he had brought down the wrath of the Authorities upon his head and shattered their family in two.

They sat at the table late into the night sharing stories and reminiscences of the life they had led in those childhood days. Nicholai told them of his godfather, Tasha and Minka, who had nurtured him after his mother's death.

"Aye, she was always a fragile woman, too delicate for country life. She was often unwell, but very elegant and talented. She could play Chopin so beautifully at Christmas, to lighten our hearts. Not like the folk ballads we sang. Something more sophisticated and refined. She had beautiful hands which drew magic out of that old piano, not like it is there, but properly tuned and highly polished. That kind of music left with her, and no-one else uses it," Said Dimitri, with undisguised admiration in his voice, as he remembered a strange exotic creature who had landed up with Stefan from Moscow. They all were silent, thinking of the life they had led.

"And you Nicholai, do you remember your time here? Young and fearless and full of love for the horses." Said Beta guilelessly.

Mikhail's face darkened, here she was again encouraging Nicholai to engage with the animals. He thought in fear and foreboding.

"Actually, Dimitri, it is about the animals that I have come. I feel I owe my godfather and mother a huge debt for looking after me so well during my time in the United Kingdom. I would like to repay them, in some small measure, for being such a loving family. I wish to take home some breeding stock and I know I could do no better than to buy them from you. I have already seen the horses in the fields and they are fine animals."

"Oh, so you do intend to leave then." Sneered Mikhail, partially mollified by the news.

"Of course." Said Nicholas reassuringly. "And I also have another debt I must repay but I will tell you more in the morning. If you don't mind I think it is time for sleep as I have been on the way here, oh, it seems forever," And he yawned.

"Oh la, I see you have not changed." Beta said. "Go and get your beauty sleep." You will be all the better for sleeping in your old room." And she busied herself with providing a stone hot waterbottle for his bed.

Mikhail was disturbed at the new turn of events. Life moved slowly around him and mostly he was content. He knew he was respected as a horse breeder and he worked hard to gain that respect. His father was a taciturn and hard taskmaster, so he was not allowed to feel that he counted for much. He knew his father could not manage the farm unaided but it was never acknowledged between them. It rankled with him that his help was taken for granted but he had hoped to be in charge of the farm one day and had bided his time. He knew the farm wasn't officially their own but had felt fairly confident that it would one day be theirs. IF, and only IF, Stefan did not return to claim it again. Now here was Nicholai, Stefan's son, appearing out of the blue with some obviously spurious story of horse dealing. He tossed and turned, thinking about this new situation, but could not decide what to do.

To trust or not to trust him.

For the moment. he decided to co-operate. After all he should not antagonize Nicholai too much. Their old sibling rivalry had broken through with startling speed and he needed to disguise any animosity he felt.

They had not enjoyed their childhood together although he was the elder. He resented the time his mother gave to Nicholai's education when he was her son. He only remembered Nicholai's mother as the beautiful pianist. He could not remember her activities in either the kitchen or the dairy. Beta had seemed run off her feet by this precocious brat and, in his child's eyes, he instinctively understood the preference in his mother's love.

The next morning Nicholai woke with a sense of contentment he had not felt for a long time and he remembered where he was. The memories he found all around the room brought his childhood vividly to mind. The sense of space and proportions were different, as he adjusted all his memories, that had Alice in Wonderland proportions, to the reality he had now re-aligned them to. But the horses held their spell for him in just the same way, they always had.

He looked out of the window and saw them frisking and bucking around the field. Throwing their stiffness of the night from them. Far away, almost as far as he could see, the steppes stretched until they were swallowed by the dark line of forest bogland trees. The steppes had lost their covering of snow but everywhere, there shimmered snow melt that lingered over the grass. In higher knolls, the grass had begun to green up but it still presented a very wintry picture.

He jumped out of bed and decided to take a traditional shower and clattered down the stairs into the back yard. He found the pump, just where it used to be, and tearing his soiled vest and pants off, he worked the handle until the water poured forth and plunging under it, shouting with vigour as the water cascaded over his lithe young body in all its manly glory.

Beta, busy in the kitchen with breakfast and bacon about to be cooked to feed her men, screamed in mock horror as he dashed back into the house, but he only laughed at her as if he was still 10 years old!

She had watched him under the pump and her heart contracted. Oh, how like his father he was, as she remembered him, and she ached for the passage of time and her lost youth. She had settled for a family life when Dimitri had courted her, but in her youth, had known the wild stirrings of passion for Nicholai's father, before he went to sea. But she had made her choice to take his brother out of good sense and self-preservation, when Stefan was gone. Later, when he returned with his exotic wife, she was disciplined into obedience and accepted her role gratefully as dutiful wife.

The young Stefan had let his heart rule him completely as his Moscow wife, Marieta, had no idea of country life. All her experience had been of a spoilt, indulged only daughter of a Professor of Music at the Ballet and she had been a talented musician but what use was there for a musician there in the wilds of the Steppes. That Stefan had been infatuated was clear, but within months, he had transplanted her to this remote land. Listlessness followed the birth of Nicholai, and Stefan was forced to return to Moscow for his wife's health.

Babeta had lived in repressed agony at seeing the emotional turmoil that Stefan was experiencing. The only outlet she had for her confused and subdued spirit was to see to the upbringing of Stefan's son. Her first son was brought up with the traditions and expectations of a Russian kurnak but his official father Dimitri was the second son.

Stefan had chosen to serve his country in the Navy and it was this break with the country that had enabled Dimitri to be in charge of keeping the traditional ways on the farm alive.

The unhappy outcome of Marieta's depression resulted in Stefan returning to Moscow to his father-in-law's house. The care that was needed to help his wife resulted in their son, Nicholai, remaining on the farm. This arrangement had suited everyone. Everyone but the older boy, who sensed the emotional whirlwind that was blowing around him.

Strangely, although Dimitri loved his son, he could not show any natural expression of that love. He kept a tight rein on him fearing the volatility and lack of responsibility he saw in Stefan's misdeeds.

Cast adrift by both his parents, Mikhail's resentment grew as the years passed.

Nicholai meanwhile had lived a life of healthy exuberant activity. It was clear, from an early age, that he had a natural affinity with the horses and spent many wild rides with these sturdy breeds. Beta, with a guilty glad acceptance of the role his mother should have undertaken, made sure of an education for the boy and also oversaw his musical appreciation. She was so absorbed in her duty to Stefan that she was oblivious to the alienation of her own son, from his cousin.

War had come and Marieta came back to the farm and seemed better able to cope with the son she had conceived but not nurtured and the two women waited for the two men to return. Dimitri had been drafted into the Army, to handle the horses working the guns, and it was a harsh life for him. He returned hardened in body and spirit and found relief in listening to Marieta on her piano.

Stefan had returned politicized by his experiences and had found work as a junior lecturer of marine engineering in Moscow. They returned to the city where he gave voice to his resentment by speaking to his students against Stalin. This was not countenanced by the University Authorities, so again they had returned to the farm, where his father had infuriated the Party by publishing a book and, most damning of all, he had published it abroad. This was too much and the Politburo under Stalinist rule, had sent him to Siberia.

They had all been up for hours seeing to the horses, clearing out stables, and breakfast was taken after all the essential chores had been seen to. The smell of bacon frying gradually permeated the yard and there was no need for Babeta to call them in. Soon each one of them had finished their duties and came into the kitchen. Nicholai, freshly laundered by Beta, was looking altogether more bright-eyed than he had appeared on the doorstep the previous day. The slough of days on the barge had been washed away at the pump and sleep had restored his spirits.

"Good morning, Nicholai." Said Beta with a twinkle in her eye, "Are you refreshed from such an invigorating shower?"

And he laughed. "You see I didn't forget the old ways. How many times did I grumble at the dunking you gave me when I had been out in the paddock with the horses, and you scrubbed me down, I don't suppose I am any different now?"

"Erm, not quite." She said, a frank smile on her old face. "Now come and eat one of your favourite breakfasts." As she piled his plate with all the traditional food of the farm. Soon the other men were sitting at the table and the talk turned to the horses.

"How many mares do you run?" Asked Nicholai.

"At present about 30 but there will be more when spring arrives as we have about a quarter of those in foal."

"Do you have your own stallions or do you take them to stud?"

"A mixture of both as we have many other farms breeding good horses."

"Well, I don't believe they could be finer than those I saw in the fields. Perhaps, Dimitri, you will show them to me when you have time."

"You were serious then about taking the horses to England?" Queried Mikhail.

"Of course, I don't talk idly of these things, but I do have something else to ask you."

"Ah, now we come to it," Said Mikhail and he folded his arms, tight-lipped.

"I don't know what I am going to say which makes you so suspicious."

"Well," said Mikhail, "I suppose you want to reclaim the farm."

"Hush, hush, Mikhail, said Dimitri. let the man speak!"

Nicholai looked from one to the other, so alike yet so unalike. Dimitri and Babeta had welcomed him warmly but here was Mikhail openly distrustful of his intentions.

That Mikhail was jealous of his claim to the farm was clear, and he must not antagonize him over that. His own father's life was at stake and he had no wish to fall out with his cousin.

"No, let him speak frankly. Said Nicholai. It is right that he wonders why I have returned but let me make it plain. I do not mean to stay forever in Russia but I do hope to stay here for some weeks, not here at the farm, but in the country, but I will speak of it again. For now, perhaps Mikhail, you would show me your wonderful horses and agree about which you would be willing to sell me.?" He had held the olive branch to his cousin who then had no reason to refuse. They walked together to the paddocks side by side whilst Dimitri and Babeta watched.

He shook his head sadly and said, "There's no love lost there; so, unnecessary and upsetting, but there has always been discord between them, even as children."

She said haltingly. "You are right and you have always known it. So many things are left unsaid and we cannot always help our inclination." Looking at him for forgiveness.

He looked at her frankly. "Don't I know it," He said harshly. "But I have always known it was the price I must pay for your acceptance of marriage, and I have always loved the boy dearly. No-one could have done more, I think. I have kept the farm for him to rightfully inherit but now here we have a legal wrangle which can only be resolved by frankness."

She looked back at him in relief and wonder. "You mean, you mean." She faltered.

"Yes. He said softly. "I have always known the boy was Stefan's but I was his father by name and by right as I brought him up to be the fine Tartar horseman he is."

She hung her head. "I am ashamed." She murmured. He touched her gently on the cheek.

"Oh, Beta, don't you think I always knew you would choose Stefan before me. How could I compete with the young handsome dashing Naval engineer, this plodding man of the soil that I am. Beta don't you think that I also saw him as a great hero and felt I could never compete with him in anything, least of all the woman we both loved."

There was silence in that homely kitchen that Babeta had carefully tended all these years. She looked at him in dawning realisation that here was the man she had loved all these years, who had given her a home and rescued her from her shame, always aware that she had deceived him, but never admitting that he had known of her deception.

"Dimitri," She said uncertainly. "I am sorry for all my silence, but I have always tried to be a dutiful wife and I have been happy and content in my life. Sometimes we have to pay for our mistakes and work at helping others along the way."

She was silent then continued. "That is why I was so anxious to help Nicholai, who was not mine but who had also been cast adrift by circumstances and I am sorry that I didn't see how that affected Mikhail. Yes, you have been a good father to him; he couldn't wish for more because he is happy and proud in his home and animals, but I have never really acknowledged your part in this, Dimitri. Please forgive me because all this time I have looked elsewhere when I had grown to love you without realising it." And she hung her head.

With two strides, he had taken her little round dumpling body in his big calloused hands and hugged her as if he would never let go.

****

Mikhail walked with Nicholai to the paddocks and there was stiffness in every stride. They walked quite apart and there was no sense of affection between the two men. Nicholai tried to draw him out and allay the distrust he could see was in every line of Mikhail's body.

Nicholai looked at the horses, assessing these beautiful animalsThey were a breed called 'Don' that had been the backbone of farming life. Strong and enduring, they had pulled the guns and supplies of the whole Russian Army but were not built for speed. Their strength was in their broad deep chests and sturdy flanks and they were capable of long distances on little maintenance. They made excellent carriage horses and life in the steppes couldn't function without them. The two men examined the mares and Mikhail pointed out the merits of all the beasts

Nicholai asked to ride some of them and soon they had saddled up and were galloping across the plain. They spent the rest of the day looking at the merits of one horse against another. By the time, they had returned to the farm, there was a professional respect for each other's expertise and they returned to the kitchen with more relaxed steps. A truce had been forged as Mikhail accepted, that he was about to strike a very profitable deal.

They returned to the farm and their evening was one of congeniality, and everyone was at their best as they remembered moments in their life together so long ago. When the vodka was produced, the toast began and the kitchen was alive with jollity. Soon someone suggested they try the piano and Nicholas remembered the song he had played at Christmas, about the snow sweeper, and before long they were deep into their Russian ballads. All else was put aside until the morrow.

Nicholai awoke again to the watery sunshine but he had little inclination to enjoy it as the brightness of the light brought back the excesses of the evening and he had a bad head. He groaned and turned over. "Oh no, go away sun." He groaned, but knew that the other two men would be already out caring for the animals and other farm matters. He dragged himself out of bed and clattered down the wooden stairs out into the yard, this time to douse his head in a long moment of cold reality. Partially restored, he made his way to the outbuildings and watched the two men brushing and combing and feeding those animals in the barn. One of the mares had foaled in the night and a sturdy young colt was busy suckling at his mother's teats.

"What a fine new addition to your stable, he remarked. Any complications?"

"No." Said Dimitri. "These animals look after themselves in such matters and we have only provided shelter for them. The winter has been long and the grasslands provide little nourishment yet. We have had a large bill for fodder this winter as we are behind in getting the animals out into the paddock."

"So, if I relieve you of some of your stock, at this moment, it will help you, I hope."

"Yes, but some of the animals need more attention than others and I am not sure how you mean to transport them." The merits of each of the horses were aired in slow and weighty fashion and each man gave his own discourse on the matter.

They talked about it over breakfast, they talked about it over supper, each relishing their own knowledge on the matter. The winter had been harsh and the opportunity to be men with other men, talking men's talk, was far too enjoyable to be hurried.

****

As the Easter vigil drew near, Tasha was more than a little relieved to see that Nicholas had sent him a telegram regarding some horses. He was mystified about the content but was reassured that he was well and had reached Samara.

The most perilous part of his journey was to come but at least part of their plan was on target.

He looked again at the mention of horses and read that Nicholas was buying horses in Russia! Was this an insane fancy or was this a device to get his father out of Russia? He thought nostalgically of his own homeland

and the lovely horses he had known and envied the young man his opportunity to possess something so fine from Russia, but was this with the Chevaliers' money? He couldn't reconcile the buying of horses with their mission and continued to puzzle over it.

****

Nicholai spent days riding the awakening grasslands and grooming the horses; Seeing to their welfare and getting to know the characteristics of the horses he was buying. Giving them special attention and brushing them till their coats shone. Some were wild young colts that knew no master, but with patience and instruction from Mikhail and Dimitri, these began to answer to his voice and allow a bridle and saddle to be put on them. They were not yet broken but they began to understand the domesticity of the older horses and were familiar with thc workings of the farm. Sometimes he would ride out with the older horses and run with the colts on a bridle with the older mounts. Everything he could think of and could see the other men doing to tame these lovely wild animals. Mikhail had begrudgingly to admit to the skill of his cousin in the saddle. He had a fearless, relaxed way with these animals which was not part of his own way with them.

Mikhail knew that his own approach to them was harsher and the animals knew the difference. He deeply distrusted his cousin's empathy with the young mounts as he knew that it could never be his own way. Discipline, and knowing he was master, was the only way he knew to bridle the wildness of these strong horses and it had never occurred to him to love them. They were a livelihood and he had to ensure they were in the best condition to be sold on.

One morning a neighbouring farmer in the co-operative came to see what was happening. He had agreed with Dimitri to help entrain the animals, when they had to be loaded, and the next day a Letter of Compliance came for them to sign.

"Good morning, Comrade." Said Igor Petrovich. "Those horses look fine today. Have you been spoiling them instead of attending to the other needs of the farm?" Smilingly Nicholai looked up from brushing one of the bays.

"Hello Igor." Said Dimitri laughing, "This is the work of my nephew, Nicholai. Do you remember this young man as a child? He lived with us then if you can think back fifteen years. You know, Stefan's son." He turned to Nicholai.

"Do you remember Comrade Igor Petrovich? You used to play with his boys and sing in the fields with his sister."

The young man looked at the grey-haired bull of a man and Nicholai tried to envisage those childhood days. Time had changed the man he saw, as much as his own appearance had changed, but he remembered the timbre of his voice and remembered the man as he had been.

"Indeed, I do," He said and smiled broadly. "and I remember chasing the goose around the yard and how you plucked it and drew it in the yard with all the feathers flying!"

Igor shook his head. "Yes, you boys got me into a lot of trouble that day, for the feathers were for my wife for a mattress and half of them flew away in your naughty games!"

"Oh, boys will be boys." Said Nicholai, not realising that his saying was not from his Russian past and he had spoken in English. Igor looked at him in astonishment!

"Well this is strange indeed. How have you come back to Samara after all these years? Where have you been living all this time?" The questions kept coming and Dimitri knew that his neighbour had really come for a chat and to spread the news of Nicholai's arrival.

Dimitri said, "Questions, questions. Why don't you come into the kitchen and share some food with us, or at least take coffee?" He ushered Igor into the kitchen and he sat down to share their meal. Babeta set another place for brother Igor. "He is eager to hear all about Nicholai and family."

Nicholai explained. "I live in England now with a friend of the family that Papa knew from the War and who felt indebted to Stefan for saving his life when their ship was torpedoed. So, I owe my godfather a great deal." He paused. He needed to gain the man's sympathy without mentioning any political reminder of his father's banishment, although he was fairly sure that his father's position was known.

"We live in the South of England, where many horses live wild. I thought it would be wonderful to take some of our native horses back to that region, to breed them, as a little reminder of home. A thank you, to my Papa Tasha and Mama Minka, for all their care of me after my mother died."

"Ah your mother, such an exotic creature but wonderfully gifted on the piano. Died, you say? But where?"

Nicholai drew breath. "After…after we left here, we went to live in the South of France, near Montpelier, where many Russians now live. But she didn't seem to be interested in anything and soon I was left alone."

"Somehow," He continued. "my Papa Tasha heard of my orphaned state and took me to England, where I have been for the rest of my life."

Igor stared in amazement at the change in Nicholai. "Well you have turned into a fine young horseman!" He exclaimed, "for I had seen you riding across the steppes and you were made for these spirited animals."

They sat in silence while they ate the breakfast and then Nicholai asked. "And what of your daughter, I seem to remember, Nina?"

"Oh yes, indeed, a fine young woman, but very headstrong. She has persuaded me to let her study to be a vet so I hope all the Government's money will not be wasted. Most of the time she is in Rostov but will be home for Easter. Will you be staying until then?"

"Perhaps," Said Nicholai cautiously. "I am waiting for all the paperwork to be completed before I would think of going."

Mikhail had come into the kitchen and now said. "But Nina is very busy isn't she, with all her study, and doesn't find as much time for old friends." He said in a growl to Igor.

Nicholai looked at him and knew immediately that Mikhail's heart was engaged there. That's one young woman I will not be sweet talking. He resolved. I have enough antagonism from that quarter without causing any more.

"Well, whatever I can do to further your project, I will do what I can." Igor assured them. Dimitri outlined Nicholai's plans to buy some horses.

Igor knew as well as Dimitri that this opportunity had come at a very welcome time. The new Agricultural Policy had been to encourage these farmers to turn more of their grasslands over to the plough. The recent bad winter had left them short of fodder to see them through until the new grass came.

They needed to sell some of their horses pretty soon and this was a heaven-sent opportunity to get a good price for them.

But they were canny traders and they did not express their worries openly as they held out for the best price. A bittersweet moment when a figure was agreed.

"They are fine animals and they should be recognised as such." Said Igor enthusiastically. "I will do what I can to help, Dimitri." He repeated.

He turned to Nicholai and casually said. "Whilst you are here perhaps you might like to look at my animals too. You would be broadening the hereditary base for breeding from them if you are serious about that."

So, that's what he's after." Thought Mikhail. "The old fox." But had to agree with his suggestion as a bit more variety in the breeding stock would help maintain the quality. Mikhail conceded the truth of his neighbour's suggestion and was not about to contest the point, especially as he had intentions for the hand of Igor's daughter. This was his hope but he was by no means certain of Nina, as she had not given him any promise. Month by month, as she studied in Rostov, she grew further away from him in spirit.

He certainly didn't want his cousin to butt in there! He thought fiercely.

"Next month she will be home as it will be Easter, or Spring Festival as we now refer to it, and they are allowed a rail voucher to return home for the festival. Will you be here then?" Enquired Igor.

"Well the rate the Authorities work I most probably will and I would love to join in the traditional ways. It is one of the things I most remember about my childhood here."

Before Igor left he had agreed to help entrain the animals when they were to be loaded. With that, Igor bid them farewell. "Don't forget Nicholai, do come and look at my stock as well." He said on parting, and Nicholai wondered whether he should steer clear of that complication.

His instinct told him that here was his greatest danger, and perhaps temptation. He had spent three months longing after a blonde-haired beauty. Perhaps it was time to remember the charms of the dark, well rounded, lovelies of his childhood; But his natural curiosity and friendliness won out over caution, and he hoped that his Export Licence and veterinary papers were delayed so that he could join in the celebrations.

He could sample the simple delights of the coming Festival, couldn't he? Changes had been wrought to their lives in the past decades but they were still country people and celebrated the seasons in due time. Whatever the dictates of the Regime, they knew it was fitting to give homage to some unknown force that blessed them with a good harvest, and the winter had been cruel, giving them every reason to celebrate the arrival of Spring. They needed to re-affirm the year's cycle and commit their seed to the yielding earth. The universal cycle of energy affected them all, and many marriages were arranged at this time.

They decorated the church, they decorated the trees, they decorated their horses and their womenfolk and, in the ways of old, they planted their crops for the coming season. When all was done, they gathered in the village barns and ate the last treasures of their winter store and, if some still celebrated in the church, in the old way, well, most right- minded folk turned a blind eye to the practice, as long as no fuss was made of it.

Soon the music began, and the dancing, and the menfolk twirled and strutted, these cossacks of yore, and Nicholai joined arms with them to high kick with the other young men and sing their songs of old.

The maidens of the village wove their ribbon dances in and out of the makeshift square and the old men and old women clapped their hands in joy. Soon the maidens separated and in turn invited the Cossacks to join them in the dance. Nicholai was drawn in by a smiling maiden with a lovely laughing face. He was entranced by the rhythms and the gaiety of the occasion and soon found himself rotating amongst all the other dancers. At last the music finished and he was facing a young woman of his own age, a little older than the others, and recognised that it was Nina. Ah, here was a complication, for she was looking at him with such inviting eyes. All the other dancers were being ushered into the barns where trestles were laid with the new white bread and wine.

He went to speak but she spoke up first. "You must be Nicholai, I would know you anywhere from that cheeky smile. Welcome home." and she planted a kiss on his cheek. He quickly looked down not daring to respond to her invitation.

"My, you have grown up Nina, what a fine young woman you are! Am I to congratulate you as Mikhail's intended?' And he looked her blandly in the face, not daring to meet her eyes as he was aware of how easily he could have her favours.

"Huh, Mikhail might think so, but I have my studies to finish first before I make up my mind and you are, after all, my first playmate." And Nicholai was well aware of the implied invitation.

Damn! what could he do? It was the last thing that he intended but his self-imposed faithfulness was finding severe strain in the light of this lovely girl standing in front of him. He hesitated, wondering how he could proceed and saw, with relief, Mikhail coming swiftly towards them.

"Ah, Mikhail, I see you have come to claim my dancing partner. I apologise for monopolizing such a lovely dancer. We have just been reminding each other of our childish selves. That we were playmates in the distant past. But those times have long gone, have they not?" And he looked at Nina and firmly extended her hand towards Mikhail to lead her into the barn.

She stood still for a moment, contemplating him more closely. Finally, she said. "Whoever holds your heart, I hope she appreciates it." And he nodded, gratefully acknowledging her defeat and allowing his cousin free rein to woo her. For a moment, there was a fleeting regret but he was amazed to find that her reminder of another woman had awakened all his longings for Carole, far away.

He hitched up his newly acquired Cossack trousers and, in his smartly polished black boots, followed them into the barn.

****

Otto Strauss was enjoying a coffee on the waterfront of Istanbul. Bright craft of every kind bobbed and swayed in the morning sunlight. It had become much warmer in the past few days and it was pleasant to watch all the commerce of the East and West, plying their trade in front of him. He had managed a few really good deals in the past month and was happy to continue his vigil, observing and noting any unusual cargo coming through the Bosphorous.

He was able to ascertain that things were certainly moving out of the Black Sea, with more than usual amounts of heavy cargo, and the number of military ships seemed increased also.

He had, this morning, received an unusual request from Nicholas, who seemed to have taken more than a passing interest in his buying and selling instructions. He had wanted Otto to find a suitable ship to transport horses from Leningrad.

This surprised him but he could see that such a cargo would need grooms to look after them and all that entailed. His admiration for the boy grew as he saw Nicholas's strategy developing.

Nicholai and his uncle had agreed their sale of the horses by the end of the week and all that remained were the details of commerce and paperwork, but officialdom liked to grind slowly. The co-operative nature of their modern farming methods had resulted in many more layers of permits, and an army of bureaucrats to stamp ever more paperwork, and he must have patience for the wheels to turn. He decided that the trip to Samara, to finalise his plans for the horses, would be the moment to lay before Dimitri, his other reasons for his journey. One word to the Authorities and he could be done for, but he needed their help, and hoped they would be his allies in this other venture.

Dimitri and Nicholai set out for Samara. They were in light-hearted mood and talked eagerly about the coming sale.

They also talked of the celebrations and Dimitri joked. "So, you enjoyed all the festivities of the old ways? What about the young women? Did any of them catch your fancy enough to stay here with us?"

Nicholai laughed, "Aye, they were all handsome and, indeed, I could have been tempted but I find that my heart has already been taken by someone I have left behind, so my new home holds my future." Dimitri nodded, re-assured that Nicholai was not about to re-assert any family claim he might have to the farm.

With all the permissions and licences duly stamped, they returned to the farm, the light-hearted mood of their outward journey having been replaced by a more sombre and reflective one. Nicholas held his breath before turning to Dimitri with the real reason for his journey.

"Now that we have agreed terms for the horses, I want to tell you about my hopes for the future. The deal we have signed is independent of anything I might ask you now, but I hope your memories of your brother Stefan will sway you."

Dimitri listened intently for what Nicholai was about to say. He knew instinctively that this would cost him more than money, and held his breath. Nicholas continued. "My main reason for coming to Russia is to try to get my father out of the Gulag and Russia."

"Good God, Nicholai, do you know what you are saying?" Dimitri said harshly.

"Yes, I do. It will be very difficult but I believe that my plan has some chance of success."

"I have made my plans so far with the sole purpose of providing an escape route for my father and by using him as a groom for the transportation of the horses. I have documentation which will provide for him to accompany the horses to Leningrad, but I cannot rely on too much help from a weakened man and will need strong arms to back me up. Do you think you might aid me?"

Dimitri took several minutes to answer him, "And what should we expect for such a risky venture? This will put all our lives at risk."

"Well, for me," Nicholai said, it is a matter of family feeling. "I have been asked to do this by people who believe in my father's work and want to use him to speak out against injustice; but I do it to regain my father and I don't think he can last much longer if he stays there."

"Are you saying," Dimitri repeated. "that you want to take him out of Russia, not just back to the farm?"

"Indeed yes, I don't think he would be much use on the farm, would he? Anyway, you deserve to hold the farm that you have built up."

"I would like to think that my father would respect that and I certainly would reject any claim that I might have on it. It might be due to me by inheritance but it is certainly yours by right of common justice because you are the one to have tilled the soil and kept it alive all these years. I would certainly be prepared to sign away my claim to the place but can only promise to try to persuade my father to do the same."

Dimitri was silent and they went on their way. Nicholai did not force a decision and they sat side by side, hoping that they would come to an agreement.

"May I give you my answer tonight when I have spoken to Mikhail? He is young and strong and would be very useful, but we are risking our lives here, and I think that we must be given more facts before we say anything more. I certainly have obligations to my son but I also have 'issues' with my brother, which go back a long way. If I could be certain that he would deal fairly with us then I am inclined to help you, but it is not just my help that you want to enlist, is it?"

"No, it's not and I might be putting you in more peril than you are prepared for, but I have given my word that I will venture this gamble so, either way, I shall try my luck."

Dimitri was pleased that he accomplished such a good deal for the horses and he had been happy that Nicholai had been fair in his dealings. They had arranged for the horses and foals to be entrained at Samara, when the foals were less dependent on their mothers, but were still suckling. That way they could get the maximum profit for the animals without too much expense keeping them in fodder. They had agreed one stallion, two fillies, two geldings and two mares in foal making seven beasts and he began to think how they could be tended during the journey.

The request that Nicholai now put to him was somehow, what he had anticipated all along. Dimitri knew that this was the greatest gamble of his life. If Nicholai signed away his future rights to the farm, then Mikhail might eventually inherit and he need say nothing more. But the boy was impatient and would sour, if his hard work and inheritance were not fully recognized. He already showed signs of resentment and needed to be given hope that the farm would be his sooner rather than later.

What it needed, and he now readily admitted it, was for Stefan to acknowledge his ELDER son, Mikhail's prior claim to the farm but that would be opening up past wounds and brand Babeta a harlot. Could he risk that all the accord that he had built up with his wife, would be shattered by this gamble.

He must speak to both Beta and Mikhail but what they would say, he did not know.

Nicholai kept his word and asked the lawyer to draw up a Renouncement of Title to the farm, to be signed when Dimitri had decided, and held by the lawyer until his return. The days dragged on as his uncle, aunt and 'cousin' thought about his proposal and Dimitri held back his knowledge of past secrets from the two men as it seemed that Mikhail's fervent hope of inheriting the farm would be realised without opening up the realities of the past.

CHAPTER SIX

The Drive

The purpose of Nicholai's visit was laid out for them to discuss and it was a subdued breakfast next day after the family had thought about his request. There were practical considerations that had to be solved if they were to leave the farm. Whilst the present batch of mares had foaled, they would be more independent of supervision when they had been weaned. The next mares to foal would be next month, so they had a month between the two batches of foals to be born which would give them about one month's respite between the two sets of mares foaling. If the men were away, Beta could supervise the horses' progress but would need a farmhand to deal with the unexpected, and it was agreed to bring in one of the sons of their neighbour Igor, to help Babeta with the heavy work. With Dimitri and Mikhail away, she was freed of many duties in the homestead and would be more available for help with the horses.

If these practical matters were seen to, it remained for them to decide if they were willing. Dimitri acknowledged that he must pay his dues to Stefan for leaving to follow his dream of a life at sea. This had allowed him the chance to secure Babeta. He had faced the reality of her condition when she had accepted him. Now it was important that Dimitri and Stefan settled things between them about the inheritance When he had told Mikhail all he wanted to know of the proposition, his son had seen the advantage of securing the farm from Nicholai, but was indifferent to his uncle's fate but if it got him what he wanted as a result of the rescue, he was willing to try.

He was young enough to be excited by the challenge and had everything to gain by it except the gamble with his life. But youth did not see the dangers as their elders did. A sense of adventure and greed held most sway with Mikhail and agreement was made between the three men to attempt the rescue. This had involved taking horses from their herd to sell in those far places. Any trading of horses was always welcome east of the Urals, as the harsh conditions aged the draught horses very quickly, and a constant supply was always needed.

Babeta was horrified at their plan and the danger it posed, but her latent love for Stefan held her from openly opposing her husband. She must leave it to the men to decide and do her part in keeping the farm going.

****

They left with the dawn with three pack horses each and they headed north for many days. They headed for the boggy forests to the north of the steppes and followed the ancient paths through the forests. The grip of winter in the forest was loosening as they saw evidence of the emergence of wild life. They had taken rifles in their packs as there was a chance that they might encounter wolves. There were animal signs for them to track to add variety to their supper, all the time watching for the re-emergence of the black bear that roamed in these regions. For many miles, they could see the Ural Mountains ahead of them with Siberia beyond. They reached the Railhead of Ufa and went to find a corn merchant that could sell fodder for the horses.

Near the railway was a large livery stable and tavern attached, which serviced the logging merchants and carrier trades from the main railway station. They housed their animals and went into the hostelry. Soon they had spoken to the Stationmaster and had asked him about rail times and onward travel on the Siberian Railway. There were wagons being towed that contained livestock and they gleaned information about any trade to be had further east and the restrictions placed upon the movement of horses, either East or West.

Eastwards, horses were in demand as they were constantly required in more remote areas. Hardy animals sickened quickly in these forbidding regions, but in summer there was a great need to use all the daylight they could, for the warm weather was very fleeting. They decided to take a train east until they came to Omsk, and wished to ascertain the procedure for entraining the horses and what checks they might encounter.

They embarked the horses and saw to their fodder and bedding straw. They travelled with the beasts to ensure their safe arrival. Next to the boxcar was a slightly separate area where they could bed down with the beasts but protected by a side stall to prevent the animals trampling them in their sleep. They had bought black bread and sausages and plenty of vodka and baked potatoes off the train platform, so had enough to carry them onwards. The three men were muted in their conversation, as they had planned their journey beforehand and were intent on their goal. It was to be a risky business and it was best if they did not engage too closely with any other passengers.

Two days further East, they arrived at Navotbirsk, which was a busy staging post from all directions. Here the train waited to pick up passengers from Mongolia and the north, and they had several hours to kill. The bar and provisions station was full of passengers and market traders looking to purchase from the train and they let it be known that they were horse dealers. Soon interest was shown in their mounts and there were serious buyers from the Gulag area. They were eager to replace their broken horses with new mounts and haggling began. They learnt which, and where the section was, that they were seeking and laid their plans.

Babeta was anxious about their progress as she had heard nothing from them.

The young lad from the neighbouring farm was coping well with the horses but she knew there would be a testing time.

She had been instructed to hire help to drive the animals to the railhead at Samara to take the horses northwards. Then to meet the Siberian railway going westwards, to the port of Leningrad, where they hoped to embark for the U.K. If everything went well, Dimitri and Mikhail would meet the rail cattle train from Samara to take them further to the sea port with their onward travellers inside the freight cars. She knew that this would be the riskiest part of the journey and she hoped and feared the outcome. Oh, how she longed to see Stefan again but his safety in England was more important than her wish to see him. She knew that her life with Dimitri would be happier now that they had come to their mutual moment of love and respect and she prayed it had not come too late for them.

From Navotbirsk, they took the horses north to the Gulag 4. They had met the wagoner at the station and he was guiding them to the camp. They rode companionably on, with a fair amount of vodka being exchanged on the way. They laughed and joked and spoke of the hardships of their lives. They exchanged experiences of working the horses in this land and the hardship the horses had to endure and their capacity to survive.

"I suppose your prisoners are even more feeble than the horses in these regions, I don't suppose many of them last long."

"That's true, but occasionally one or another lasts longer than we ever imagine."

“Really.” Said Nicholai. “Is it because they get lighter duties or what?” He urged the man to explain and air his experience.

“Well, it’s really hard to say, but some, seem to be able to stand it more than others; really seem to relish the hardship.”

“What kind of man would that be. I wonder?” Mused Nicholai.

“For instance, we have one famous prisoner, who came as a dissident 14 years ago, and is still here. I don’t suppose he will last much longer, as I can see the fight going out of him. Seems to me he’s served his term. Been like a living death these past few years.”

Nicholai’s heart contracted in pity but he held his voice steady.

“I don’t suppose it is any picnic for you stuck up here, year in, year out. Where do you come from?”

“Oh, I am a horseman through and through, from Astrakhan.”

“Really, do you ever get home or are you here with a family?”

“Well I do have a family here but I hope to end my days, home in Mongolia.”

“Well if you ever come to our part of the world, you are welcome.”

They continued on their way with Nicholai sowing the seeds of the man’s longing for his home in the south.

Later they found a wayside eating house of poor quality, but it had beer and wine and vodka and a vegetable stew of some kind to keep out the cold, and black ersatz coffee.

“I suppose you don’t get much in the way of luxuries here? How do the women stand it?”

“Oh, my lady is okay. She has known much hardship in Uzbekistan so she doesn’t complain but the odd luxury is always welcome. Why, have you anything to sell?” He asked, sensing a deal.

“Well, I come across interesting items, something to please the ladies. They are always grateful for any little item that takes their fancy, if you know what I mean?” And he winked.

He fished in his jacket and, like a conjurer, he fished out a pair of tights.

“This little item came my way when I traded a few bottles of vodka. God knows where he got them, but they are the latest thing for women in the West apparently.” He paused seeing the man’s interest. “They would certainly keep her far warmer than long hose as there are socks on them as well and, for a special outing, she would be the envy of all the other women."

"Here," He said, handing the tights to his companion. have these on me and see what she says. I have several more if you want to trade them amongst her friends."

"Do you ever trade anything else?" The wagoner asked, innocently.

"Well, I get the odd thing or two and I am always aware that cash is not always the best way to trade. Times are hard and the Government…he paused dramatically. Well let's just say they grind a man down with their rules and regulations. How is a man to live, eh?"

The other man grunted and it sounded like agreement but he was obviously cautious.

Nicholas let the subject drop and they continued on their way.

Sometime later, the party calculated that they would be unable to return to the railhead before nightfall.

"Do they have a hostelry nearby the camp?"

"Well they have a small hut for visitors to the prisoners but it is very plain. Look why don't you come and meet my wife. We will be glad of the company in this God forsaken place."

"We will be very grateful to you for your kindness, and perhaps we may have something to brighten your evening." They all nodded and agreement was reached that they would come to his home as soon as they had settled the horses.

Nicholai, by now, was very tired. He felt he had come so far to help his father leave the country and now here, on the brink, he felt at breaking point. He knew he must drive home his sales pitch and come to the crucial moment in the negotiations. He was sure he had laid out a temptation for the driver but would he put self- interest before his fear of the Authorities. The unusually long time in the saddle had tested his riding skills to the limit and there were many moments when his horse had stumbled and he had nearly come unseated.

His uneasy relationship with Mikhail had turned into a truce of sorts but he was very unsure of how his cousin now regarded Nicholai. Self-interest was uppermost in Mikhail's mind, he was certain, but how that would serve Mikhail best he could not tell. Nicholai had tried to show his good faith by renouncing his claim to the farm but was that enough for this cunning farmer. He was acutely aware that he did not trust his cousin entirely, and Nicholai felt he needed to watch his back.

Dimitri was another matter. He had warmed to him, in equal measure to his distrust of Mikhail, and felt that he was the authority here. They shared a bond that was due to Nicholai being Stefan's son and, in rare moments on the journey, Dimitri had spoken of Stefan in his prime. It was obvious that he had hero-worshipped

Stefan as a young man, but somehow there had been a rift, because he clammed up when Nicholai asked too many questions. Families, he thought, there were so many things he did not know about them.

His memories of the farm had been golden and he had returned expecting a welcome. He had forgotten the enmity between Mikhail and himself and he supposed his most treasured memories were of the horses and dear Babeta, and he was now seeing the past through adult eyes and it had changed his view of things.

He helped stable the horses and made himself presentable for their hosts. He had taken Dimitri aside before they left for the carter's house, to let him know what he planned. He urged them both to be ready for any overtures he might make to the drover and to appear disinterested in any arrangement he might make. Above all, it must be seen as a gesture of humanity rather than, their original purpose for being there.

Their parts, were to play the good guests and entertain their host with good cheer, but to be vigilant about their own drinking, as they would need to be fit to ride.

They arrived at a small modern wooden housing unit among a smattering of similar structures. There was a small front space, which could be a garden, and behind, several barn units that housed some horses and tack rooms. There were rusty farm machines scattered around a working pump and trailers ready for use, in a corner of the yard. Beyond was the semblance of a kitchen garden and beehives onto the open tundra. Wild flowers were beginning to show, yellow and white, and silver grasses blew in the breeze. At this late time of day, the light slanted across the landscape and blues and yellows, silver and peach, painting it with the early evening glow. Flocks of wild fowl flew towards the west and starlings set up their evening calls.

Thousands of them wheeled and turned, rose and twisted, adding thousands more to their evening dance. The melody of the keyboard wrote its song across the sky until, with the speed of an instant, they fell to earth among the silver pink reeds of the waterlands. Their twitters reached a crescendo of sound until, again in an instant, they were silent. The sameness of the landscape by day had become the backdrop of sky and clouds for this breathtaking symphony. They stood and watched, held spellbound by the glory of the spectacle.

A large red-faced woman of about 45 stood in the doorway and welcomed them into their home with her husband Jan Gorki. Inside a large fire was burning, in a slow burner, with sods of peat burning inside. She had made the barrack like building into something resembling a home, with bright rag rugs and woven coverings, in bright colours, and any article of value had pride of place on the hearth or the table top. A large samovar stood tall next to the heat and ersatz coffee bubbled away gently.

After initial shyness, she was very happy to have visitors especially when Nicholai used his same charm on her, as he would with Babeta. He had a natural affinity with women, whether they were young or old, and she was soon blushing at his compliments. Hospitality was simple but sincere as Jan asked after news in other parts.

"Summer has come late for us in the Steppes with the snows lasting well into April and we have had difficulty feeding the young colts and fillies as we have been unable to turn them out to forage. The grass was only just coming through the snow melt" Said Dimitri.

The drover said, "Yes it has been a cruel winter here also, so we are glad of any little luxury we can buy."

"Well I have a few small items I can show you later, but I think Sasha is ready for us, yes?" She nodded in smiling agreement as, like any good cook, she did not want the meal to spoil.

They returned to farming talk and Mikhail said. "Do you have need for many horses here? Where do you usually purchase them?"

"Well most of them come from Mongolia but the fine horses you have brought will probably draw better in the dray, so will be put to carriage work. We never have enough of those as few traders get this far."

"No," Said Mikhail, "We would not normally stray so far but we have been forced to sell our horses to conform with the new directives for ploughing the grasslands."

“Well we will certainly pay good prices and make it worth your while if you are able to drive them so far.”

“Well that’s useful to know. We must exchange ‘terms and conditions’ for further trade.” Said Mikhail seeing future prospects for his herd.

They had entered into banter with Sasha as, in happier times, they might laugh with Babeta, and they praised her wonderful steaming dumpling and reindeer meatball stew.

At this point, Nicholai produced a bottle of Bourbon.

“Now this, my friend, is a special bottle, traded for many of my most precious commodities. You don’t see American Whiskey very often this side of the Urals. May I offer you a glass and may I ask you what you think of this drink of moonshine, drink of the devil.” And he poured generously for his host and his wife.

“It will not be the first time that I have tried whiskey as I met Americans in Berlin when we finally made it to that city with the gunners.”

Dimitri said, “Ah! you were in the gunners too. I was also, and served in the War. What regiment did you serve in?” And away they, went happily reminiscing about their war service. The others listened, interested in the talk about the many tragic incidents they experienced. Quietly, he encouraged the talk and poured the whiskey, with generous measure for their host.

"Ah, many good men were slaughtered in those dark days but some who survived, seem to have fallen foul of our own rulers." Said Nicholai.

'Aye, but a man has to live." Said Jan, half apologetically.

By now their host was in generous mood and Nicholai changed the topic.

"Now Jan, we have talked too long and ignored your lovely wife. Perhaps we should show her some of my merchandise to thank her for such a wonderful meal." Jan gestured his agreement and Nicholai brought out some exotic soap and toilet water made in the South of France. "This was traded from the same man that sold me the Bourbon and I wish to give it to you in thanks for such a lovely evening."

Sasha was so pleased with her gift that he asked her how she liked the tights.

"Oh, she loves them." Said Jan laughing. "You can sell me all the rest of them. I can get all the wives to buy those and whatever else you have to sell."

They spent the next hour trading satisfactorily. All this time the three men made show of their different watches, Rolex, Omega and Breitling. At this point, Nicholai pulled himself upright in his chair and in a deliberate whiskey laden voice, said, as though something had just occurred to him.

"You know I was rather moved by your story of the prisoner that had survived so long. Perhaps he is an old soldier and has fallen foul of the Authorities, as many do… He lapsed into silence while they waited for him to speak … I wonder if it were possible to finish his agony by taking him off your hands. What do you think his life might be worth?" He lapsed into silence again. The men continued drinking, and Nicholai returned to his thoughts, until he shifted again and appeared to regain his focus.

"What do you think any man's life is worth? You know, I feel like trying to help him, for an old soldier's sake. They gave so much and were left with so little. Would it be possible?"

"Well." Jan said slowly. "I know the Boss is always angry at the fellow's continual agitation of the other prisoners. Perhaps something might be arranged, but it would not be cheap as it would have to involve the Governor as well."

It was clear to Nicholai that this was not the first such transaction that Jan had made and he breathed slowly out and affected to be indifferent to the offer. "Well, it was just a thought." He said. "But I can't imagine spending too much for such a gesture." He sank back in his chair. "What does it take to release an old soldier who's not got long to live?"

Jan looked greedily at the fancy watch that Nicholai was careful to show off. "What about your watch for a life? Rather appropriate really; The beating of a heart for the beating of a watch."

"Oh, what, well I don't think …I didn't think that …"

"Go on." Said Mikhail, suddenly entering the conversation. "You talk of fine gestures but you are talking of an old comrade here who might be able to live out his days in peace. Give the man your watch and make good your fine words!" And the antagonism of before surfaced in reality and was not play acting.

Jan Gorki looked at the two men and speculated that he might raise the stakes now that honour might be involved.

"Yes, if you give me your watch I will try to negotiate his release with the Governor and he will want some payment too, of course.

'Well." Said Nicholai uncertainly. "I didn't…I couldn't…"

"Go on." Snarled Mikhail. "Make good the offer you so grandly expressed." He said scornfully.

He seemed cornered by his own grandiose gesture and looked down at his shoes. "Well, OK, OK, let me see. What about, if we see in the morning what reaction you get from the Governor? Obviously, he may not wish to trade, so let's not be too hasty." He said, as if boxed into a corner.

Jan sensed he had the man over a barrel, as there was obviously a bit of antagonism between these two men. His sense of doing a deal was excited by the prospect of trading such a worthless bit of shit for such a fine watch. It did not occur to him that this might be the purpose of the visit. That he was on the wrong side of the deal and that he could have struck a much harder bargain.

They agreed to see what Jan could arrange and to meet before their return to the railhead, which they insisted could not be delayed much longer.

****

Commandant Sokorski was fed up. He had spent all the previous day trying to keep the lid on an uprising in the Gulag. He was short of guards, short of food, short of horses, and a recalcitrant work force. The Politburo was making the management of the Gulag impossible by starving it of administrative finance, and containing the prisoners without adequate security to maintain his authority. He did not wish his camp to suffer the same fate as others had done in '58. No, here he was, trying to fill his quota of orders for the Navy. So many spares needed, it was ridiculous. Why did the submarines need so many? Spare parts? My Arse! He thought There were enough spare parts here to build a battleship! But it was not his business to question the military. Just fulfil the order. Yes, but with all the unrest and other difficulties, how was he going to do that?"

He was angry that one prisoner could have such influence over the minds of so many men and he didn't see what he could do about it. That rabble-rouser Baronski, was still causing trouble, the longer he was here the worse it had become. He had thought the man's energies would be short-lived and they would hear no more but the longer he lived the more his influence had grown.

When Jan Gorki came to him with a trade, he couldn't believe how timely this might prove. He saw the advantage of getting rid of his problem and making a little profit on the side. He pondered the idea all morning to find a way to get this troublemaker out of his hair, without the authorities becoming suspicious. Some of the prisoners could be relied upon to cause trouble, whatever the provocation, but were unable to cause much harm because they reacted to events rather than planning them.

His thoughts kept returning to the problem until he had decided how it could be done. The question was. How much could he gain by the deal

Jan awoke with a sore head the next morning but knew it would pass. He had enjoyed the horsemen's company last evening and had been pleased with all the goods they had traded. The novelty cards, cigarette lighters and condoms would be easy to make a profit on in this sex-starved environment. Pictures of naked women in provocative poses always sold to these desperate men and the condoms, God only knew what they did with these, he didn't want to know, but he always had a ready market in the official camp brothel.

The other item he wished to buy was a more difficult trade. He had admired the variety of watches they all wore and knew that they would cost the horse trader more than he wanted to spend but this little side issue would help to obtain one of them at least. The only question was, "Could he get both of them for the price of the prisoner? He mulled it over and thought how he could achieve that without too much cost to himself.

He knew that the Governor would be agreeable, if it was to his advantage, as they had done deals in the past, but how much would it be worth to release the man Baronski. Each man had something to gain from the deal but who was most eager for the trade?

Nicholai, Mikhail and Dimitri returned to their night shack amicably. Nicholai knew that the two farmers were happy with their horse trading and would return home with a good profit. He smiled at the enjoyable banter they had exchanged and the profit they had made on all their goods.

Mikhail, for once, was in ebullient mood, seeing the possibilities of future trade opening in front of him.

There remained the exchange of the prisoner. The bait had been laid and Nicholas knew that the drover, Jan, was very interested but it required all his patience to 'land the fish' and patience was not his strongest talent. It had taken all his nerve to restrain from clinching the deal that evening, as it was far from certain that Jan could make good his boast of being able to deliver the prisoner. All his strivings of the past four months had led to this moment and he paused on the brink of what seemed an abyss of uncertainty.

Dimitri pushed Nicholai on the arm playfully. “Keep heart, you did well there and I am sure you will succeed tomorrow.”

He shook his head and in the dejected mood that had come upon him suddenly, like a blanket, said. “Well, I was pleased with the trade but I am very afraid of tomorrow, we have come so far and we are almost there but not – quite – yet.” And he paused in sombre thought.

Mikhail was surprised at his father’s show of affection and his anger grew at this usurper to his father’s affections. He couldn’t quite believe what this man’s intentions were. Surely, he would not have come all this way just to rescue his father? All his instincts told him that there was more to this business than Nicholai was telling and his father was just a pawn in the process. With all the native cunning, he had divined the truth of the situation, of which, even Nicholai had originally been unaware. He was a pawn on the chessboard and far more powerful people were moving the pieces.

For him the overriding reason had been one of honour but it had somehow been twisted by others to make him feel used and abused by them all, and he needed to keep focusing on his primary task. The months he had spent on this venture had stretched and strained, pulled and tightened every sinew and, although he did not know it, he was almost beyond his strength to achieve his heart’s desire. Mikhail saw only the outward demeanour of the man, Dimitri looked deep into his psyche and saw, what he had seen many times before, during the war, with his soldiers. Here was a man hanging onto his resolve by a hair's breadth and he pitied him.

Here was a leader for sure, but Dimitri also knew that such men pushed themselves further than anyone else, and did not know their own breaking point. He hoped that Nicholai could hang on, for he saw and admired the spirit of the man.

****

Governor Sokorski was in a better mood when his wife saw him next. She had feared that his return would be as gloomy as the last time she had seen him. She set his meal in front of him and smiled uncertainly at her husband.

"Thank you, Tatiana, He beamed. I have a little present for you here." And he produced the pair of tights he had bought from Jan.

"Oh, what are these?"

"I understand they are like long hose but they have socks attached to make you more cosy."

"Oh, I see, you mean like stockings and pants, all in one?"

He laughed, "Exactly, you see I do think of you sometimes and I thought these would keep you warm.

She simpered at his jocular manner and could read all the signs of marital affection. What next, she thought.

He went to his drawer and said, "I also have something else for you to try. These are the latest kind of protection with built in fruit flavours." She looked at them in astonishment and he said coyly. "Perhaps we might try them together." and she knew that Spring had worked its usual effect on the governor,

Later, he was ready to do battle with the prisoners and his lunchtime activities had rejuvenated him in mind as well as body. He had planned a disturbance to be created by being extra hard on certain men, enough to trigger a reaction. Whilst dealing with this, the prisoner could be allowed to slip away during the distraction, by being detailed to help the carter with the latest body to be buried. There had been a death overnight and the carter had to take the corpse to the burial ground outside the camp. He could be encouraged to make a break for it. When this was done, Governor Sokorski would have peace at his work and passion in his home and he could enjoy a summer of love. He had confirmed the procedure with Jan Gorki and was glad to think he would be rid of all his troubles.

****

Nicholai was waiting to see Jan again as he was still in the dark about his proposition but, at last, his plans were being acted upon. His months of self-discipline and single-mindedness were being carried forward by other hands more eager than his own. They wished to get rid of this awkward prisoner and Nicholai had been able to agree terms with the carter.

He had been told to be ready with the others at the cross roads outside the camp, amongst a clump of trees, with their packhorses, at 5.30pm. The prisoner would be delivered to them in exchange for two of the watches, the Rolex and the Breitling. Nicholai had fought to keep the second of the two watches, to keep up his charade of being caught in his gesture of humanity to pay more than he wanted to, but in the end, a deal had been done.

Now all he needed to do was alert Mikhail and his father to be ready as well, and be sure to have provisions for the return journey. They went to the carter's home for one more visit to thank their hostess of the evening, and took their leave of them both. The exchange would take place when the prisoner was in their hands and a place in amongst the trees was agreed upon to leave the watches.

Nicholai, Dimitri and Mikhail were all ready to leave and had followed the instructions of the carter. They had purchased a long hessian sack and were waiting at the clump of trees. The day was now far advanced and the prisoners' supper was due to be served.

The time ticked past and still the men were on the work party. Sometime later they filed back into the camp under guard and Stefan was detailed to help Jan take a body out of the camp to the cemetery.

Nicholai spied the cart coming slowly out of the camp just as the alarm sounded within. The carter continued his journey outside the camp until they were about 100 yds. from the trees. At this point the man turned the cart round and began to head back to the camp, pausing briefly to allow his assistant to dismount, but with difficulty. They spied a man slowly moving towards them, taking cover every 10 yds. or so. By now the carter had covered half of the ground back to the camp and was beginning to quicken pace.

As Nicholai waited, he saw that Stefan might not make it to shelter before the carter was inside and the alarm would have been raised. He shouted to Mikhail, "Come with me and keep low; we must help him before he is spotted." They covered the 50 yds. between them, crouching amongst the marshy tufted cottonweed, to reach Stefan. As they did so, they could hear the commotion in the camp and saw that the guards were busy running around inside the gates where the carter had disappeared.

They grasped with both pairs of arms under his armpits and dragged and half carried the man between them. They reached Dimitri and flung the sack over Stefan's head and body and pulled up the string. Hefting him like a sack of potatoes, Nicholai and Mikhail put him across the front of his son's saddle and, in the same moment, Nicholai was upon the horse with his bundle in front of him. Within minutes they reached the track, and slowed until they were out of sight of the camp so that they did not alert anyone to their presence. Whilst all the guards' attentions were firmly fixed on the trouble within the camp, the horsemen hoped to reach the cover of a small coppice of trees.

No hurry could be exercised whilst the guards were still in sight, but they quickened their pace after one mile, eventually finding shelter within the sparse tree cover. They stopped and Nicholai jumped free of his mount and went to open the sack. He had already reassured the prisoner that they were friends and not to struggle but no other words were exchanged. Now they looked at the man inside the hessian bag and saw that he was only half conscious.

"That's taken all his strength, Dimitri. What should we do? We cannot continue in this fashion." Dimitri looked at his brother with concern but saw that the prisoner did not recognise him. Stefan had stark cheekbones and sunken eyes and skin drawn tight over what spare flesh he still had on his face. It was obvious he was in a state of semi-consciousness and would be unable to help himself.

"We must take it in turns to ride with him but he must stay in the sack. Put him up here in front of me for a while; he weighs so little it will not trouble the horse too much. If we take turns, we shall make satisfactory progress." With worried frown, Nicholai agreed that they could not help the man, as they would wish, until more distance had been covered.

On and on they went, hour upon hour, changing the mounts for his fragile body, until the moon rose over them. They had covered perhaps half of the distance to the railhead and would need to reach there by 8.00 am. They again looked for some much-needed protection in this barren land and came upon a small bluff, with the slight cliff facing southwards, giving them partial protection from the keen Arctic wind that would get colder still as night progressed.

They managed to make a small peat fire and boil some water before the moonless Tundra gave way to dusk. Any larger firelight would give their position away to any pursuers. They had twelve hours of night, at this time of year, before the daylight broke again but they needed to rest as well as looking after their horses and captive.

Nicholai carefully lifted his father from his horse and felt how cold he had become. He realized that his own body warmth had been his father's blanket and his father desperately needed more protection than he could give him.

Dimitri called to Mikhail to hobble one of the horses' front legs and get him to lie down. With the knowledge of an old campaigner, he put Stefan beside the horse and covered them both with a horse blanket. He had needed to keep himself warm many times in this manner, when he had been with the gunners, as the horse instinctively knew that there was a mutual dependence to be had in these severe conditions. The man and the horse shared their body heat to survive.

They settled down after watering the horses, gave the half-conscious man a warm drink, laced with vodka and tried to sleep. Six and a half hours later they were awoken by a skein of cranes flying overhead and realised it was time to re-mount. They knew that sooner or later they would need to push their horses to the limit before they were safe.

Nicholai rose, his worries still large, as he could see how frail his father was. He looked agonizingly at the sleeping man and when Stefan woke there was a glimmer of light in his eyes, but still no recognition. Nicholai knew that his father did not know him. Best not, he thought, for all their sakes. Stefan did not need to know who his rescuers were. From now on, Nicholai must take care to keep his father in ignorance of that fact, because if they were caught, that knowledge would hang them all.

They rode and they rode, southwards over the tundra, which became, not the monster of the night, but a living breathing vital thing, as flocks of birds of all kinds flew in their pre-determined flights across the golden dawn. All, seemed to have purpose and the desert, in front of the travellers' eyes, became a food table for the myriad birds of the wastelands. Mosquito and gnats, dragonflies and damselflies hovered over the semi-frozen marshlands and gave sustenance to all the creatures living there. The fish and the frogs, the hedgehogs and the water voles all provided links in the chain for others to devour and these humans too were part of that enchainment, to be slaughtered at the will or whim of others. All they could hope for was God's blessing and more reason to flee than to be pursued.

****

Governor Sokorski was satisfied. His trigger for the dissatisfaction had been to work the men for longer and present them with awful food until they had more reason than ever to feel they were being starved to death. In truth, that had been the case for many months as the supply chain had continued to be inadequate. They had all been systematically underfed, as rations ran out, but this latest deprivation was exceptionally harsh and he knew that it would result in desperate action. He had picked particular prisoners for this treatment because they were still strong enough to rebel and they had not disappointed him. He gave three hours for the riot to run its course with much banging and anger expressed before he sent in his extra guards to stamp on them. Before the day was over there were two men dead and another in a sorry state.

When he was finally told that the rioting was over, it was dark and his actions would await the morning.

Next day when he made a Report of the riot, he simply had to fill in the names of the dead and include Stefan Baronski as ringleader, and the matter was closed. He would write an unofficial letter of justification to his superiors and maybe the affair might focus their minds on the explosive situation that had developed and the Authorities own part in causing it; the Military Ordinance camps had all been put under extreme pressure to deliver all the requirements of their Government. These had been much more demanding recently with greater expectations and deadlines. He hoped that the workload would slow down for a while to enable the men to keep going. A 'tinder keg' in more than one sense of the word

He congratulated himself on a day well spent and hoped to enjoy his Breitling, with its state of the art gadgets, for many years to come.

Jan was also content. He had successfully acquired more working beasts for the punishing schedule they had been working to, all this year.

He had once again, put his Governor under an obligation, so felt his life to be more tolerable than usual.

For once he had a loving wife, who was pleased enough with her man to allow more privileges than usual. The present of the toilet water and soap of such an exotic smell, had quickened his senses and, together with the other fancies, had given him more than usual excitement.

He thought about the traders and decided that, one way or another, he would keep the trade links open for future dealing, and he wrote a letter of thanks to Mikhail to keep the young man keen enough to venture the journey again.

Beyond that he did not question as he had seen enough of men's motives to know that it was better not to ponder further. All he knew was that his life had been made more joyous for their visit.

CHAPTER SEVEN

Realisations & Revelations

Nicholai, Dimitri and Mikhail, together with their charge, arrived with an hour to spare at the railhead. They did not wish to be amongst the other passengers until they were on the train but they needed to see to the horses. They had ridden them hard and they needed to be fed. They stopped at the Livery Stables and called for mash and hay and milk, to add nutrition to the horses' diet after their long journey, but did not overfeed them as they would be cooped up for several days of travel westwards. Whilst Mikhail saw to the horses, Dimitri and Nicholai unpacked their baggage horses and the bundles upon them. The thickness of the hessian disguised the man and when they bought plenty of hay for the cattle truck, the bundles were indistinguishable from each other.

Nicholai went to the Station Master to have his tickets stamped and with 20 minutes to wait (officially), he went into the Way Station and bought more sausages and black bread for the journey. He also managed to purchase some eggs, although they were limited to one per passenger, fruit and vegetables were non-existent but were supplemented by several tins and jars of assorted pickled cucumber and beetroot and pickled herrings. Satisfied that he had all they would need for immediate use, he returned to the Station yard with his purchases and ordered coffee for them all.

There were several officials and dignitaries about to alight and some peasant women and men plying their meagre goods along the route. Without haste, he looked along the platform at the assorted waiting passengers and saw no obvious curiosity in their faces. Of course, by now he was what he looked, a scruffy hardened plainsman, returning home with his horses, and there was nothing in his demeanour to think otherwise.

The minutes ticked by and he sat with the dregs of his coffee, apparently whiling away the time, but all his senses were aware of the ebb and flow of the Station activities. A quarter of an hour after the train was due, an order in the signal box resulted in a green light appearing from the East and three minutes later the train rolled into the Station.

In the barn, the father and son were alone for the first time for many days and Mikhail was talking enthusiastically of their trade with the camp. Mikhail said, "That was some journey wasn't it Dad. I never dreamt that Russia was so vast and how different the people could be."

"Aye, there are so many of us from East and West and we have covered but a small part of Mother Russia."

"Well, I for one, would like to see more of it." Mikhail said enthusiastically.

"Do you my lad? Dimitri growled at his grown- up son. "Well, what about your passion for your horses?"

"Well, of course, my horses mean a lot to me but I have made some more contacts here if I want to trade with them, and perhaps I should see more of the world." Dimitri was silent. This seemed such a departure from anything his son had ever expressed as an ambition.

Am I getting old? Do I not remember clearly how Stefan had been in his young days? Did he not wish to roam when he was young? Well yes, fleetingly he had. But when war had come to change all their lives, Dimitri had seen more of the world than he ever wanted to see again, and had been glad to go back to his farm. Perhaps he had imposed his dreams and ambition onto Mikhail and now his rightful father Stefan, was pulling Mikhail towards him.

He drew breath sharply when he thought of the consequences. He might lose his son and his farm and he was horrified. They had risked everything by helping Nicholai to rescue Stefan and now their hearts desire was almost achieved. Their own farm, his son (no not his son, he remembered) was exhibiting all the dreams of youth to see the world, that Stefan had shown. But how could he hold Mikhail back? If he went, what would it do to Babeta?

Now they had reached an understanding, would she be heartbroken if her son left home to roam the world? He felt confused and was still deeply troubled when Nicholai came to tell them that the train was arriving.

Stefan awoke and moved his limbs cautiously. He was aware that the perpetual ache in his muscles had eased and that he was lying on soft bedding. It reminded him of his childhood when he had slept over the stable in the hay loft. All the smells of home assailed him. The straw, the smell of horses and the sound of their champing, and the rattle of harness. He must be dreaming, he thought, relaxing into the straw again, and went fast asleep. Later he woke and someone was feeding him some milky gruel, which he supped gratefully.

Later still, Stefan awoke to darkness and was able to absorb the sounds of a train rattling over the rails. He tried to sit up and realised he was restricted by some blanket or bedroll. It can't be a dream. He shook his head to clear his muddled mind. There are too many things here that are real. I can feel my limbs, I am restricted. I can hear a train rattling over the track. All the other sensations are, yes, the sensations of my youth. but I am not in a barn, I am in a train. But why?

He tried to focus his mind but it refused to give him the key. He drifted off to sleep again and finally some six hours later woke to a slanting early morning sun, rising through a crack in the timbers, a freight truck!

Stefan smelt the air and heard again the snorting of animals and the clinking of harness, and recognised the sound of a train cattle truck lumbering westwards. How had he got here and how had he left the Gulag?

He heard the murmur of soft voices and 'Lord be praised,' the smell of coffee!

He struggled to get up but again found himself too weak to move from the restrictions that bound him. He grunted, puffed and panted, and he heard someone come to him. A hand touched him gently.

"Don't fret, you're in good hands, you do not need to fear." And the man pulled some coarse cloth from his shoulders and allowed him to reach forward to touch his captor.

"Where am I? Who are you? Why am I going?" he said in a rush, fearfully.

"You are in a train heading West many miles from Moscow." Said his companion. "We are well-wishers, hoping to take you away from your old life and when you have eaten and drunk something we shall tell you more of our plans. Rest now and we will bring you some food."

He fell back and stared at the roof. Things were returning to his memory, of a ride over the pummel of the saddle and then sitting in front of different riders. Were these the men?

He could not make head or tail of his thoughts. Soon they brought him some gruel and coffee and he fell immediately into another deep sleep. Occasionally he cried out in tormented dreams and a man shook him awake and bathed his face before he fell asleep again. The next time he woke, the young man, who saw to him most of the time, leant close to his ear. "We have stopped to take water on board and will be checked by the guard. Do not make any movement or noise. All our lives may depend on it." And he realised that they were his protectors.

When they arrived at the junction with the southern train, the men were relieved to find that the cattle trucks from Samara had arrived and that Babeta was there with the lad Petr from the neighbouring farm. They had managed to load the horses and had travelled north to join them. They had expected to say goodbye to Babeta for a while but she insisted upon travelling with them. Dimitri did not argue. He was as pleased as anyone that she was there and thought that perhaps she could knock some sense into Mikhail.

Every other day Mikhail slept in the other carriage with Nicholai and they helped each other tend the mares. He could see that Stefan was still very fragile and must be kept from exerting himself. When Stefan was with the two men he had seen the family resemblance and surmised they were brothers but more than that he did not begin to understand. Stefan, who began to take more notice of things, sensed that the older two men were unhappy about something and there was much friction in the air. Years of living closely with other men, made him acutely aware of these undercurrents.

Danger passed and the train rattled on. They had come to a large junction and the train had taken on extra carriages, some more cattle trucks, and he saw that two of the men had left the carriage. They were in a railway siding for some time and the men seemed to be mucking out the carriage and putting down more straw. They brought seven more horses to the cattle trucks and took the others out of the train. There was another carriage, which appeared to contain some of the horses too. In his carriage, there were pregnant mares with not long to go, who regarded him with calm eyes. They did not appear to be frightened and he knew that they had accepted him. He was aware that his presence might have spooked them until he understood that the horses sensed his fragility and were not frightened by him.

The youngest man came back and climbed into the carriage. The other two men and, he sensed, a woman, were in the other cattle truck. He asked no questions but was content to let the train rattle over the points. taking him, he knew not where. Periodically, the train stopped and officials looked into the truck but mostly it was a cursory glance. He knew now to be very still and to hide under the straw when they came by. Stefan was aware of kind hands washing and stripping him and he felt the smell of coarse linen on his back and familiar trousers and boots. He was assailed by the smell of horses and the familiarity of the clothes. They listened to the hiss of the water and clank of the overhead pipe as it replenished the water for the steam engine. Voices could be heard moving along the outside of the train and two men pulled down the door to the cattle truck.

"Papers please." Said an official and Nicholai handed him his documents.

"Do you want to check the horses? Do you want a hand up?" Nichollai extended his right arm and bent to help the official on board.

"No, no, that's alright." The official hastily replied, as the smell of horses assailed him, and moved on, handing back the documents to Nicholai.

He watched the Officials retreating and called to the driver. "May we have some water for our horses, when you have finished your refuelling for I don't know when you will next stop?"

'Don't worry, I will make sure that you are supplied. Our next stop will be when we cross the River Onck, and you will have time to muck out the truck and give them a walkabout."

Nicholai offered him a cigarette, as he seemed an obliging fellow, and was inclined to talk.

"Those are fine horses you have there, it would be a pity to lose one of them for lack of care."

"Yes indeed. I appreciate your thoughtfulness." He hesitated. "You seem familiar with their requirements?"

"Well, I wasn't always on the railways and some of my time in the army was looking after the gunners' horses and we had to entrain them at times."

Dimitri, who was listening to their chatter, joined in.

"I was with the gunners, and what regiment did you serve in?"

"Oh the 7th Cossack Brigade, although they were no longer called that by the time I served."

"Ah, so you are from the Steppes also?"

"Well." He hesitated. Yes, a long time ago but life has changed a lot since then." And he finished his cigarette and added." That should be nearly ready if you want to get some water."

Nicholas was already at the Water Station anxious to fill their containers and soon they were on their way.

When next they stopped, Nicholai said to Stefan that the horses were to be exercised. "Do not leave the carriage for any reason as we will take the horses out for some exercise."

Days seemed to pass and still Stefan slept and ate and slept again, until one night he heard the whimpering of one of the mares and he saw that she was about to drop a foal. He continued to listen to the animal but did not go out into the main truck. He knew from his time on the farm (How did he remember that? he wondered} that horses usually foaled at night and that they were best left to do this themselves.

He looked across at the young man who had been sleeping in the same stall as himself and their eyes met. There was such a moment of affinity that he gasped. Did he know the man? Who was he? He couldn't remember but somehow, he knew that they shared some part of his past.

He drifted off to sleep again but was woken later when he heard a scuffling and knocking and realised it was a foal trying to stand. The miracle of new birth: Within a few minutes the foal was on his feet, albeit rather unsteadily with the rolling train, but nevertheless able to skip and, soon after, suckle its mother.

This marked a turning point for Stefan. Somehow, the awakening of new life in the horses had awakened new life in him and he was able to stay awake much longer. The mares seemed to accept his presence with the foals and they did not try to protect them from him and he began to see to their feeding.

Father and son worked to make the horses comfortable while Nicholas laid fresh bedding for the mares. They had two foals now in the truck and there was little room to allow them to move but they were placid enough.

He was aware of turning off the main route and heading South West and that a large city lay to the North. Dimly he was aware that they had passed

Moscow but he didn't know why. His strength was very quickly dissipated and his initial enthusiasm needed to be curbed. He helped and rested and helped and rested, not knowing where or why they were going West but knew that he was going to safety.

****

Months of travelling had taken its toll of Dimitri and this crackpot idea of Mikhail's was just too much. His nerves were irritated by the prospect before him. For years, he had planned their future and now, when the farm was within their grasp, his son was wanting to go off on some mad adventure. He was also tormented by the thought that his real father would take Mikhail away from him.

He had brought up and loved the boy as his own and, at the first opportunity, he wanted to do what Stefan had done and throw away the farm and all his hopes. It was not right! How dare this happen when all he had done was help Babeta in her distress and take on all the responsibilities that should have been Stefan's. Round and round his thoughts ran until Dimitri thought he was going mad.

"At last." Said Nicholai, to his father. "We are nearly at Leningrad." He hoped that Captain Aaronovich had been given his message and that the 'Ice Maiden' had arrived to transport the horses.

He felt that most of his worries were slipping away but he had become aware that Mikhail and Dimitri were arguing over something and he couldn't begin to understand what the trouble was. He had thought that his own animosity towards Mikhail was bad enough but he could not imagine what had got into Dimitri. Nicholai began to think there was something wrong with his cousin. He seemed to have that capacity to rile people with his obstinate streak.

They arrived at Leningrad in early morning, their point of embarkation for the United Kingdom. Nicholai was aware of the dangers they still faced but, so far, their false official papers had been faultless. MI5 had supplied an extra passport for his father but it had been made up on the basis of an ageing interpretation of Stefan's features and was now very far from the mark. His father's gaunt features were nothing like the man that stared out of the picture.

The three salient features were still intact, the strong nose, wide forehead and piercing blue eyes, but the ravishes of skin and beard and expression gave the photo a completely false impression of blandness.

So far, they had not tested his credentials, as Stefan had remained hidden on the train, but now he needed to slip off the train and act in the capacity of a hired hand at the docks.

The two cattle trucks had been shunted off the main line and were manoeuvred onto the quay, into the cargo bay.

Nicholai needed to sign them off at the Customs Office and arrange their onward passage. Then they had to wait until the 'Ice Maiden' arrived. All, was fine in theory, but still required the final transfer.

Inside the two cattle trucks, the people waited, and again Stefan heard raised voices in the adjoining one which had been placed alongside his own. He awoke from sleep and listened to the tone of their voices. Somewhere there was a woman's voice mixed into the sound and he was taken back to a moment that had happened to him when he had argued with his brother about leaving the farm for the Navy, so many years since.

He now understood that he was not only re-living his own past but the past of his brother and it dawned on him that he was listening to Dimitri, and Babeta. Suddenly his memory came flooding back and he knew who his rescuers were. He flung his arm over his eyes and the tears flooded from him and he wept as he had not wept since his wife had been ill and all his previous life rolled past his inner visage.

"Oh fool." He exclaimed to the four walls of his truck. How could I not have known? For many minutes, his tears flowed, but when they were spent, a calm descended upon him. He had re-aligned his thought processes to include Dimitri and Mikhail and yes perhaps Babeta, but that left one more. His comforter in his nightmare sleeps. He did not know who he was and yet he bore a strong resemblance to the others.

Who could he be? Did Dimitri and Babeta have another son? He tried to remember but his brain refused to make the connection.

****

The 'Ice Maiden' had arrived and Nicholas had finished the paperwork with the Customs Officials and the Port Authorities and had his Bills of Lading verified. The addition of foals to the original order had to be noted and the Official had duly inspected the cattle trucks. He had affected an anxious pose about the mares and foals, emphasizing the mares' protective stance and stressing that their inspection must not frighten the mothers.

This guaranteed a cursory inspection of their temporary home as even hardened customs officials did not wish to be trampled and he gave them a generous tip in appreciation of their considerate handling of his horses. Bribes were never given, of course, or received, but a few 'thanks' were unofficially given.

Paperwork completed, Nicholai went to a quayside café to await the others. He sat in the pouring rain looking out at the dockside with its jumble of industrial detritus and it was a shock to Nicholai after the wide-open countryside that he was leaving. He reflected that he had half fallen in love with the place again, although the life had been so hard.

He thought of the people he had met, the kindness of his uncle and aunt, and the antagonism he had felt towards Mikhail after all these years. He knew that it had been a privilege to come back to this country and see it with adult eyes. Nicholai idly thought, that he would have to weigh his reflections of Russia against England one day, but for now he was just glad of the journey he had taken.

As he sat watching the rain beat against the window, his attention was drawn to a fat little man waddling across the space in front of him, directing a porter to take his 'cargo' to the No. 5 Docking Point, and sounding rather hysterical, even over the rain.

Nicholai watched absent-mindedly the pantomime in front of him. Suddenly his attention was caught, sensing that there was something familiar about the man's actions. He began to smile and watched the performance with increasing interest. That man was a gem! He sighed with pleasure and relief and saw that he had 'the cavalry' riding to his aid!

He watched the man more steadily now and could see that he was putting his cargo in the space immediately next to their Cattle Truck. He had been directing a huge lorry to unload what appeared to be cabins or, as he looked more closely, seemed to be wooden stalls and a great quantity of straw bales and sacks of animal fodder. Mikhail had come to see what the fuss was about and when he could see what was being unloaded for them, directed the man towards the café.

Nicholai called the waiter over and ordered two more coffees.

The rain coated man made slow progress through the puddles of water, with his black umbrella waving precariously above him. His mackintosh had seen better days but the suit beneath showed a glimpse of sartorial elegance of a more flamboyant nature, with a wide tie of Italian silk in hues more appropriate to the Mediterranean. He opened the door to the café and looked around, casually spying Nicholai at a window table. He went to the counter and was directed to his table.

In a loud voice, he hailed Nicholai, "Am I speaking to the owner of those dreadfully stinky animals over there?" And he gestured towards the dockside.

"Yes, you are, and who wants to know?" Said Nicholai in his most truculent manner.

"I am the owner of those pallets I have brought you and would hope that we can conduct our business quickly, as the ship is due to sail"

"Alright by me." Nicholai replied gruffly. and the man sat down with his face partly to the room and partly overlooking the dockside.

"Well my fine friend, you've certainly exceeded my expectations. Congratulations." He said in an altogether softer and more friendly tone, which quite belied the look on his face.

“I’m not done yet, but it’s good to see you. You’re the best teacher I ever had and I have thought of you often in the past months.”

“We have little time to speak now but I will be with you on the journey. Suffice to say that I have brought some provisions and grain and bales of straw for your horses on the boat home. These will be put into the next stall to them, for all your need. I have also brought harness and slings for the new born foals to keep them from harm if the sea crossing becomes rough. You will note, for any emergency, that the middle bale of straw has a cavity inside to which your ‘item’ might wish to avail itself, if necessary. I shall be in 1st Class all the way and you, no doubt, will be in steerage.”

“Do not attempt to come to me. Someone would inevitably smell a rat, old bean.” He said ironically, taking a large sniff at this disreputable fellow he was speaking to. Weeks of living with the animals had left Nicholas far removed from the elegant young man of the London social circuit. His hair curled wildly around his neck and his face had the wind hardened redness of the Siberian Winter. Only the midnight blue eyes danced with merriment as he relaxed his guard at the posturing of this fine actor, Otto Strauss!

“You can come to me if there arc any problems. At 6.00, 12.00 and 6.00 again, I will partake of a cigarette on the stern storm rail, so can be contacted there at those times.” He stood up and passed a Bill to Nicholas, and gestured for him to sign it. They shook hands. “Good luck my friend.” Whispered Otto.

He waddled out of the door and Nicholas wondered when he would see him again. He had liked the man enormously and felt he had made a friend for life, but was brought up short when he remembered that he was only another pawnbroker and there must be no sentiment to their relationship.

Stefan was greeted by his rescuer, who sounded much more cheerful than he had heard him, and tried to respond with friendliness. He wished to remember more about this man, and was intrigued to know the reason why they had not revealed themselves to him.

He had been able to feed the mares and quieten them after the customs officials had been to inspect the horses. There just remained a visit from an official vet to pass the horses fit and they would be done.

Stefan had begun to groom the mares to keep their coats in good condition and also to reconnect with his past. It had given him something to do while he was waiting, all cooped up in here. He had forgotten how much he had loved these noble beasts and they gave balm to his soul during this transition. He greeted his friend, who said, "I have brought you a treat here, bratwurst and bread, or in American, a 'hotdog', and smiled at his father, his face alight with familiarity that Stefan had hitherto not had eyes to see and, at that moment, he knew who this young man was.

"Son, son?" He cried uncertainly. and Nicholas folded him into his arms. They clung together knowing the precious nature of this moment.

He shook his father gently and said. “There will be plenty of time to talk more, once we are on the boat, but we must say goodbye to Dimitri and Mikhail and Babeta.”

“Babeta!” Exclaimed Stefan. “She is here too?” confirming his thoughts about the other helpers.

“Yes, they have been seeing to the other horses. Dimitri and Mikhail have helped me to bring you here and we must thank them.” “I have renounced any claim to the farm, as your son, but now I am asking you, to also forego your claim to it. Do you think that you are ready to make a life with me in England and leave this place forever?”

Stefan thought deeply about his words then said, “Yes, that is fitting. If they were willing to give up so much for me then I must reward their loyalty with this act. Dimitri was always the one who loved the farm and I have been selfish all these years in not acknowledging that fact, and Babeta has always been good to me and to you, and she would never leave her home.” He paused for breath and continued.

“Yes, I must cut the ties of home forever, to make a new life with you. But do you want this broken-down husk of a man dragging you down?”

“Oh, father,” And again he took his father to his breast. “I am not the only friend you have in the West, believe me. Your friend from the war, Commander

Tasha Counterniev is there to welcome you as he has a debt of honour he wishes to redeem, I think?"

Memories flooded in thick and fast and he sat down suddenly as he remembered the awful nights at sea and, as he thought of the journey they were about to take by sea again, he quailed. But his natural love of things maritime overcame his fear.

This talk had been an emotional rollercoaster for them both. Nicholas realised, thankfully, that his father was regaining his senses but that such a moment had brought his emotions to chaotic levels and he urged him to sleep once more.

All the animals had been embarked and were quiet and safely in the stalls that Otto had brought and all that needed to be loaded were the bales, including the one with the secret compartment. They would then be ready to sail. The five of them were at last on the quayside together.

Nicholas gave his hand to Dimitri to thank him. "Uncle, you have served us well with your loyalty and I have done what I promised." "But before I go, I am concerned that something ails you. I have watched you becoming troubled about something. Is there anything I can do to help?"

Dimitri looked at Nicholas and he said sorrowfully. "There is nothing you can do. Mikhail is more like his father than he realises. After all these years, I have treated him as a son, and now he has tasted the roaming life, he wants to go away and see the world. All my hopes of owning the farm and passing it on to its legitimate heir are being frustrated by his wilfulness."

Nicholas turned to Mikhail and raised his arm to place it on his shoulder.

"Don't you touch me, he spat. Don't you ever touch me again. He drew a knife and stood with it facing him fiercely. Don't you see how my father treats you. With more respect than he has ever shown me."

"But Mikhail, he has always loved you and by agreeing to this venture Dimitri has now proved it by giving you your heart's desire. My father and I have relinquished our rights to the farm and it is now yours, in law as well as in justice, and you have no reason to doubt your father's love for you."

Babeta, who had been listening to this exchange then spoke.

"No, I don't think he has, but if so, then I am to blame. Dimitri has done everything that a father could do for his son, and I now acknowledge it. But blood will out, and I see in him the restlessness of his…" Nicholai moved to silence her, as an appalling thought came into his head.

"Hush Babeta, it is not necessary." and he turned to, his cousin, thinking to placate him. But the moment and gesture had come too late. As Nicholai turned to his cousin, Mikhail brought the knife down towards him.

Seeing what was about to happen, Dimitri thrust his left hand out to divert the blow, which glanced down Nicholas's face from cheekbone to chin, tearing the flesh to the bone and continuing down his father's chest.

Horror was on the face of all of them as they realised the seriousness of the blow.

Slowly Dimitri slid to the cobbled quay "No, Mikhail, no, you must not." Sinking further into unconsciousness he said, more faintly by the word, "You cannot kill your *brother*."

Babeta and Stefan ran to the fallen man and Mikhail stood there sobered by his angry deed.

"Father." He called in anguish.

Stefan turned on him angrily. "Father indeed, he was more of a father than I could ever have been. But, yes, I will acknowledge you as mine. You, who have all the characteristics of this selfish wanton wreck of a man that I am, that you see before you. Selfish, proud, arrogant and uncaring. I have destroyed the lives of everyone I should have cared for most. Aye, I acknowledge you as my son, because you have the mirror image of all my faults. Now, I renounce you, as the son I disown, as I must admit these faults in myself."

"Go to your true father who has nurtured you all these years and pray to God he is still alive, and let us have no more of this family feuding." And he sank down exhausted by his emotional outburst, beside Nicholai, and ineffectually tried to stem the slowly spreading tide of blood.

****

Otto had been very pleased with what Nicholas had been able to tell him about his journey and it confirmed, at first hand, many of the stories he had heard on his stay in Turkey. He was sure that Stefan would also have more to tell him when they returned to England, but for the moment he had to see to their bodily needs, which were considerable, but perhaps, not life threatening. He had been watching the family say their farewells as he inspected his cargo being loaded, and he had expected Stefan to be loaded with the bales.

When he saw the altercation between father and son and Mikhail draw a knife, he was transfixed. Surely at this late moment they would not fail. As the son struck out he realised that he needed to act quickly. He ran to Stefan to staunch Nicholas's wounds, then turned to Dimitri. He still had a pulse but was haemorrhaging blood over the quayside. He called to the sailors watching from the ship and told them to alert the captain. Whilst the sailors were distracted he grabbed Stefan and pushed him into the bales of hay, which were just about to be loaded.

Mikhail and Babeta were bent over the wounded man, that Otto did not know, so he turned to Nicholas and helped him to his feet.

“Hang on Nick, ol’ buddy.” He said in English and hailed the captain, who by now was on the gangway.

“Hello Sir, I’m afraid one of your passengers has met with an accident. Perhaps you can take him to sick bay to stitch him up.”

“This other gentleman will need hospital, so perhaps you could phone for an ambulance.”

At this, Babeta appeared to regain some awareness of the situation and she thanked him.

“I don’t know what happened here, and I don’t want to know. Otto said. An ambulance has been called. Suffice to say, Nicholas will mend and is on board. As for the rest, I think you will have all the assistance you need, in this accident. And he looked her in the face. It is up to you now.”

Babeta nodded and understood that this family quarrel would go no further and that whatever happened only medical help had been called.

Quayside brawls were common enough and it was left to the injured parties to explain what had happened but, by then, the ‘Ice Maiden’ would have sailed.

EPILOGUE

The old man sat before the fire and waited for his son. He had dozed in front of the warmth, that spelt luxury to him, and fretted about his son's arrival. Soon he dozed again until he heard the latch click on the door.

Stefan saw his beloved son come into the room and he smiled, "Oh, there you are, I wondered where you had gone." He said querulously.

"Don't worry Papa, I won't be far away, you are safe here. There is nothing to disturb you."

Nicholas went into the kitchen and made his father a cup of malted milk and a piece of bread and butter. He saw that his father's face was filling out and that his cheekbones no longer had the tautness of stretched skin, as he had first seen him.

They sat companionably together in the early morning and were content to sit there, two invalids together. It would have been difficult to know who was the weaker of the two, when they had first arrived at this little Victorian house at Wandsworth, south of the River Thames in London, Now, the natural powers of youthful recuperation had outstripped the old man's strength.

Gradually, the younger man was regaining his health, but it would take many more months, and maybe years, for the livid scar on his face, to fade.

They had been brought here by a Customs Cutter, up the River Thames from Tower Bridge and left to make whatever life they could together.

Their sea journey had been fraught, as the young man had been unable to see to the horses, but Stefan somehow had made contact with Otto and help had materialized. The day to day necessities of their cargo of horses was seen to by silent hands and, as soon as Nicholas had been stitched up by the ship's surgeon, he was able to feebly see to their charges.

Otto proved to be surprisingly adept with the horses as unbeknown to Nicholas he had grown up on a Texan ranch which was his home if ever he had a chance to call anywhere home, and, between them, they had arrived up the Thames to Battersea. He had ensured a smooth transition to land and secured the services of Sir Charles's network. Now time must heal the infirmities of the two men.

That morning Nicholas had walked to the river, as he had walked to the river every day since his return, and he saw the young woman leave the boat. He hesitated again, as he had paused every day before, afraid. Then, when he saw her leave Chelsea Harbour, decided to leave a sign. He went across the river and along to the houseboats and crafts moored there, walking down the pontoon and onto a large river cruiser moored there. He turned the key in the lock and stepped inside and the smell of her perfume assailed him.

ABOUT MEL FLAVELL

Mel Flavell was born and bred a middle Englander and spent most formative years from the Welsh Marches to the Fenlands of East Anglia. Educated in Birmingham and Southampton, in Art and Design and Economics.

Time, working in London gave a true love of our capital city Now living in Dorset, may sometimes be seen tramping the hills and valleys or enjoying the seashore of Southern England.

Occasionally may be spotted on Westminster Bridge with backpack and banner to add voice in support of the helpless against the politicians and the powerful.

This is Mel's first book in the trilogy *The Baronski Testament*

AUTHOR'S NOTE

Many of the names of Russian cities have been changed either for artistic purposes or by government decree, e.g. St. Petersburg - Leningrad - St. Petersburg.

This story was given life by the memory of meeting a little old lady, dress in black who lived in an adjacent flat in a terrace of flats in London where one summer, the author once lived with her flatmate. This lady was one of the diaspora of refugees that had fled to London from the ravages of European wars during the first half of the 20th Century.

For a time, this lady became friends with the two girls and once showed them an invitation to a Soiree at the Russian Embassy! She suggested that the two girls might like to accompany her to this event. Intriguingly, this never happened, because the girls were posted elsewhere with their jobs and never saw the little old lady again.

In their innocence, had they stumbled on someone, something, that might have changed the course of their lives? Who knows. With hindsight, and many years later, this Russian emigre was the inspiration for my first novel.

ACKNOWLEDGEMENTS

To Coggi and John, my first mentors.

To Vivian and PaTrisha-Anne for making sense of my scribble.

To all my friends and family who have a love of the magic of words, for their encouragement and enthusiasm.

To my son, Paul for not giving up on my resistance to all things digital, and for helping me to climb to the clouds.

THE PRISONER AND THE PEARLS

32483567R00210

Printed in Poland
by Amazon Fulfillment
Poland Sp. z o.o., Wrocław